Bolan knew he was looking at unfinished business

He let the AR-15 fall to his side as he checked the night, listening to the silence after the roar of the vehicle was eaten up by the dark.

Bolan walked, intent on giving the blackness around the perimeter of the slaughterhouse a thorough scoping for any armed stragglers. Some horrific chain of events had erupted, a magnet of death cast his way by fate. He didn't know who was who, but he suspected black ops, answering to some rogue faction higher up the food chain.

Twenty minutes later he walked through the screen door of the diner. As the hinges squeaked, he could feel the tension. "It's me," he told the survivors. "Stay here. I'll be back."

And the Executioner went in search of answers.

DON PENDLETON's
MACK BOLAN®

Dark Truth

A GOLD EAGLE BOOK FROM
W❂RLDWIDE®

TORONTO • NEW YORK • LONDON
AMSTERDAM • PARIS • SYDNEY • HAMBURG
STOCKHOLM • ATHENS • TOKYO • MILAN
MADRID • WARSAW • BUDAPEST • AUCKLAND

First edition May 2002

ISBN 0-373-61484-5

Special thanks and acknowledgment to
Dan Schmidt for his contribution to this work.

DARK TRUTH

Printed in U.S.A.

Evil is easy, and has infinite forms.

—Blaise Pascal
1623–1662

It doesn't matter where evil comes from—drug thugs, a dictator, the quiet guy next door who goes berserk and kills his co-workers or a covert NSA agent. Evil is still evil. I'm in the business of slaying monsters in human skin. It's more than a mission. It's a calling.

—Mack Bolan

CHAPTER ONE

The killing never bothered Sam "Wildman" Dean. It was business, plain and simple, any ghosts lingering in memory of the dead shrugged off as nothing more than cash on the hoof.

Eight years and change, the body count nearing the midcentury mark, and he figured he was among the hallowed ranks of first-class professional guns for hire, up there with the coldest and most lethal assassins the CIA produced, even if he spent most of his life on the back of a Harley-Davidson and didn't look like much more than a grizzled, scummed-up water buffalo. Success in his eyes pretty much boiled down to never getting bagged by the pigs, ultimate victory a middle-finger salute to society at large while riding on in the wind, a freebird fat in cash, circling the next walking carcass. Blood on his hands was the sweet fruit of a contract murder, to be damn sure, and with the sort of brazen bulldog style he showed off when it finally went down he sometimes imagined—in fantasy fueled by speed and Jack Daniel's—the roaring accolades of well-heeled citizens who wished they had the pair he did, but instead handed off the money and shivered in the shadows while he did their dirty work. An award-winning performance year after year for his real-life role as a hired killer, no shit, visions of glory topped off with nubile babes in the prayer position while their menfolk stood by, choking on envy and impotence, wishing all to hell and back they could be larger than life like Wildman Dean.

If nothing else, the grand finale of blowing away the mark always washed down the bitter taste of raw contempt he felt after nailing down the deal on the front end. It was damn near as good as the fire of bourbon or whiskey burning down his throat and swelling his ample belly with the warm glow of reward for a job well done. They paid him, simply because they didn't have the guts to pull the trigger themselves. But their cowardice seemed to only feed his own sense of superiority. Such was his lot, he figured, the last warrior from the old days when ships were made of wood, men of iron. It was a straight world, stem to stern, these days, computers and the politically correct threatening to send the final few real men, he thought, the way of the dinosaur.

Which was in large part why he stayed in business.

Most of the doomed along the way had been citizens, bogged down by that PC mentality, those walking dead in their straight world, before, of course, he did them a personal favor, the way he saw it, and put them out of their own misery. On the flip side, where he had encountered guts and glory, at last count a dozen kills had been bikers in rival gangs, usually Pagans or Hells Angels who crossed a brother Trojan in a meth or gun deal. When a hit was contracted for biker competition, it had always gone down as two or three heads for the price of one, since outlaw bikers leaned toward the herd instinct, and would also rather rule in hell than serve in heaven. Meaning they always went out with a roar, weighted down with enough lead to sink a small boat on their way to hell.

Citizen, biker or pig, the numbers, anticipated or otherwise, never tweaked a nervous bone in Dean. He was the best at what he did, balls to the wall all the way, and he never left home without his .44 Magnum Smith & Wesson pistol or the backup M-3 A-1 sub-gun, which was stuffed in the satchel now fastened to the sissy bar of his customized Sportster. The big piece, snugged in shoulder leather under the loose-fitting sleeveless denim jacket touting the Trojan colors and filled with six hollowpoints, was the main weapon of choice. From his first kill on, Dean had liked his hits full of noise and mess aplenty, big gaping holes in the body, lots of running blood for pigs and coroners and forensic geeks to wade through and hopefully slip on, all arms and legs windmilling, he imagined, as they flopped down in the gore to ruin cheap suits that probably cost society's underpaid slaves with badge a month's pay. As far as he was concerned, sound suppressors and a mere one killshot were for candy-ass spook types.

The flashing neon sign lit up the desert night like some beacon on a landing zone for wayward aircraft. Homed in on the Howling Coyote through the smear of bug juice on his goggles—the sign on this lonely wood-and-adobe outpost in the middle of north-central Nevada also boasting the best steak and prime rib in the West in smaller winking letters—he eased off the throttle, swung into the lot. Blowing up some tumbleweed in the wake of his rolling thunder, he parked on the far blind side of the plate-glass window, dropped the kickstand and killed 1200 ccs of rumbling iron beast.

It had been a fairly short but hard run from the Trojan clubhouse outside Reno, flying along I-80 at close to ninety, jacked up on two fat lines of crank before setting out, just to help shave the mental stretch of time and distance. Swinging his large, beefy bulk off the hawg, draping the goggles over his satchel, he took a few moments to get his bearings. Flicking a couple of insect carcasses off his beard, squeezing a few drops of cold sweat out of his ponytail, he counted three battered pickup trucks that looked thoroughly abused by the ravages of desert travel. Then a vintage Ford Galaxy, next to what looked to him like a Japanese shitbox—completely out of character for this neck of the woods—and finally spotted her older-model Trans-Am at the far end of the lot. The Jeep Cherokee he let his eye fall on last looked fresh off the assembly line, a picture conjured up of some urban cowboy out to indulge a nine-to-five fantasy about the wild Wild West. He stood his ground, grunted, cooling off in the chilly desert air, his heart hammering as the meth kept coursing through his veins. Just after midnight, and it looked as though quite the crowd was gathered at this lonesome eatery, local desert rats and citizens alike passing through, chowing down right before last call.

All things considered, it sure wasn't the best place by his grim reckoning to conduct their business, with diners shoveling food into their mouths in stoic silence. He hoped she at least had the good sense to claim a cubbyhole far enough away from potential ears. The hit, he hoped, should be easy enough, but with something like this he could never tell, and he sometimes wondered if his luck would sour due to unforeseen events beyond his control.

But this particular client, or so he wanted to believe, was smarter, more savvy than to get reeled in by something like careless talk or cave to a case of bad nerves if the heat came scorching her way. She was a former old lady, after all, knew the ropes when it came to living on the edge, skirting the law, thumbing her nose at the rules straight society had to live by. Indeed, he remembered her as stand-up, tough as the day was long, one sweet mama, too, in the looks department, if memory served him right. But she had gone straight, just the same, having caught a high-calorie taste of legit riches on the other side of the tracks.

Things happened, people changed, for damn sure, and what man could ever really get a fix on what made a woman's heart beat anyway? In his experience, they were like the wind, shifting allegiance in the direction of wherever the breeze of opportunity blew. Still, he wanted to think the heart and soul of the lioness he knew from the old days still pumped the blood of a righteous outlaw chick in her veins. Back then she had belonged to Willy "the Terrible" Tuggell, before, of course, she up and split the Trojans, he remembered, gone shaking what he recalled were ample goods for the high rollers in a Vegas strip joint. Seemed she'd met and married some suit who supposedly did classified work out here for any one of many spook projects that had slews of locals all over the state up in arms about strange lights in the sky, the lunatic fringe sounding the hue and cry about alien spacecraft hovering over or whisking across the skies of nuclear testing sites and military bases at light speed. Seemed she wanted out, tired of clean living and the missionary position maybe, but she wanted to bail with the whole cash enchilada before moving on to whatever she considered greener pastures. So she had reached out to Willie by phone, roughly a week ago, calling out for the only kind of mothership rescue that made sense to her, the former old lady stating she needed help in making a clean break, needed her problem solved in permanent fashion.

The good Trojan brother that he was, Dean told Tuggell he'd take care of it.

He gave the darkness beyond the Howling Coyote one last search, the desert going on forever, it seemed, until it was swallowed up by humpback hills that looked more suited for the face of the moon. He was feeling his nerves suddenly, wondering against his will if something hinky was about to go down. He decided it was only the meth talking to him, simply demanding a couple stiff shots of Jack to smooth out the tweak. Or was someone out there, watching him? And if they were, why? Was that a vehicle in the distance, south, headed that way? Between the meth, the ride and the pitch blackness, it was near impossible to tell. Before he could look any longer to make a decision either way, it appeared a chain of hills swallowed up whatever it was. A check of the sky, and he saw a few clouds skirting along, passing beneath the moon.

Shadows from above, nothing more.

He marched ahead, swung open the front door, the cowbell announcing his entrance and serving to also flare up meth-sparked nerves. A quick look around to count the numbers, he took in the sparse crowd. Beyond the chest-high partition that appeared to separate the smoking section from PC diners, as he caught a whiff of burning tobacco to his immediate right, and he counted four citizens right away. A brunette in a denim blouse that molded a pair of sweet mounds, not shabby at all from where he stood, but with two boys most likely her brood, the kids forking up steak while she kept a glum eye fixed on her beer. He scanned the main dining room around mom and kids. On the far side he found a balding citizen in long-sleeved white shirt and glasses, too busy carving up a slab of prime rib to look his way, pegged the guy for a traveling salesman. The bar, he noted, ran down the north side, from the main room to the edge of the beaded doorway leading to the smoking section. A lean citizen in a crew cut was nursing a beer behind the bar, and Dean caught him throwing the evil eye his way as if like he was something the guy had just stepped in.

"Closing in thirty minutes," the citizen called out.

Attitude. Implication that biker business was about as welcome as a nest of diamondbacks.

"So, that's thirty minutes you're on my time and money, partner," Dean said. "You're not too busy, how 'bout two shots of Jack, a Budweiser. Make sure it's the coldest bottle you got. And some privacy."

The scowl frozen on his face, the citizen barked out across the dining room, in the direction of what Dean assumed was the kitchen. "Betty! Customer."

A chubby blonde who'd seen better days in his estimation popped through a doorway downrange. She growled, "What?" Followed then the head bob from the bar, frowned his way with a face he figured had cracked a few mirrors in its best days, then strode with purpose across the room, grumbling something to herself he was glad he couldn't hear. Aware at least two folks were eager to serve and get him on his way, he held the surveillance pose, further checking out the four-star restaurant rave north of Vegas. It was Western decor, as expected, walls hung with saddles and lassos, oil paintings of cattle drives, ghost towns and rugged landscapes, as if amateur artwork this side of finger painting, he thought, was meant to add scenery to what struck him as just another dismal saloon. He smelled the cigarette, heard a voice from the past quietly call out to his right, "Hey. Over here."

Wildman Dean turned, found her sitting by herself in a booth butted up against the window. He was stepping into the smoking section, still taking in his surroundings, his brain talking to him that something didn't feel right, when he spotted the citizen glancing his direction. The brief look shot his way threw Dean off his stride, made his racing heart lurch.

He was a dark man, white obviously, only he could have been some foreign import, Italian or Arab perhaps, Dean thought, judging the black hair, lean face with its slightly swarthy complexion, which could have been simply flesh burnished by the elements. Something, though, about the guy he couldn't pin down, the way he sat, cool and in control of the moment, sure of himself, the dark man having some way of noting his entrance, but without directly looking at him. No, he decided the citizen had looked "through" him, Dean feeling sized and measured in one eye blink, not worth another look. He felt the scowl coming on, ready next to bore the guy with some no-shit stare he didn't quite feel for some reason, when he caught the lady of the hour looking at her watch.

Time to get down to business. Good enough. As hoped for, she had staked out a roost, far enough away from eavesdroppers where they could talk, in hushed tones, at worst, but guaranteed some privacy. Settling into the booth he let his stare wander past his buxom client, wondering what it was about the dark man that troubled him. Figure it was just the lightning midnight ride, gassed on meth, paranoid fantasies about cops and double crosses dogging his thoughts. Nothing too much in the mental and emotional department some Jack, cold cash and a quick bloody hit couldn't tame. Say the guy down there, he thought, was in fact more than just another citizen, even a cop. Hell, he had that look, eyes that could see it all without looking, for one thing. Only it was something a little more in those eyes Dean couldn't nail down. But what? The eyes of a killer? A hardass, just happened to stumble in here on a lark for a quick bite?

Screw him.

Law or not, how much of a threat could any guy eating salad—might as well be eating quiche far as he was concerned—and nursing one small draft, hardly touched, no less, possibly pose to Wildman Dean? Worst case, he would only move closer to that number-fifty ghost, even if it was a freebie.

TINA WAYLAN THOUGHT if it all wasn't so pathetic she could have just written it off as another gruesome Jerry Springer episode. Sipping her beer, she chuckled with quiet bitterness at the hideous image of herself and her AWOL husband shrieking obscenities at each other as the crowd hooted and chanted, those pitiless spectators of inhumanity wishing only to incite a spurned wife to shed blood for their viewing pleasure.

But this was her life; the unthinkable had happened to her and her children. And she would walk in front of a Greyhound bus before her sorry circumstances became a freak show for public amusement. She had two sons, ages eight and nine to consider beyond her own dismal plight. Bottom line, she was a mother, first and last, and without them she realized she was, indeed, lost for good. And without her, as bad and as ugly as life had turned, the two of them might as well just march out into the desert, fend for themselves as long as possible, until they were consumed soon enough, of course, by slow, cruel death, courtesy of Ma Nature. She erased the mental picture of Bobby and Tommy on their own as soon as it tried to take shape, aware such grim dwelling might possibly drop her into some abyss of even darker contemplation. She was a fighter, damn it, always had been, and as long as she was breathing she could at least hope for a better tomorrow, some sort of intervention by a kinder fate perhaps. But only if she stayed strong, she believed, didn't crumble to some bout of cancerous self-pity, some long-running loathing of herself and circumstance crippling any chance she might have of finding a way out.

Glancing up from her beer she found both boys peering at her, wondering perhaps in their own innocent way about this injustice, unable at their tender years to fathom the senseless cruelty of the adult world. Even more sad, she suspected they would someday look back upon this time, and hate the monstrous perpetrator who was their father. No, they couldn't possibly understand what had happened—not even she could believe it—but they knew something was terribly wrong, the walls of their world closing in to crush all hope and dreams.

That the here and now was some dark, malevolent spirit demanding their despair, or worse, God forbid. Yes, only the strong did survive. It carved a knife through her heart as she read the pain and confusion in their eyes, before they went back to working quietly on their T-bones, mashed potatoes and green beans. God only knew when they would eat this well again.

Which made her hate him that much more. He hadn't even shown the guts or decency to do it in person, opting to deliver instead the punishing blow over the phone.

Small comfort they owned the mobile home near Battle Mountain, had a roof over their heads for the time being. The immediate survival task involved money, since the bastard had made sure he'd paved the golden road for his new life, nearly wiping out the family savings of twenty grand, with Mr. Benevolence leaving all of three hundred dollars and change in the dust of his custom eighteen-wheeler. As if he was doing the three of them some grandiose favor by seeing they wouldn't starve in the next few days. She heard the vicious string of curses rearing up in the black caverns of thought, but shut them off, telling herself she wouldn't become bitter or vengeful, no matter what, no matter how tough life got for the three of them from there on. Why was she surprised anyway? He was gone for two, three weeks at a time since nearly the beginning of their marriage, making runs to the big cities east, phoning home when the mood struck him. The concern about her loneliness was easy enough to read through, some chime of laughter in his voice warning her he was out there having a big old party, just checking in to make sure the little lady was holding on, sticking to the role of good mother and faithful wife. Hadn't her girlfriends warned her about Tony? Did she blame herself now for getting duped by her own desire in the beginning? What she felt next sickened her, made her even wonder about her own sanity. Ten years of marriage, and some wistful corner of her heart still wanted to cling to the good memories, as if remembering alone would make everything all right, bring him back, it was all just some bad dream.

Recalling, such as the first time she'd seen him swagger into the Vegas casino where she'd been a cocktail waitress, when she was younger and could get by on looks alone. What a fool she'd been, and now two innocent lives were made to suffer because she'd been blinded by love or lust, which left her wondering if the two were simply one and the same. Bastard. Back then, he had been all smiles and charm, the big spender, drinks for everybody, keep the chips coming, Tony long on wit and even longer in the love department. Handsome as the devil, she had thought the first time she'd laid eyes on him, smitten right away even as her girlfriends pleaded he was all wrong, Satan's spawn in human skin. Sure enough, it turned out he showed a streak of hell in him no amount of her love and devotion would ever cure. Well, if there was any justice in life, whoever he had left her to shack up with would shove the same amount of bitter fruit down his gullet, leave him choking on the pieces of his own shattered heart. And if he came crawling back, groveling for a second chance, that he had changed his philandering ways…?

Not in this life, or the next. He'd made his choice; she had pride, if little else right then. She was moving on, no matter how dark and uncertain the future loomed.

"Tina? A minute, if you don't mind?"

She read the apologetic look over her shoulder, the owner, she was sure, ready to once again tell her how sorry he was to let her go. In some strange way, bordering perversion almost, given her own dire straits, she understood his position, didn't take her firing personal. Jim Lake had a business to run, after all, and he couldn't afford having her boys running all over the restaurant, her attention torn between keeping them under control while waiting tables, messing up orders all too often lately in the whole process of keeping it all together, pulling double duty as mother and employee. His claim for her dismissal was that business was too slow to keep her on, but she knew better. She was something of an embarrassment—she was sure of it—which only threatened to inflame her anger and resentment even more.

Keep it together, she told herself, don't let them see you crack under the strain.

It wasn't in her nature, she knew, to cast blame, much less outright curse the rumor mill, the whispers and looks she'd caught lately making her feel that she'd been branded as pathetic baggage, all the good folks wondering whether it was something she had done to drive away a husband and father. Eureka Springs was a small community, population 231—now 230—and rumors about her husband's bailout had floated around her for two weeks until she'd broken down, confirming the horrible truth to those she worked with. Hard to deny it anyway, since she'd been forced to baby-sit her sons every shift since Tony had ridden off into the sunrise.

"Eat up," she told her boys, quiet, making sure she kept any pain or anger toward circumstances out of her voice. "We're leaving in a few minutes."

She drained her beer, stood and managed to keep the trembling from suppressed anger out of her legs as she took the few steps to the bar.

"I'm really sorry I had to do this, Tina."

"Business is slow, like you said. Nothing personal. No hard feelings."

He had grace enough not to pursue it, or mention the other problem.

"The meals are on me," he told her, then poured a draft and put it on the bar in front of her. Drinks on the house, too, a little parting gesture to ease her pain, or salve his own guilt?

She was surprised at how strong her voice sounded, even as hot tears welled up behind her eyes. "Appreciate that."

"Listen, you need some money, I can float you a few hundred."

"We'll manage."

"If things pick up…I'll call you. You're a good waitress, Tina, everyone likes you…but I can't have personal problems following you in here."

"No need to explain, Jim."

"Anything you need…"

"I'll let you know."

He reached over, gave her shoulder a gentle squeeze, as if to reinforce the point he was in her corner, despite the firing, the fact she'd been abandoned by her husband to become the local pariah. As soon as he was gone to do whatever he did to close down the restaurant, she found Betty by her side.

"Lousy break, huh? I'm real sorry, Tina. Him and Angelo," Betty groused, firing up a cigarette, "big restaurant owners, all the heart and soul of a rattle-snake. You know," she said, lowering her voice in that conspiratorial tone that made Tina wonder how much gossip old Betty might have spread about her predicament, "if you ask me, I'm thinking Angelo's the one probably twisted the screws and got you canned." She wondered about that, too, why Angelo in the past week had paid her more attention than ever, the polite inquiries about Tony, the kids, Mr. Compassion. And she had caught, more than a few times, the way Jim's partner looked at her recently, his eyes betraying the kind of hidden motives that had nearly seen a platoon of lawyers shut the place down a few months back. "Did the same thing to Marta when she wouldn't sleep with the porky creep. Heard they paid her off to keep her old man from raising enough hell to take this place and send them packing like whipped dogs, like they deserve."

"I'm not looking for revenge."

"Didn't suggest you were."

"Angelo's married. I'm sure he's not interested in scorned goods." She knew how defensive and lame that sounded, given how her instincts had warned her Angelo was just another shade of Tony, but she felt compelled to say something to try to salvage a moment of dignity.

"Think that matters to him? Men." She stabbed out

her cigarette, a thick cloud of smoke shooting over the bar on a gust of a clearly bitter breath. "Listen, I can help you or the boys any way, hon, gimme a shout." A pause, then said, "Anyways, I gotta go get dinner for handsome over there. And I ain't talkin' about that biker trash neither. God a-mighty, if I was ten years younger and twenty pounds lighter, I might have a shot. Guess a girl can dream, even at my age."

Curious, when she was alone again, she looked toward the smoking section, but already knew the one in question who'd gotten Betty stoked up in romantic fantasy. He came in maybe thirty minutes ago, every bit as tall, dark and handsome as Tony, she had thought at first impression, but more athletic, graceful, as lithe as a cat. And there was something in his eyes—she'd seen it and it took her breath, as if he'd walked a thousand terrible lifetimes, only carried his own ghosts in a class she'd yet to see in any man. Something, yes, in the way he had moved, then sat, confident in himself as one hundred percent man, but far from any arrogant front Tony put on for the world, not even a hint of some macho need to prove himself. Before some foolish flight of fantasy could take root, born, she realized, out of self-pity and fear of tomorrow, she looked away. Her sons were her whole life, the only men that could matter in her personal corner of hell. Somehow, as surely as the sun would rise, she would prevail, pick up the pieces, forge ahead. No options left.

The untainted had been dumped on the scales of life

or death. They were counting on her to find the answer.

FEAR PREYED on him without letup, had been, in fact, since bolting the accounting firm of Reiss, Bentley and Barklin in Chicago, a dead-of-night departure, meant pretty much all along to leave his partners high and dry. The very thought they would, no doubt, curse the day he was born when the clients in question came calling almost made him laugh.

Well, shit happened.

Eventually they would find themselves forced to explain a missing six million dollars and change to guys in silk suits who had trusted the firm to clean up enough cash over the long haul to fill an armada of dump trucks. Crooks, the whole lot of them.

Little wonder, though, he found his nerves talking to him in loud decibels, he thought. Two days on the run in his Toyota rental, a briefcase with the two hundred grand he'd emptied out of his legitimate account, and it was understandable why he was jumping at shadows. Why every stranger, also, posed a potential threat, with maybe some lurking, faceless hit man hunting him at every turn, meant to squash him like some insect underfoot. After, of course, the hired killer retrieved their money.

Well, he'd made his choice to abscond with their funds long ago, a decision he now saw as destiny preordained, carved in stone due to the disrespect and contempt he endured from the immediate world around him. No turning back the hand of time—there was nothing left to do but keep on running.

And spend their illicit dollars like there was no to-morrow.

Funny how it all had come to pass. Looking back, the decision to do it leaped out of nowhere to consume his every thought and desire, fueling him with a living fire, the whole idea taking shape with just a tad of scheming in the genesis phase. Truth was the plan came raging at him with a life of its own, crying out from some dark, angry impulse, and right after his second wife sashayed out the door, the greedy whore promptly marching in yet another round of lawyers for the raping. It had sure seemed the right thing to do, his conscience telling him it was simple justice to get back all that had been taken from him, to wade right in there and find he had the right stuff to make it big in a world that had snubbed and talked down to him all his life. In some way, he had been surprised at his own grim resolve, a toughness he never knew existed inside a basic yes-man cocoon. But he had pulled it off, succeeded, a thief in the night. So far.

It was easy enough to rationalize taking money from criminals, even if it was far more dangerous than picking the pockets of Harry Homeowner. Telling himself during all the months of pilfering there was no way the Mob could possibly miss a measly few million. Doctoring the books, skimming a chunk here and there, funneling it over the course of two anxious years into an offshore account. Of course, he had long since decided the Bahamas was too close to the scene of plunder, any menacing pursuit a mere hop, skip and jump away. So he settled on Honolulu, at least for the time being, some distant point across the ocean where he could hunker down, fall into his new identity, make sure his back was clear and free of gun-toting shadows.

Free-floating bile in his stomach, it was nearly impossible to keep down the prime rib unless he ate bites not large enough to satisfy a rodent. Damn, but it felt like some invisible carnivorous bird was perched on his shoulder, waiting for him to break down, confess his sin, weep himself into total submission, beg for that savaging of his flesh to begin.

No way, he'd come too far, risked it all, earned the right to live the way he choose. Robert Barklin sucked in a deep breath, flooding out the sudden rush of queasiness damming up his throat. He couldn't afford to break at this point, not now, aware his very life could be riding on the line. All he had to do was get to LAX. A week ago he'd purchased a ticket for Hawaii through a Chicago travel agency, paid for in cash, an assumed name going into their computer. The way was ready, escape a mere handful of hours off in sunny Southern California. From there, once he was squared away in his island paradise, it wouldn't be much trouble to have the funds from the Bahamas wired to a numbered account he'd arranged through a banker who likewise, he knew, had some shady tales to tell himself. Having friends in high places, he decided, even of the white-collar-criminal variety, looked set to pay off.

Relax, take another deep, slow breath, he told himself. Let the fear go. Let it be. The future belonged to him, an open gate of white light calling him forth to taste nirvana on Earth. He'd sure as hell paid enough dues to grab up his own slice of heaven, wherever he landed. He was a man, by God, no longer to be browbeaten and bullied by women who were never satisfied no matter what. Not to mention no more kissing butt on a daily basis, sucking up to all the slick ones who had more money than God, even dared to flaunt their ill-gotten riches in his face like some badge of courage.

Like he was their peon, barely fit to scrape the gum off their shoes.

Well, it was his turn to live large, laugh at the world, and all the way to the bank. Robert Barklin was flying on to paradise, and no one was going to stop him.

So why did he feel so unsure of the moment, weighted down with gnawing fear, a twisting ball of guilt in his chest that wouldn't unwind?

It was one guy, making him feel that way, and he couldn't quite pin down why.

He didn't want to look back toward the smoking section, but he couldn't help himself, drawn to check out a face that struck him as carved out of granite. First time he saw the man, he thought he'd spotted a look in the eyes, forged by some fire he found himself imagining could only belong to a killer. Or was paranoia getting the best of him, threatening whatever determination he clung to? One guy, a party of one in the smoking section, had his nerves jumping through his skin like an endless string of firecrackers. He looked away before the guy caught him staring. He was sure the dark man was either a cop—an FBI agent most likely—marched out by his partners, the Feds having picked up the scent of his flight. Hell, he imagined his own fear had trailed him from Chicago like a bad stink, a malingering odor pointing the way directly to this hole in the middle of Nevada. Or was the stranger something worse, far more diabolical than a mere law-enforcement officer? The dark stranger had some cold, supremely confident manner Barklin didn't trust himself to study any longer.

Barklin choked down another bite, mentally wrestled with finishing his meal or just paying the tab, resuming escape to paradise. The juicy meat then started washing away the sick feeling, once it settled firm in his stomach, allowing him larger bites as he kept digging in. He chose to stay, finish up this last supper, determined not to stop and eat again until he was safely in the air and well over the Pacific.

ERNIE COLLINS FOUND more holes in their plan than the internal revenue code. The whole scheme sounded shaky, not to mention dangerous to his health, two of them poised to go through the front door, two more charging in through the kitchen. That was assuming they stuck to the few details he'd overheard. Say some hero mucked up their play and they were forced to kill a cowboy who'd seen one too many Charles Bronson movies? Once—if—it turned bloody and they were

looking at death row, what would stop them—four total strangers—from executing everyone inside, then
putting a bullet through his own brain to silence one
last eyewitness?

Too late now—there was no choice actually but to
follow through, since he'd sold his services only yesterday, agreeing in a moment of greed and desperation
to fulfill his part. Now that the moment of truth was
staring him in the face, he determined to go through
with it, if only to suck down a couple belts of booze
once inside, get his nerves under control while he
scouted the place, then trooped back to report back on
the numbers, mood inside, where the owners were, like
that. Or so they had defined his role as something of
a recon stooge.

The real trouble, he was afraid, would start once he
returned to the van to sit tight and supposedly watch
their backs while they took the place down. This was
Nevada, the Wild West, and folks out here tended to
arm themselves. The whole thing now took on a dimension of insanity he would have never allowed himself to get talked into in the first place, if he hadn't
been sitting around the previous day, smoking grass
and chewing mushrooms with a couple of those UFO
kooks who had been kind enough, just the same, to
give him food and shelter. Nevada was getting spook-
ier with each passing day, but he needed a little more
time to hole up, maybe con the more gullible cult
members into showing him where they kept the guns
and whatever cash was stashed at the ranch.

Man, sobriety had a strange way of bringing on the

grim doubts of a reality check. For instance, he wasn't sure exactly what the four men in black had in mind, how they planned to pull this off without firing a shot if a cowboy or two took exception to getting robbed. A dump like this, how much cash could possibly be squirreled away to begin with? What if someone panicked, and there was a mad rush for the door when the hardware came out and folks were getting screamed at to shut up and get on the floor? What if one of the two owners locked himself away in the back office, dialed up the cops when the first scream broke out and an obvious robbery was going down?

If he was afraid of the immediate future, what would or wouldn't happen, he was even more scared to death of what the four men in the van would do to him if he didn't follow through with his role. He took a moment, just the same, to pause at the front door, trying to will away the trembling in his hands and knees, but gave it up, figuring only some booze could help win this particular mind battle. A look over his shoulder, and he imagined he could almost hear the four shadows inside the van cursing him to get on with it. Two basic facts sent him marching inside the restaurant to case the joint, fulfill his obligation. One—they were armed to the teeth, and he wasn't. Two—he'd taken their money, three hundred dollars in cash, far more than the chump change he'd fled Bethlehem, Pennsylvania, with about one year ago. It was a bad time back then, sure, running west from about six wants and warrants, one of which was for grand theft auto. Even still he suddenly wished he could go back somehow, face the music, but feared the four strangers far more than the bondsman he'd skipped out on.

He wondered who the four men really were, had never heard them call each other by name while in their presence. They didn't look like any wild-eyed, pissed-off-at-the-world armed robbers he'd ever come across. And anyone he'd ever known for any stretch of time was either a hardened criminal or well on the way. These guys were pushing forty easy, maybe fifty, clean-cut types all around, looked fresh out of suburbia, U.S.A. Go figure. And why, precisely, had they sought him out? Ask a basic question, and he was stared down with eyes that warned him it was best he kept his mouth shut. They didn't need to fill in the ''or else'' part.

Best just to get it over with. So he went through the door, flinched when the cowbell jangled and he felt all eyes look his way. Right away, it all looked and felt wrong. A biker and his old lady, looking up from their table, a bearded one-percenter who clearly had bad news written all over him as Collins felt himself treated to full hostile scrutiny.

Three steps next into the smoking section, homed in on the bar—oh, God, let there be quick service and Wild Turkey—and Collins felt a rush of heat flash into his head, his strides faltering, pulling him up short as he met a pair of eyes he figured had melted ice in their day. Somehow, he walked on, turning away as soon as the stranger eating by himself looked up, inspecting him, measuring. All the way to the bar, Ernie Collins kept hearing a voice of doom in his head, warning him the guy was trouble. He knew a cop when he saw one.

CHAPTER TWO

He was no cop, but he could see where the nervous types with something to hide could make that mistake. There was, however, photo ID complete with proper credentials declaring he was a special agent of the U.S. Department of Justice. It was tucked away in a thin wallet stamped with the Justice seal, inside pocket of a white windbreaker about one size too large, situated just beside a Beretta 93-R that hung snug from a shoulder holster. The Justice ID packet naming him as Mike Belasko was official.

It was also bogus.

He also wasn't psychic, much less able to read minds, nor did he consider himself some superior judge of character, since human nature in his grim experience was as prone to sudden and violent change as the weather. Someone had once stated, he recalled, a man's character determined his destiny. That, he believed, was especially true of Animal Man. If fueled by insidious motive and hidden desire, he had seen more times than he cared to count how man could become a monster. Bulldozing over society at large. Consuming the innocent, never sated. Bloodthirst, avarice or pure want of only the self expanding a sickness of the soul, with no limits or restraint until all life was devoured. In short, a runaway train of greed and lust for power, rampaging on to crush and to take, leaving behind nothing but grief and death.

Such was his experience, more than a few hard lessons about the dark side and some heartbreak earned along the way. And the man sitting in the corner by himself, nursing a beer, working on his salad while waiting on the main course, instinctively knew he was under the intense mental microscope of two dark forces simmering with shadowy agendas.

First the biker. Bugged-out eyes, two pinballs had ricocheted from face to face, wall to wall, the one-percenter most likely jacked to the ozone on meth, he suspected. Worse still, the biker was lugging a big piece of steel beneath the grease-stained denim vest, as he had taken into account both the bulge and the familiar vicious, predatory look of a stone-cold killer. Then a desert rat, the latest midnight arrival. Mop of curly hair like sprouting weeds, now moving double-time for the bar, Weed acting ready to bust out of his skin, pants on fire unless he doused whatever flames of fear and agitation seared him inside with a quick medicinal shot down the hatch.

Two bad seeds, in his estimation, his own radar for trouble locked in, watching them without watching, instinct doing all the work, the inner man poised for the poisonous fruit to fall from the tree. And the way he'd felt their eyes initially boring drill bits into him, well, he could almost hear them wondering if he was a local, state or federal badge.

Officially, yes, he was a Fed. Unofficially, and known only to a select group, the man named Mack Bolan was about as far removed from being a law-enforcement officer as the moon was from Earth.

Truth was, the man who had also become known as the Executioner had seen more than a few hard days on the wrong side of the law. That seemed another lifetime now, when he'd been hunted by officialdom for taking his unconventional war and shoving it down the frothing maws of the savages. Legitimate, courageous and well-intentioned law could perhaps reach out and reel in the cannibals with red tape and Miranda, but it could never score permanent victory, certainly not in the way of Bolan's ultimate cleansing fashion that cut out the cancerous human tissue from the uninfected body whole. A simple and direct approach, fight fire by dropping total conflagration on evil. End of discussion.

Bolan had long since come in from the legal scorching heat, the soldier now sanctioned by even the President of the United States to work as part of America's most covert counterterrorist arm, known as Stony Man. Organized crime, terrorists, tyrants, every ilk, shade and shadow of thug and traitor, the Executioner was often given a pass by the Man himself to keep the free world from being eaten up by its enemies.

Right then the soldier was supposed to be on R and R. Just off wrapping up a foray halfway around the world, Bolan had pretty much been ordered to stand down, take a few days for himself. That came straight from Hal Brognola, the big Fed at the Justice Department who oversaw Stony Man Farm and doubled as liaison to the President. So take a short breather. There were—and would always be—flashpoints around the globe, already heated up to critical mass, with cannibals aplenty waiting for the Bolan touch.

At any rate, the Man from Justice had told Bolan the cyber-sleuthing intelligence team at the Farm was cooking up another mission, but it might be several days in the brewing before the green light flashed from the Oval Office. Get in a car, Bolan's old friend told him, breathe the air, go see America. So be it. Why not?

So, he'd landed at LAX, rented the Jeep Cherokee and started driving east by northeast. Breathing all that fresh air away from the killing fields. Unwinding, sort of. On hold, but reining himself on a personal leash. It had been a military flight dropping him off at L.A., meaning the war bag with hardware and high-tech goods didn't require a customs search. The mere fact that weapons and gear were stowed in the SUV only served as another reminder it would be time to go, march back out there to face down a new monster soon enough.

Not by any stretch was it Bolan's nature to stop and smell the roses, fill up the idle time with, say, normal activities and pleasures other folks enjoyed, perhaps even took for granted. Sitting still or taking in the sights was for the other guy. Even then, he was grimly aware another bunch of savages was out there carving up humanity. That knowledge alone—and being a warrior, first and last—kept him restless and hungry as a shark to go wage the good fight in his War Everlasting, as soon as possible.

At that moment, thanks to Weed and the one-percenter, Bolan hardly found himself nurturing any peaceful, easy feeling. Something smelled, and it wasn't just the riffraff who hadn't, according to his nose, seen a bath since Paul was a tax collector for the Romans.

The way it stood was something of a fluke, what had been an aimless sightseeing tour of the desert West that finally steered him to the Howling Coyote. Rolling down I-80 the billboard had leaped out at him in the headlights, claiming the best beef in the West. Hunger pangs then got the better of Bolan, since he hadn't downed a square meal in days.

But now that he was here, watched and watching, he sensed something both sullen and sinister in the air, even felt himself boxed in to some extent by a cast of characters, not all of whom he could safely reckon catered to the dark side.

Beyond the seedy duo, there was the middle-aged, moon-faced guy who looked like a businessman away from home, nondescript from all outward appearance, but lost in some turmoil that would make even the most insensitive and ignorant of cable talking heads wonder. He certainly struck Bolan as being as nervous as Weed, even frightened of something or someone. The soldier had caught the guy checking him out, three times at last count, a darting furtive look, there then gone. Yet more sizing, wondering who or what he was, maybe questioning why he left the windbreaker on, zipped halfway down. Much the same way the biker and Weed tried to read him. Only Businessman's lips would flutter on, as he stayed crouched against the wall, hunkered low in the booth over there—a bomb shelter in the middle of nowhere the way he acted— the guy talking to himself every few minutes or so, a silent running dialogue with some ghost in his head.

Accidentally, Bolan also overheard what he assumed was the proprietor telling the lady with two sons how sorry he was, reading between the lines that she'd been fired for reasons left only to his speculation. Eyes to himself, Bolan had found himself admiring her quiet way, the complete lack of bitterness and resentment in her look and voice, even as some terrible misfortune clearly weighed her down. There was a strength inside her he recognized in one eye blink, either natural or earned by coming out the other side of tough luck, the spirit moving her in calm reassurance that tomorrow did, indeed, take care of itself— or at least showed the good ones the way. Whatever her trouble, she was a carriage of dignity, two lives, at least, beyond her far more important than her own suffering.

Maybe Hal was right, he considered. Go see the face of America while not under fire. Reaffirm a value system, a basic honor and decency he'd spent a lifetime fighting for. If nothing else, the lady reinforced a personal philosophy of Bolan's.

Which was not all warriors carried a gun, or went to the kill-or-be-killed mat with the forces of evil.

Sometimes the so-called normalcy of perceived civilized life and daily routine carried its own burdens and troubles enough to force a man or woman to stand up and choose.

Welcome to the real, the other but so-called normal world, he thought, sorrow cutting a slice through his heart as he glanced over at the woman and children. Aware, even more intensely right then, that the warrior spirit could shine through, in all walks of life, that it all boiled down to basic character and guts in times of trouble. That good people still breathed the same air, held on tight, struggled, suffered and kept on trying even against the long house odds. It felt real good, almost sweet to smell a rose or two right then, even if somewhere down deep the soldier might feel himself languishing in on-call status.

The soldier then overheard the biker tell his bleached-blond lady friend, "Nice surprise, Rhonda. Looks like square living's kept all the right parts together. That nine-to-five bread keep them juices running hot as the good old days?"

"I see you're still the same sweet talker."

"Regular prince. Here to rescue a damsel in distress."

Bolan felt the mean eye once more as Prince Scumbag glared his way, making certain Bolan maintained full concentration on his salad. Then a long hard pause from that direction, the biker killing his shot, helping himself to one of the lady's cigarettes. Weed meanwhile plopped down on a stool, scowling all around for service, one leg bouncing like a spring. The soldier detected high anxiety—natural paranoia—in Weed's eyes before the guy zeroed in on Bolan's waitress as she whipped around the corner of the alcove leading to the kitchen. Bolan's prime rib trailed a wisp of steam behind her as she rolled into the smoking section.

Antsy as he seemed for a booze fix, Bolan found Weed running a long search around the restaurant. His eyes darted from face to face, but the soldier briefly wondered why they bypassed him when only moments ago Weed looked set to faint as Bolan met his eye. The fear coming from that way was suddenly as glaring to Bolan as the neon sign out front.

The waitress brought the soldier his meal with the same smiling eyes she'd taken his order with. Easy enough to read between the lines, as she set down the plate, but Bolan found himself grateful for a friendly face among the somber, the angry and the tweaked. She lingered a moment, wanted to know if he needed anything else. As Bolan quietly told her no, and thanked her, the biker and Weed were barking for drinks.

"Hold your horses!" she rasped. "I only got two hands and two feet!"

"No shit. Think you can get your lizard-hide butt in gear for another Jack and Bud with the same enthusiasm as you showin' your hormones?" the biker snarled, throwing Bolan a look meant to challenge any chivalrous stand. Bolan felt the angry scowl tug at the corners of his lips, but decided to look away, content for the moment to maintain peace on Earth. Normally rudeness wasn't any cause for alarm, much less a call to arms, considering the roads he'd traveled, but he could always make an exception to the general rule. The waitress spouted off a few curses on the move, all fire and brimstone, telling Bolan she was more than able to fend for herself.

"Shot of Turkey there, honey," Weed told her on her way in for the liquor racks. "A nice fat one, if you don't mind."

"Double's five bucks, big-time."

"Whatever. I see my fingers on the other side of the glass, no tip."

"Like I was expecting one."

Touché, and Bolan almost smiled, then went to work on his meal. He listened as Weed turned conversational.

"Owner around?"

Something in the voice, prying, a sly inquiry, shot Bolan's antenna up.

"Why do you ask?"

"Maybe I need a job. You need a cook?"

"Already got one," he heard his waitress fire back, Ms. Hostile in high torque, as Bolan watched her drop the shot glass on the bar, spilling a little firewater down the side, bringing on the expected scowl from Weed.

But Weed bit his tongue, more concerned with killing the drink, then making a dramatic face as if he'd been in dire straits for the magic elixir for days. "Maybe you need another cook. Maybe he gets sick sometimes. Or too hungover to come in."

"Angelo doubles as cook we get shorthanded in the kitchen."

"This Angelo around? Maybe he's a little more pleasant to talk to."

"Forget it. Both them are back in the office or kitchen, closing up."

"Both of them too busy for me, back there with this one hotshot chef, that what you're saying?"

"Too busy tonight, and for the rest of your life. You don't exactly strike me like you just came behind the line of some four-star establishment. In fact, I'd say you probably don't know a burger patty from a buffalo chip."

Weed snorted, made some phlegmy noise in this throat, then dug into a pocket of faded blue jeans ripped out at the knees. One more long look around the restaurant, and he made a show of rifling through the bills before he peeled off five dirty ones. He slapped Washington down on the bartop, growling, "Whatever happened to service with a smile?"

"Whatever happened to basic everyday manners and class?"

"Up yours."

"Back at ya."

Weed muttered to himself, Bolan watching the guy as he nearly ran from the bar, through the main room and out the door. Another bite, then Bolan looked out the window, but saw only a fading shadow, broken up in an ominous jagged silhouette by the flashing light above, as Weed vanished down the far side. The soldier carved off another chunk of rare beef. He was waiting for the rumble of an engine that would signal Weed was on his way.

A full minute or so passed. The expected noise never came, but Bolan hadn't seen him drive in, either. Maybe Weed had walked...

Something felt wrong, something out there in the dark that put him on edge. The Executioner sat in deliberate grim silence for a long moment. He couldn't quite say why, but suddenly he wasn't hungry.

"HERE COMES the puke."

Kyle Braxton shot a look in the rearview and nearly smiled at Weatherspoon. Puke, huh? He liked that, somehow a perfect fit for the piece of trash chosen from the whole raggedy lot of the lunatic fringe out in the desert. And just as that UFO cult couldn't possibly know they had been under constant surveillance by Big Brother for two years—both landline and cell phones tapped, state-of-the-art laser parabolic mikes able to pick up a belch from two miles or more off, with a prototype NSA eyes in the sky capable of seeing right through their very roof, thanks to infrared X-ray laser—their stooge would never guess in his wildest peyote hallucination what fate awaited him.

The puke was dead meat when this wrapped and they had absconded with what they'd come here to take. Bunch of nuts out there anyway, he thought. Who would possibly miss one more loser of the disenfranchised? No one. Well, they could watch the skies at night for strange lights all they wanted, he thought. Maybe get lucky, spot or even film what even he suspected existed in the classified Hangar Thirteen, nestled and under armed guard in the base of the Shoshone Mountains. But he didn't have time or the inclination to fantasize over wild rumors. The four of them were there to deal out a grim reality, and in the name of national security. Still, out of twenty-nine crazies out there in the dilapidated rathole they passed off as headquarters and commune, and he had to wonder why the former chief of security had singled out this one particular sorry sack. Just pick a human scab, one sacrificial lamb as good as another? And why had the ex-chief hinted only yesterday—when the details for this bloody chore were nailed down—at some future plan to use the whackos? Well, orders were orders, he decided, and they were simple enough.

Braxton cocked and locked the Uzi submachine gun, slipped on the black ski mask, then settled the com link in place, adjusting the throat mike. Two spare clips snug in his waistband, good to go. A quarter mile or so south of where it would all happen, the van hidden in a cleft carved between two hills, Braxton spotted their boy coming out the front door. Fading out of the dancing halo of white light, swallowed by the pitch blackness, he made out somehow their stooge swiveling his head, stumbling along, thought he even heard the guy cry out. Jumpy and afraid, that much was obvious. And damn well he should be, as Braxton checked the troops.

Ski masks dropped over identical crew cuts and clean-shaved, fairly handsome mugs that could have made them spit-and-polish poster recruits for government issue. Outfitted in black, head to rubber-soled combat boots, com links fastened. Four clones, all of them roughly the same six feet of lean wire and sinew, except for the hardware. One Glock 17 with threaded sound suppressor for Burton, who would lead the back-door charge, Christensen watching his rear, the M-1014 HK-Benelli combat shotgun in 12-gauge sure to choke back any scream at just one blink. Next he caught the cold glint of the white orbs of Weatherspoon's eyes in the rearview as he cradled the AR-15.

The puke's heavy breathing hit the interior as he hopped through the open side door. ''You got problems, gentlemen. There's a cop in there. Look, man, whatever you got in mind...''

''Shut up a second and slow the hell down,'' Braxton rasped. ''Suck some air, son, pull yourself together and give it to me straight, top to bottom, wall to wall. I want numbers and positions.''

Between bouts of wheezing and ad-libbing, Braxton listened to the puke's scouting report. He heard about the alleged cop first, of course. Big guy, sitting alone, far north corner of the smoking section, couldn't miss him, the puke embellishing some point about the guy having eyes like death or chips of ice. Then the biker, the stooge spouting how the Harley trash acted juiced out of his skull on speed. Two problems, right off the top. It went without any discussion, with a new dark mood from the troops speaking volumes how the biker and this supposed cop with the death eyes had to be brought under control right off, within a heartbeat. It was all going to come down to split-second timing anyway, Braxton knew, quiet communication between the two teams, watches synchronized when they split up. Then their stooge ran down the rest of the numbers and positioning, claiming their two main marks were in the kitchen or the office, shutting the place down. An idea leaped to Braxton's mind, something that would grab everyone's attention right out of the gate, put a freeze through any cowboy looking to be some kind of hero. Braxton asked the puke if the mom and kids looked to be finishing up their meal, and ready to head out the door. Puke couldn't say.

It didn't matter either way, he reckoned, if he hauled in a human shield or two to make sure some hero didn't get froggy. The standing order was to not leave behind a single witness.

Braxton found the puke peering around, noting at last their faces were concealed. Braxton grinned through the slit, decided to give the guy a little false hope. It was going to be one hell of a sadistic outing anyway. He could be certain Martin Harrison, aka Jim Lake, and Angelo Balducci, who in a former life was Agent Anthony Baldone, weren't about to give it up. They knew the drill from personal experience. And Braxton was counting on, even looking forward to dishing out persuasion by way of some serious pain. So why not, he figured, fuel the beast inside, gear it up even then, hand off a fat lie and allow the stooge some sense of security and well-being as if he was just along for the ride?

"That's right, son. They can't ID us, everyone simply goes home."

"Man, just do it and get it over with. I been thinking, how much of a score could you take from here anyway?"

"It's not about money, son."

"What? Then if it ain't a robbery…"

Braxton took a small handheld radio from his pocket and dumped it in the puke's lap. "When we go inside, push the button on that and let me know if any late-night diners pull up. One more thing." The smile disappeared, Braxton letting the stare bore into the guy. "We come back and you're not here it would be better for you if you just found the highest, nearest cliff and took a header. You'd find a quick suicide far easier, and way more preferable to what I could do to you. We clear?"

"Like crystal, man."

"Good boy. Tell you what," Braxton said, turning the ignition key halfway, then twisting the knob to the radio. He kept the volume down to less than a whisper. He ran the dial through the soft but whining static bursts common all over Nevada, given any number of classified frequencies not even the FCC or the government-affiliated Interdepartmental Radio Advisory Committee knew existed. Braxton put on the grin once more, as he found and settled on a classic rock station. He looked over his shoulder and told the stooge, "Just relax, son. It will all be over soon enough and you'll be on your way. Like the song here says—take it easy."

CHAPTER THREE

He found his partner, once again, searching for bo-geymen. Three nights in a row now, taking out the trash, and it was becoming a freakish routine, border-ing the pathological in his eyes. Spooky how the man went off by himself, sometimes thirty minutes or more, before Harrison came out and caught him watching the desert. If it wasn't for the glowing eye of the Turkish cigar, Martin Harrison would have missed him altogether, a nearly invisible block of stone, cloaked in a blackness every bit as ominous, he thought, as their collective pasts. He took a moment to study the dark shadow with gaze fixed on some distant point in the desert. Then, before he was aware of it, realized he was examining the night himself, compelled to wonder about shadows and potential danger out there, or maybe contaminated, he thought, by the man's paranoia, wondering next if the hills did indeed have eyes. All things considered, a case of nerves was understandable, given what they knew and had seen. It was why he kept ''the leverage'' no far-ther than a short trip back to the bar. These days, his partner, however, believed all the edge they required came by way of a .45 Colt and a 12-gauge Winchester pump shotgun. It took some convincing, but Harrison had finally talked him out of skulking around the restaurant, handgun shoved in his waistband for all to see, driving away what little business tromped in as of late. So he relented, eventually after some heated give and take, but only if both weapons stayed on the premises, back office in a liquor cabinet. Unlocked, just in case those bogeymen stormed the palace.

That particular ominous scenario wasn't beyond the realm of possibility, he knew. Indeed, if he was honest with himself, it was perhaps the reason he'd let Tina Waylan go. Despite the smoke screen about lack of customers, he knew he'd be unable to live with himself if he bore witness to one more single drop of innocent blood shed. Since the truth was both fearfully and jealously guarded from customers, employees and local acquaintances, not to mention lurking shadow men, he figured their new lives were pretty much a charade, albeit a most dangerous game. Bottom line, he could only hope the whole aim and goal of hiding in the open, under their very noses, provided armor enough against dark knowledge and bogeymen. No one but he and his partner knew the hazardous, potentially lethal course they ran if the shadows decided they would no longer be held hostage by the leverage.

A little more than fourteen months ago they'd both walked out on the Orion Project. Not something anyone—civilian labor, nuclear physicist, aerospace engineer or intelligence operative—did without being reminded of the dotted line they signed on their contract the day they landed at Nellis. Subsequent check-ups followed any termination or retirement, hardmen in blacksuits sometimes even paying a former employee a personal visit in the dead of night. Then there was the usual phone tapping, bugs planted, the whole nine yards of surveillance that might leave a man wondering if he could even trust his own wife and children. On that score he was grateful, if nothing else, there was no bloodline, content to some degree to languish in restless-bachelor status.

There was guilt enough already to spin off on every point of the compass.

And if an ex-employee thought it might be slick to write a book or woo Geraldo with fantastic tales of what went on at a base so classified it wasn't named, numbered or even listed as a black project at the Pentagon? Talk about ultimate reprisal, the average citizen would never believe the extreme remedy for silencing loose tongues. It was something any civilian would have sworn could only happen in Red China or some Third World backwater where anarchy and wholesale slaughter was the rule and not the exception. But he knew the stark truth, an eyewitness that Big Brother did in fact have a license to kill those who were liabilities to national security. Like those associated with the project who found they weren't able to control loose lips. Such as trespassers who had been clearly warned by the posted signs authorizing the use of deadly force.

No formal resignation had been involved that day, but words of warning had been issued from the other side. Harrison had to wonder right then if it had been foolish to let them know on the way out the door exactly what he was holding on to, just in case one of them had a strange fatal accident in the days to come. Or even if they started finding hardmen sitting at the bar, nursing a soda for hours on end, crew cuts who didn't know much more conversation than monosyllabic grunts. The kind of guys he'd seen march two college kids, not much older than twenty, out into the desert for seeing something they shouldn't have—

Too late now to cry over the spilled blood of the innocent.

Quitting as special operatives for a classified arm of the National Security Agency wasn't something either one of them had done on a whim or in hopes of following some rainbow to the horizon of another career. They might have pooled some of their money, landing the restaurant, starting over, so to speak, but the way things stood—grimly aware of who and what they'd turned their backs on—they had agreed the best place to hide was right out in the open. Something public, with folks usually hanging around, local regulars who came in, might miss one of them and sound the alarm if there was a strange and sudden disappearance by one or both proprietors.

Occasionally he thought about someplace far away. Tahiti or Nepal, for instance. But it wouldn't have mattered anyway, he knew, if they'd vanished to some remote corner of the world. They could hole up on top of the Himalayas and damn near touching the stars, or live on the run, changing cities, hotels and identities as easily as normal folks changed clothes. Special Security—which he'd come to think of as Big Brother's SS—would track them down sooner rather than later, and it didn't matter if it was the Ramada or the Sudan. The way his partner had been acting lately, Harrison started wondering if the man knew something he didn't about any renewed clandestine surveillance effort.

Harrison dumped the plastic bag in the back of the pickup truck, a bottle rattling as it landed on the bed. He watched as his partner flinched at the noise as if it were a rifle shot. "I liked you better when you were hitting on the hired help."

"I liked myself better then, too. Easier to deal with threats of lawyers and harassment suits than to come here every night and wonder..."

He let it trail, but Harrison knew the line of thinking so well he could almost hear the cryptic dialogue in the man's head. "It would have happened by now."

The cigar tip winked back. "Wish I shared your confidence. I didn't mention this, Marty, but they've been following me around the last week. Out in the open, not caring if I knew I was watched. The usual black van, tinted windows so you can't see them. No plates, sometimes I find them outside the house, first thing in the morning like they've been sitting there all night. Even have my wife telling me her cell phone's making all these strange clicking noises soon as she gets on it. Strikes me as a little more than the standard drill when one of us drops out. Y'know, I've been thinking, one call and we can end it. Just give it to them.''

"And end up like a couple of our former colleagues?''

"You're talking about Lawler.''

"And Walters. How many brand-new cars you ever heard of have their brakes go out? How many times can one of us get wrapped around a telephone pole at eighty?''

"My whole point.''

"They murdered two kids that we know of. I know of at least six other suspicious deaths.''

"Which you have documented. Not really much by way of evidence, if you ask me. And who outside of us or them would believe it anyway?''

"It's enough to keep me thinking I can go to sleep tonight and wake up tomorrow. Don't forget, I also have a lot more on them than executions of 'government employees.' ''

"The foreign-subcontractor angle?''

"Make the problems they've had at Los Alamos like Chernobyl to a flick of a cigarette lighter.''

"You at least reconsider the gun thing? This late at night, out here in the middle of nowhere. Knowing.''

"I'll think about it. But, if I agree, only when everyone else has gone home.''

He couldn't be sure, wrapped as the man was by the dark, but he thought his partner was nodding in agreement. The cry of alarm, though, with the cigar tumbling for the ground, was unmistakable, alerting Harrison to some danger right behind. He whipped around, spotted the two black shapes at the edge of the building. Armed, nothing but the whites of their eyes shining at them from the gloom, making him think they had materialized out of thin air.

"Appreciate that little piece of information," Harrison heard the one with the pistol say. "Inside, gentlemen. Angelo first. Get your ass in gear back there."

For a moment Harrison was sure his partner was going to flee into the night, taking a step in the other direction, then the hardmen in black with the shotgun warned, "Run, fatso, and I have no problem shooting you down like a dog. You know what we want, ladies, so let's make this nice and easy for everybody concerned."

Heart racing, Harrison waited as his beefy partner waddled past, what felt like agonizing minutes later. Even with the threatening edge in his voice, the gunner made it sound as if there was hope. Hand it over, life would go on, no harm.

Or so he desperately wanted to believe, but Harrison knew better, and his worst fear was confirmed moments later when he trailed Angelo through the screen door. They weren't two steps into the kitchen, and Davie the cook—married with children and recent transplant from Denver—froze over a rack near the dishwasher, eyes going wide at the sight of two armed men in ski masks. Davie was mouthing what looked to Harrison like "What the hell?" when he heard the chug. Angelo made a strangled noise, jumping at the sound, but the bullet whispered past his point march and drilled a ragged hole between Davie's eyes.

THE FIREWATER DID next to nothing to smooth out the jagged edges. Sorry truth was, it seemed to only jack up the fear, paranoia and agitation he felt coiling like a rattler, and tighter by the second in his chest. Then he decided any mounting dark mood, any snake in his belly had little actually to do with the raw electric spark of meth still snapping in his blood. Hell, no, it was something about the dark guy, sitting there in heavy silence, locked in grim thought about something. Waiting? Plotting? He saw the citizen working on his prime rib but acting as if he didn't care one way or the other about eating, while having glanced, not once or twice, but three times out the window. Searching for what? Or who out there?

Rhonda's waffling—what hit him as bizarre and infuriating behavior, chick ducking any questions put to her about their business—also stoked the recharged mean streak inside, until he found his head buzzing with a hornet's nest of bad images and dire thoughts. For one thing, why the hell was she having so much trouble looking him in the eye? Why was the dark man burning up pictures of cops and guns and badges, stuck in his face, and with near lifelike crystal clarity? Why was he all of a sudden hearing the judge's gavel pounding and seeing iron bars slamming before his eyes? Why was he imagining, worst of all, the whole damn booth itself was one giant Old Sparky, set to fry his bacon? And just what the hell was going on back there now in the kitchen? Sounded like the roof was coming down in chunks, some heavy crashing thud, there then gone, which had his butt jump a couple inches off the seat.

It was all Dean could do to keep his voice lowered, as he pinned Rhonda with an angry eye and edged close to her face. "I don't think I like what I'm hearing, Rhonda. I ride straight here from Reno, pretty much at your beck and call, bat out of hell, Willie telling me the whole week how you been whining about the old man. You telling me you have the envelope with half the bread in your car ready, and now you're sitting there, talking at me how maybe you should just maybe divorce the guy."

She gnawed on her cigarette, nervous eyes darting away from his face. "Okay, so maybe I'm having second thoughts."

"Doesn't sound like you, not knowing what you want."

"He hasn't been bad to me, or cheated, or anything like that."

"Hooray for Mr. Civilized."

"You don't understand."

"Damn right, I don't. How much you say you brought?"

"Half."

Three grand, way short of his normal asking price of ten. But they'd agreed already to price over the phone, coding it, of course, in lingo that any listening ears couldn't make sense of or use in a courtroom. Besides, it was something of a favor to Willie. Now this, bitch not knowing whether to crap or get off the seat, jerking his chain, talking lawyers, divorce. Hardly any real solution he could see.

"It's like this, baby, I'm here now. You got it, you give it up, let me take care of business. Lot cleaner and more easy than giving some shyster a fat cut. You feel some guilt after, go to church. I mean, what the hell happened to you, anyway? This ain't the tough chick I remember. Yeah, what," he said, when she flashed a sulky look. "Gonna tell me you got too much to lose, you've changed, all that crap. I don't buy it. I want an answer now. Yes or no."

"WE'RE IN. One chef du jour down, tonight's special in the oven."

Braxton was hugging the south wall, just beside the door, when the quiet confirmation from Burton sounded over the com link. From his position he couldn't see who was what or where, angled as he was, downrange from the window. If the puke had gotten it wrong, he would enjoy kneecapping or castrating the guy with an Uzi burst. Maybe both, what the hell.

Business first, pleasure later.

He keyed the button on his com link, Uzi coming up in the free hand. "Three count, then go, starting now."

One.

Braxton grasped the doorknob, twisted. On two, he found a sudden stroke of luck, a trump card to use on any wanna-be heroes, headed right his way.

Three, and he was through the door, rolling hard

and fast, bringing up the subgun's muzzle to draw a bead on the woman's face.

CITIZEN TRAFFIC was veering all over the restaurant, it seemed, headed this way and that, boiling up yet more rage, cracking further apart what little composure he grasped. Plunged by possible eavesdroppers into steaming quiet, Dean was forced to ride it out until the moving sets of ears passed. He saw mom following kids for the door, not meeting the one last approving eye he shot her breasts. Then the giddy lizard, blowing into the smoking section, torn between showing Windbreaker more raging hormones and glaring back at the bald citizen, the guy over there standing now, calling out he was set to leave, cash in hand. Edgy. Another guy in there with something to hide?

Dean scowled away from the waitress, was glancing toward mom and brood when he caught the terror on the woman's face, saw her freeze in her tracks, reining in the kids.

Next he saw the two guys in black ski masks and guns marching out the hostages. What the hell was this? A robbery? A sting?

Whatever was going down, something exploded in Dean's brain, a bellow of pure fury in his head, unleashing adrenaline, fear and screw the world, as a primal howl of murder ripped next from his mouth. He heard some distant voice right behind shouting, "Freeze!"

Screw that. He was walking out of there, blast his way out or get killed in the mayhem.

A microsecond permitting, he would have cursed Rhonda, slapped her silly, a lightning flash of thought telling him he'd been duped somehow, set up.

Wildman Dean bolted to his feet, hauled out the .44 Magnum pistol and went for broke. Whatever was happening, if he was checking out he determined to see as many folks as possible riding the coaster with him on the way to the other side.

IT WENT TO HELL in the time it took to blink, look up and know with utter grim futility it was too late to react, make a stand.

It was way past any immediate hope to attempt a thwarting counterattack, for damn sure, or to sit there—if he was even so inclined to curse his luck—and ponder the racket he'd just heard from the kitchen, having sounded to his experienced ears like the heavy thud of a falling body. Gone far too south, also, to decide, one way or another on a course of action, what that chugging he'd barely made out three heartbeats ago really meant.

All hell broke loose, and for the first time in a long dark age the Executioner found he was unable to do a damn thing to stop it from happening.

They came charging in, four gunmen in black, eyes wild and searching through the slits of their ski masks, their moves and direction clearly mapped out and well-planned, weighed and measured going in. Then he spared a brief bitter thought for Weed, believing the guy had been a scout, casing the joint, fixing the numbers, positioning. Maybe having read into who was what, gone off to warn the hitters who was an obvious problem, and who could be grabbed up as human armor.

Two raced through the front door, while two more gunners rolled out the kitchen doorway. It was done with such clockwork military precision, split-second timing as they converged to take down the dining room, that Bolan knew they were pros of some trained and lethal variety, and not junkie desert rats or felons on the fly looking to stick the place up for a handful of cash.

Two factors kept the soldier at bay, restrained his killing play even as he stood and his hand delved inside his jacket. First, his waitress had raised her hands on initial sight of the armed ski masks, shimmied about on legs looking set to fold. Stark terror on her face, the woman teetered sideways in some slow-mo weird dance step that put her right in any line of fire Bolan might hit the attackers with and end it all before it got started. Next, but hardly least of considerations, he saw the Uzi stuck right off the bat in the mother's face. All around it was either bad luck, grim fate or rotten circumstance, but they seized the moment, had the edge, with a gunner hollering at Bolan, "If I see a gun, mom and kids are the first to go!"

The threat was backed up in the next eye blink as one of the two-man back-door team peeled off, two quick steps that found him right behind the woman and children, a combat shotgun out of Bolan's view but aimed, he could well guess, at their backs. Shotgun had secured a perfect human shield.

The one-percenter had other ideas, and the shooting started in blood earnest.

For reasons Bolan could only guess, the biker—panic or mindless rage driving him to a suicide stand—was cursing and roaring from the first look at the hardmen. He was clearly hell-bent on saving only his own rotten carcass, and Bolan heard himself cursing the bastard. Across the room, just as the biker was up and swinging the .44 Magnum pistol into play, Bolan heard the businessman launch into hysterical pleading, adding yet more angry decibels to the chaos and gunfire.

"No! Listen, I have money in the car, I'll give it all back you want! I'll work it out...."

A wailing—was that guilt Bolan detected somewhere in the voice?—all but muted as the big .44 boomed, but the gunner with the AR-15 already had the biker beaten to the draw. The first line of lead tumblers tore into the one-percenter's vest, his companion screaming next, hit in the face with crimson rain. He couldn't say one hundred percent how it happened, as he noted how Uzi fastened a cold stare his way, heard the subgunner bark another warning when Bolan's hand twitched an inch or so deeper inside the windbreaker—so close but so far away—but some indiscriminate or hasty shooting swept errant rounds past the biker. It was little more than a flashing glimpse, but Bolan caught the biker's lady friend slammed around in the booth as if she were wired to twenty thousand volts.

Bolan froze. He held his ground as the biker kept

coming, roaring at the attackers as he pounded out wild Magnum thunder. The AR-15 kept chopping him up, driving him, spinning, out into the room. Something in the eyes behind the ski mask of Uzi warned Bolan the curtain was only just going up on this psycho show.

CHAPTER FOUR

Robert Barklin couldn't—no, he *didn't* want to—believe it was happening. And to him, at a time when he was just about to turn the corner, move on, find the missing pieces that he was on the verge of pulling together, show a complete man for a scornful world at large to see.

It was an outrage, no mistaking, but somehow it all now struck him as fate about to come full vicious circle, all the bitter fruit of, at best, a mediocre, floundering existence, finally tasted, chewed and shoved all the way down his throat.

From cradle to grave, it was all gall and regret.

Bullied, in that distant youth that he suddenly yearned for, by God, as he saw a chubby cherub with thick eyeglasses. Funny how, or so they said, a man's life did flash before his eyes, a freeze frame held up before him when he faced down his moment of utter personal doom, a silent judgment before he was sent, kicking and screaming, into the abyss. So many foolish dreams ago, grabbing for that academic brass ring had seemed far safer and made more sense to him than chasing the fleeting macho glory of sports. Old habits and perspectives, though, meant to shore up lack of self-esteem, keep the world at a safe distance, died hard, but they had carried him onward and what looked like upward. Far safer and easier on the ego to spend life avoiding conflict and confrontation, searching out the path of least resistance.

Society dictated might made right, but he had always opted to let a diplomatic tongue steer the course around any unpleasant encounter that might end with no worse than the rare sharp verbal exchange. He had always treated everyone, from wives to coworkers to clients, with a mild-mannered deference he had passed off as civility and respect. Even back in Chicago, he would rather cross the street to the other side, head bowed and eyes averted, if young toughs came bouncing his way, always avoiding unfamiliar or intimidating human contact meant to do him bodily harm. Good citizen he had been—up to now—he obeyed every law to the letter, proud he'd never seen the inside of a courtroom, not even a traffic ticket on the books. He didn't gamble, smoke, use drugs or frequent bars, indulge those vices he'd seen flush careers and marriages of several colleagues and acquaintances down the toilet. Moderation and minding his own business was simply the way of the wise in his mind.

Mr. Clean? Or had he simply lacked a testicular fortitude he had always admired in others from a safe and envious distance? Strange, he thought, how all this didn't have to happen, how he believed he really didn't belong there.

It was a mistake; the gods were indeed mad. Or were they?

For instance, any exposure to violence, to the real and ugly world of everyday men and women, had always been confined to the evening news, over dinner and a glass of red wine, while Rather or Brokaw showed America war zones and unimaginable suffering in places like Beirut or Belfast, Sudan or South Central L.A., where no one in his right mind, a decent life to live, or money to burn would go to anyway, by his reckoning. Places where abject poverty and desperation, he could only surmise, could only breed rampant crime and mindless violence. Indeed, that other side of the tracks where bad things always happened to the other guy.

Or so he always believed, until now.

Call it a sick fluke of fate, plain bad luck or rotten coincidence, but there he was, smack in the midst of his own living nightmare. And in a no-man's desolation of Nevada, of all places, where human contact was scattered so wide and far Uncle Sam could blast nukes in test sites all over the state. It struck him now as way beyond unbelievable, he thought, it was injustice leaning toward the obscene.

A minute or so away from walking out the door, safe and snug in his car and on his way to paradise, and they had come in out of nowhere, armed with enough weapons, he guessed, to field a small army of hoodlums. And guys he'd never seen, much less cared about, were shooting up the place, threatening his life and limb with bullets zipping all around. Despite the fact he could get nailed by a wild shot, he found he was too terrified to move anything other than his mouth.

Barklin watched as the biker was shot up, twitching his way, a slapped-around grizzled puppet, blood flying everywhere—the woman behind him looking chewed up to red ribbons—with the biggest and loudest handgun he could ever imagine exploding rounds like rolling peals of thunder. The chaos, noise and watching violent death in full living color cleaved his senses, did a tap dance all the way to his sphincter.

So far the only lead blazing from the black-garbed foursome was eating up the biker. Maybe they weren't interested in him after all, Barklin thought. He was thinking how he had endured too much to see the dream flee him now, due to circumstances beyond his control, when it happened.

One second he was on the verge of forming a picture of his lush tropical paradise, a mental dreamland just to help him pull it together and keep hope alive, and the next thing he knew that massive handgun came jerking around to aim his way, pointed right at his face. It was obscene, he thought, the way the biker's executioner kept pouring out the lead, slicing him up, a slab of human beef to be butchered into a thousand pieces. The standing slaughter had forced the biker, Barklin realized next and way too late, to spin his direction, with death spasms causing the biker to keep on squeezing the trigger. Barklin saw the flame, heard the thunder. He thought how was it all so unjust, so close yet so far away from paradise.

For less than a heartbeat, in some bizarre freeze frame, he imagined he could almost see the bullet with his name on it, burning through the air, screaming for his face.

So wrong, so unjust. Before he could shriek outrage, the lights were punched out.

COLLINS NEARLY LEAPED through the roof at the first sound of gunfire. It was all thunder and the incessant staccato chatter of an assault rifle down there, with screaming and shouting, but voices drowned by what he imagined was some sort of all-out battle raging in the dining room. And it was all he could manage just to keep his bowels in check, certain he was now a coconspirator to mass murder. Did they execute murderers in this state? he wondered. He didn't think he was about to hang around long enough to find out.

Just what the hell had gone wrong? Gunfire erupting, only seconds after they went through the front door. Wait a second, wondering next if it was the intent by the four strangers with no names all along to roll right in, shoot everyone on sight? If so, why? A bone to pick with the owners? Again, he wondered that if they weren't there to rob the place of money, then what precisely were they after? If not cash, well, what manner of idiot did anything these days unless there was money involved? Maybe the cop or the biker had put up a fight, drawn iron and started blasting first? He couldn't say, couldn't see inside the window from his angle, but he wasn't going to stick around much longer. He didn't need answers that bad.

All that racket from inside the restaurant, blowing off the walls and roof from the sounds of it, was sure to get heard, and he didn't care if the interstate or the nearest living soul was miles away, dead drunk or indifferent. Hadn't he once heard how sound traveled far and easy in the desert? But who would prove the lesser of two evils, whether he stayed or bolted? Four nameless strangers or the cops?

Collins edged up between the seats, looked at the keys dangling from the ignition. Their stupidity, he decided, for leaving him with the option to stay put or ride on. Only if he fled, left them stranded, what then? Ditch the van? Go back to the ranch? Crawl into a hole and pull the rug over his head? Hope they didn't come gunning for him, all's forgiven, his nerves understandable given the circumstances? Would he run for the next town? The next state?

Suddenly he started thinking of Mexico, then decided to hang tight, ride out the dread and anxiety another minute or so, see who walked out the door. If his ride came out, he figured it would look good that he'd kept the faith.

THE SOLDIER SAW it coming, reacted in the only way he knew. Even though the biker was absorbing the blanket of scything lead, Bolan wasn't about to stand his ground, risking it to end up like the one-percenter's acquaintance now stretched out on the floor. Positioned to save at least one innocent life right away, he bulled into his waitress, sent them tumbling in a heap to the floor, away from any potential reckless line of fire. A scream echoed for a brief second, pricking his ears from a distant point across the main room, he judged, following a final Magnum roar.

"On your feet, let me see your hands!"

It was over, for the moment. New demands getting issued. What next?

Bolan felt the waitress shudder beneath the cover of his own weight, looked over just as the crimson sack hammered the floor. First the soldier took into grim account that mother and children were unscathed, the only sign they were worse for wear the obvious shock and terror etched on their faces. Her whole body was trembling as she mashed her sons' faces to her mid-section, Shotgun rising up from behind his human shields. Considering what had just happened, the soldier found she was holding up, and not coming apart in hysterics or flinging pleas to be spared, set free.

No, the lady had guts, and she knew they were lucky, grateful they were still alive. But for how long? Bolan wondered. Was it just a stay of execution? An inevitable course already determined for them by the four gunmen? Well, the killing had begun, and if he was any judge of character, Bolan suspected they couldn't afford to leave behind any witnesses at that point. It was something he saw in the eyes, the cold, pitiless depths betraying the inner soul of the cannibal, warning him the ski masks were merely for show, meant solely to provide a ray of false hope.

He bit down the curse, taking in the gunmen from ground level, going from each set of eyes to the next. They studied him, curious or fearful. Or simply waiting to see what he might do? All right, good enough, he determined. A chance. The cosmic dice may have rolled, crapping him out the first time, with Bolan unable to recall any moment when he'd felt so at the mercy of a dark force, innocent lives hanging in the balance, but they had not gunned him down yet.

The Executioner determined right then he would prove that to be a fatal error in their judgment.

The biker's unfortunate lady friend wasn't the only casualty, he next discovered. Bolan was standing, aware both the Uzi and the assault rifle were trained on him, when he spotted the body across the room. Whoever the man in the white shirt had been, he'd gotten tagged, frozen in place, most likely, when the shooting started. A running smear of blood, with larger gobs glued to the wall above the table, told Bolan the Magnum round had cored him through the brain. Quick and messy, but dead was dead. Belly up, he'd dropped square on the table of his last supper, arms draped out and down in some bizarre horizontal crucifixion.

The Executioner helped the waitress stand. No time to comfort her, quell her fears. He had all the living innocent to worry about from there on.

Whoever the unfortunate lady on the floor was, whatever her business with the biker, Bolan heard her gasping for air, clinging to a last breath. He took a step in her direction when Uzi snarled, "Forget her."

"I can help her," Bolan said.

"God...oh, dear, God..."

"She's beyond help," Uzi growled.

And in the next moment, the soldier saw how right that was, as he watched the light fade from her eyes.

"I'LL GIVE YOU what you want, but let the rest of these people walk out of here first."

It was worth a try, he figured, get a read on where things stood from there on, if there was any hope at all one or all of them could walk away breathing. One search of the eyes of the gunner holding the Uzi, and he knew it was a futile demand. He didn't recognize the voice, aware he didn't know the man behind the mask. But he knew the look, the same cold, lifeless eyes recalled that day when two American citizens were dragged out into the desert.

Déjà vu. Different time and place, but it was happening again. Because of him, or the lack of guts he'd shown that afternoon, more innocent people were going to die. In the name, no less, of national security.

Harrison looked at Tina and her sons, felt his mouth moving, his heart thumping with ache. He wanted to tell her how sorry he was, hang in there, it was going to be all right, when Uzi started barking out the orders. He told the big guy to unzip his jacket, use only his left hand to shake it off. Checking on his partner, Harrison thought the man was going to plead it out, eyes frantic, darting all over the ski masks. Angelo was set to crack.

"Everyone but the big guy, move out into the center of the main room. Keep all of your hands in the air. Stop when I tell you to. Everyone take it easy, it's going to be just fine. The biker was stupid, and accidents happen.''

Once Betty, Tina and boys were ushered into the center of the main dining room, flanked by Shotgun and Glock, Harrison was sure he was going to vomit, guilt churning a storm of bile in his gut, bracing him for the massacre. If that happened, there was nothing he could do, he knew, but watch, and wait for the bullets to soon tear into him.

''Give it to them, Marty.''

''Shut up, Angelo.''

His partner, losing it some more, while the big man dropped his jacket on the floor, displaying a holstered side arm, the center of everyone's attention.

''Left hand, cowboy. Use your thumb and trigger finger. Remove the piece, drop it, nice and gentle, and kick it toward me.''

Harrison saw something in the man's eyes that gave him a dash of hope. Whoever, whatever he was, it was clear he'd been down dark roads, knew by way of hard earning the kind of courage it took to come out the other side. The big man hadn't panicked or tried to hero his way through it, resorting to gunplay that might endanger innocent lives. Small hope, but it was all Harrison could find, something to cling to. The dark stranger was biding his time, searching for any opening where he could strike.

With their human chess pieces set to their liking, the big man's gun kicked and scooped up, Harrison watched as Uzi stepped around the narrow partition. A few steps closer, Uzi then stopping.

Contempt burned into Uzi's eyes. "So, here we are. Your new lives look to be treating you two pretty good since you quit the Agency. Big shots, cut your slice of the pie, restaurant owners, local celebrities, way they hear it at Special Security. Looking down on all us little people working hard for Uncle Sam, trying to keep America free and safe. Hey, Angelo, you look like you're ready to take a dump in your pants." Uzi laughed. "You don't know me, but I know who you are, read the whole file on you. Same flabby puke, same cheat, thief and liar, the way I've heard it. Doesn't matter if you work for Big Brother or hold on to the coattails of your buddy here. Let's just say I plain don't like you. Let's just say I need another example, show all these good people and your partner here how serious my business is."

The smile stretched the fabric around the slash of Uzi's mouth. The look and tone changed, reaching new heights of menace. This was where, Harrison was sure, the end would start.

"Marty, give it to them! For God's sake…"

"They're going to kill us either way."

"Maybe, maybe not. You care to take a chance? You willing to give up your buddy, Marty? Angelo, why don't you tell us where it is, save yourself. One chance. Two seconds."

"I'm the only one who knows where it is," Harrison said. "What I told you before. Let everyone here walk first."

Stretched seconds, as Uzi seemed to think about something, then nodded at the gunman with the Glock.

"I hate to waste precious ammo on a sack of feces like you, Angelo," Uzi said. "Especially with government cutbacks on the military budget, and all."

The man with the Glock took a few casual steps forward. All intent deadly plain now, his partner roared out his terror as the sound-suppressed muzzle was dropped square between his eyes.

CHAPTER FIVE

They kept their distance, AR-15 the closest, but still a good fifteen feet or so away. It might as well have been a mile from where Bolan stood.

Or the dark side of the moon.

Shotgun had claimed his Beretta, which had vanished somewhere in the waistband in the back of his black combat fatigues. AR-15 had just cracked home a fresh clip, cocked and locked, ready, even looking itchy for the next round of slaughter to begin. A closer scrutiny now of the gunners, and Bolan noted the skinny wire of com links in place. Throat mikes that had been nearly invisible at first glance, due to the initial burst of chaos and murder, were hung beside the slash of their mouths. Professionals, all around, they kept weapons poised to fire, low, by the hip. Any sudden lunge or quick kick-out meant to slash a weapon from their hands would prove nothing more, the soldier knew, than fantasy ending in fatality. That kind of nonsense always worked out there in Hollywood, but this was reality, with no second takes.

They hadn't bothered with a thorough frisk, either, but Bolan was surmising the hard scrutiny he'd already received, head to toe, had to have satisfied them the Beretta was the only weapon on his person. Unfortunately they were right, with no point in getting too close to a tiger, even he was unarmed.

Since, from the outset, it had been just some R and R cruise, Bolan hadn't seen the necessity to bring his big .44 Magnum Desert Eagle backup piece along for a sit-down dinner. Not even a sheathed blade around the ankle. Unless he did something, and quick...

The screams snapped Bolan's grim attention to the portly mass writhing on the floor near the bar, a bloody hand clutching the mangled foot. At the last instant before squeezing the Glock's trigger, the gunner had dropped his aim toward the floor. But agony, Bolan suspected, would soon become the least of anybody's problems. Angelo was probably selected as the first example, albeit on a sadistic whim by Uzi. In short order, Uzi would probably run down the list of victims, one by one, until whatever they'd come there to take was coughed up. It was simply a question of who was chosen next.

Whatever Uzi's problem with Angelo, Bolan couldn't say. It could have boiled down to simple jealousy and resentment, personal or professional, the way Uzi was swimming around in the guy's terror and pain, the gunner's eyes lit up with a sadistic joy. Not that any bone to pick or personal judgment of Angelo's character mattered in the final analysis, considering the innocent were marked for execution.

Whoever the men in black were, they wanted something from those two men Bolan believed were the owners, and it wasn't show me the money. Which told him little, but left him venturing a guess. The two men under the gun didn't strike him as criminals on the lam, two guys who had stuck it to four comrades, left them twisting in the wind on some heist or drug deal, absconding with the lion's share. Unless he missed his guess, judging the cold, methodical, military approach they'd used to take the place down and get everyone under control, Bolan figured he was in the middle of some intelligence scheme gone awry. Apparently, the men in black were also there to even up a score, or leave behind a grim lesson for others they could end up like Angelo.

Bolan could have stood there and asked a dozen questions for which no answer was ready and clear. Survival was far more important right then than knowing the truth. He needed to act, soon, but they were far from careless, much less willing to present him an opening where he could strike.

The women were pleading with Uzi to spare Angelo any more grief. Threatening more torture, Uzi laughed, flinging back pleas for mercy on his behalf. "It's only a foot, girls, he's got another one. It could be worse— something I understand Angelo was wagging around here a while back and had some husband up in arms."

"What now?" the waitress wanted to know, huddled close to the mother and children. "You going to kill him? Then kill all of us?"

"That's not my call, honey. Well, Marty? One more chance."

"Keep the three of us," Bolan called out to Uzi,

keeping his hands in plain sight. "Let the women and children walk. They can't possibly identify you."

Harrison looked hopeful, someone taking charge, in his corner. "He's right. Give a little, I'll give you the whole package. They have nothing to do with any of this."

Uzi grinned, prepared, Bolan guessed, to show off more of his sadistic streak. Indeed, the bastard was enjoying it all—their fear, the power of life and death at his command. Bolan knew he was in the presence of pure evil.

"Did I miss something here, people? I thought the side holding the guns was in the position to make all the demands?" Uzi barked. "The package, Marty. Now!"

Bolan knew another round of violence was coming. If they turned on the women and children, he would have no choice but to try. Doing something, even if it meant he went down in the attempt from a hail of lead and buckshot, was far preferable to standing by while the innocent were slaughtered. With daring, luck and speed, he might reach the AR-15 in a flying leap, go for broke.

Harrison shook his head. "Negative."

Uzi nodded at Glock, said, "Do it." And Angelo bellowed in terror, throwing out his hands as if they would shield him from certain death.

BRAXTON WAS GROWING tired of the waiting game. He barely watched or enjoyed the sight of Angelo getting checked out. He would have expected such a pathetic display from one of the women or kids, only they showed the balls, holding on, silently clinging to hope. He looked away just as Burton rolled right up to the guy, his teammate as cold as ice, squeezing off the Glock. A new round of screams and outrage erupted from the waitress as, unable to resist a last glance, he saw Angelo's head cracked open, blood and gore spattering the bar front.

"Damn you."

Braxton looked at Harrison, was forced to readjust his aim, swinging the Uzi a few inches across his body as the guy took a step his way. "Why are you making this so difficult, Marty? It's just a disk."

He then noted the big guy in the windbreaker had a new head of steam. The puke had been right about those eyes. They'd seen death, and lots of it, many distant battlefields that maybe still haunted, but had forged a warrior. If the eyes were the window to the soul, Braxton could well believe he was staring at a badass he'd have been proud to know, want to proclaim as part of his team. Damn shame this was just business. It would end up a sorry waste of life where the big guy was concerned. Whoever he really was, Braxton knew a seasoned killer, a number-one professional when he saw one. Beyond the stance, though, which spoke volumes about what the big guy might do to him if he could just get back the Beretta, Braxton wasn't sure how to read him. Guts all the way, brass balls, that much was clear. The way he looked at the women and kids, it hit Braxton as odd to the point of foolishness the big guy acted more concerned about them than having any real regard for his own safety. Braxton could hardly trust any man who walked around with noble ideas or chivalrous virtue. It was time to up the stakes.

"Maybe you're right, Marty. Maybe I can make one small concession."

BOLAN WAITED for the perverse punch line. It had gone way too far for any compromise on their part. The worst was just around the corner. It was a venom he could smell in the air.

Uzi proved the suspected terminal point with his next words, telling Shotgun, "Our business is with Marty. The big guy, the women and kids don't need to stand around out here. Take them back in the kitchen, but the big guy trailing the pack."

This was it, the Executioner knew. They were being herded up, human cattle for the slaughter, about to be marched into the kitchen, made to stretch out, face-down while Uzi turned the screws on Marty. And when Marty gave up whatever Uzi wanted? The kitchen, he knew, would become a slaughterhouse. Bolan could sense their evil intent mount like a scorching flame, believed he could clearly read the bottom line in both Uzi's look and tone.

"Let's move it, people. I don't have all night."

SHE HEARD ONE or both boys quietly calling to her, but the terror and shock had such a viselike grip on her heart and voice, she could only squeeze them tighter to her body. What words of comfort could she issue anyway? Even beyond this night, how could she ever hope to possibly erase the memories from her sons, the images of cold-blooded murder? That was assuming they were allowed to live.

They were moving ahead, her sons in her arms, Betty first, arms shaking like leaves in the rain. She looked over her shoulder, when something wanted to strike hope in her heart, catching the dark stranger's eye as he was urged to walk by the one with the shotgun. She wanted to stand there, decide what it was she'd caught in his look, but Shotgun was growling at her to keep moving.

"It's going to be all right. Just do what they want." It sounded ridiculous, her own voice of feeble encouragement in her ears, but she felt compelled to tell them something, keep them strong, that it was all going to work itself out somehow. She then discovered, beyond the furious pounding of her heart in her ears, how proud she was of both her sons. No screaming or crying on their part. She suddenly thought of them as little men, forced to grow up overnight, perhaps wondering about man's inhumanity to man. Sure, glancing at their faces, they looked worried to her, just the same, but she spotted in their eyes an innocent hope. They would walk away together, their expressions silently telling her they loved her, that their lives would go on somehow beyond this horror.

Brave little guys, she thought, fighting back the hot tears.

She knew better, suspecting the worst once all of them were in the kitchen. It made her sick with outrage. If they could so easily gun down two men, what would stop them from killing the rest of them? They were witnesses to murder, after all, those cold and lifeless stares warning her of everything she needed to know.

She was moving through the doorway with mummy-type steps, the light striking off the aluminum counters and stainless steel of hanging utensils in a bright glare that seemed to hurt her eyes. The adrenaline burning through her blood, she felt her fear plunged to new agonizing depths. She had to do something, she decided, even if it came down to begging them to spare the lives of her sons. No, she wouldn't let it reach that point of no return. It would prove suicide, but she could turn on the one holding the shotgun, charge him. In the same breath, she could yell at her sons to run while she provided a shield, took death in the face, while hoping only to God they would bolt out the back door, run deep into the desert, aware they could do nothing but try to save themselves. They could grieve later, try to fathom the senselessness of it all. But they would still be alive.

Tina Waylan couldn't be certain of anything right then, how she would manage to force herself to act, even if that meant sacrificing her own life if the ultimate moment of truth arrived.

Was there any hope beyond giving up her own life? She considered, then, what she'd caught in the look that the dark man seemed to level her way, and for her benefit alone. Had he shown her defiance? Anger? Judgment? A silent message to hold on, do nothing?

Keep the faith, don't crumble or do something rash, that he would take care of them? She was wondering about the man when she suddenly heard Betty gasp, found her balking at the sight of Davie's corpse. New terror and revulsion cut through her, bubbling up the nausea, as she saw the dark hole between his eyes, still leaking blood.

And she knew beyond any doubt at that moment, a bitter freeze going through her blood, all of them would be dead within the next few minutes.

Silently, Tina Waylan started to pray.

THEY WERE USHERED into the kitchen, hidden from watching eyes in the dining room, when it happened.

It could have been some divine intervention, but Bolan was hardly of a mind to question why a sudden window of opportunity had opened, showing him the way out. Whatever, it was the only chance he would get to save them all, now or never. All at once, it seemed, several factors thrust open the door for the soldier to bull through.

First, the sight of the dead man paralyzed the waitress, bringing her to an abrupt stop as if her own thoughts screamed at her and confirmed yet again the fate awaiting them all. Blood had pooled away from the hole punched in the man's forehead, spreading from the sprawled form as she slipped in the gore, nearly going down. Bolan sensed the anger from behind, his eyes flickering to the butcher knife on the counter, inches away. Shotgun growled an oath, and Bolan twisted his head enough to find the gunner was aiming the muzzle away from him, bringing it around to bear on the waitress.

Mistake.

The Executioner pivoted, briefly thankful that the gunner was arrogant enough to have cut the gap to his strike within an easy reach, perhaps thinking the sight alone of his shotgun would keep their fear marching them blindly ahead to their doom. One hand shooting out, Bolan shoved the muzzle up and away, while snatching up the knife, adrenaline and experience doing the work as he hauled up the weapon. The shotgun went off, but a dreaded wild killing eruption never happened. Instead, the ceiling light took the full charge of the explosion. The soldier held on to the gun, glass and sparks raining on his head.

It was an awkward angle of attack, thrusting the shotgun down with one hand, as Bolan followed through the half turn, lining up the strike. He went for the throat, knife flying around, and plunged the blade deep past windpipe, the razor's edge slicing past the jugular on its way in, and on. A human cyclone unleashing force enough behind the drive, Bolan felt the blade's point spear through bone, nearly decapitating the guy on its way out his neck for bloody protrusion. Bolan liberated the shotgun from lifeless fingers. One hardman down, dead on his feet, and falling.

"Hit the deck!" Bolan told the group, over his shoulder, then sighted the AR-15 swinging around the corner. He was unfamiliar with some of the basics of the new HK-Benelli but he knew it was an autoloader, nine rounds—now eight—in the tubular magazine.

Gas operated, utter reliability, supposedly, under the worst conditions, it was trumped as the state-of-the-art combat shotgun for the twenty-first century.

Simple enough, he knew, just aim and squeeze the trigger. The Executioner grimly intended to test it to full lethal maximum.

Starting now.

The assault rifle came blazing into the doorway, bullets snapping past his head, clanging off some hung cookware, when Bolan triggered smoke and thunder from the hip. It was a hasty shot, muzzle up and tracking on another surge of adrenaline when he tapped the trigger, but it nailed down the grim job. The spreading blanket of 12-gauge maulers chopped the hardman off at one knee, all but amputating the leg as he went down in a shrieking heap.

Two down, the AR-15 gunner losing his hold on the assault rifle, bleeding out like a burst dam, with shock then death seconds away. The other two assailants didn't know it yet, but Bolan was determined to nail whatever he left of their hides to the wall.

CHAPTER SIX

Jolted by the first roar of the M-1014 shotgun, Braxton looked toward the kitchen doorway, off to his left. Fear expanded icy tentacles through his belly as he wondered what the hell had gone wrong. He found his mind couldn't quite piece together the line of ominous thought that wanted to warn him one of his own was down, taken out by the big guy.

No way. Impossible. Or was it?

They were all seasoned pros, to a man. Shaped and forged by a bloody anvil of killing experience beyond any human comprehension, they were walking firewalls, juggernauts, in fact. Surely they had seized and held the upper hand, going in, beginning to end, dishing out sudden death, no mercy, to show even the toughest hardcase the only hero would be a dead one.

He'd heard Christensen snarling out the order for the sheep to get moving toward their eventual, inevitable slaughter. That had been less than a second ago, right before the combat shotgun blew and shot the perceived reality of his world off its axis. A moment of silence then seemed to freeze the air through the whole joint, followed up by heavy deadweight hammering the floor. He almost called out for Christensen, but his gut told him it was pointless. He recognized that voice, the big guy, the puke's worst cop terror, sounding the order from behind the wall for the others to hit the deck.

So, badass was taking a stand, and the guy sounded far from finished. Dark instinct made Braxton aware he was all of a second and one step away from losing control of the situation altogether. The tables were turned, halfway, at worst, but threatening to pin him to the wall, to be skewered by cold vengeance or impaled by way of nobility driving the guy on to save the little people, if he read him right.

Women and children, first ones off the sinking ship. Fucking hero. Just their luck.

Harrison had to have sensed the shifting tide himself, since he grabbed at the chance to make a charge. With twelve steps gauged between him and the former operative, Braxton figured he had a heartbeat or two to spare to see if Weatherspoon could haul back the advantage. It was time enough—stretching things nonetheless as Harrison cut the gap—to catch Weatherspoon surge for the opening, assault rifle stuttering and leading the way. For all of one eye blink it looked good to Braxton, hope flaring back, his man sticking true to form and training as an unflinching professional under fire.

Then number-two peal of impending doom sounded, and Weatherspoon's leg was almost sheared off just above the knee, a detonating minefield of flesh and gore, all the critical works of veins and major arteries opened like burst faucets. Braxton left him to his misery, the man toppling, wailing out his pain, assault rifle bouncing away as Weatherspoon's brain, he could be sure, tried to register the horror of it all. Weatherspoon was down, history, sure to bleed out. All the guy's misfortune meant to Braxton right then was the discarded AR-15 was simply another spoil of war for the badass to stake claim to.

Braxton knew it was time to get it in high gear. Two were down, Weatherspoon's dismemberment spouting blood enough, an uncapped human fire hydrant, signaling the man was a goner. That left him and Burton.

He only hoped it was enough.

It was simple impulse, rather than a vicious desire to strike out at the nearest visible threat, that caused him to squeeze the Uzi's trigger, aim low. He refrained from delivering an instant killing punch, his 3-round burst stitching Harrison low across the gut. As Harrison went down in a gutted, flopping heap, he waved the Uzi at Burton to move it out and up on the doorway. He had to make a statement himself, figuring Mr. Restaurant Owner and traitor-thief would hold on long enough to give up whatever he clout he stupidly believed he could hide and keep from Special Security.

First the badass.

THE EXECUTIONER BROKE stride as he closed for the doorway, combat shotgun in one hand, leading the way as choice pulverizer. He had already retrieved the Beretta, had a heartbeat at most to check on the women and children before he let it rip on the gunners beyond the door. One look shot to the rear, throwing a nod to indicate they should secure cover on the far side of the counter, and he moved ahead, aware there was no choice but to leave them behind, hope for the best. Beyond the two clear and present dangers on the other side of the wall, Bolan wondered if there could be other hardmen, left outside to secure the perimeter, watching for new arrivals, covering all bases. Common sense, though, told him they would have rushed through the door by now. And Weed didn't strike Bolan as the adventurous sort. No choice left at all, but to crank it up for a clean sweep.

On the way for his fire point at the edge of the doorway he heard the hardman with the mangled leg croaking out his agony. His head was lolling around as if fixed to a rubber band instead of bone and muscle, the whites of his eyes rolling at Bolan's approach, when the Executioner tapped the Beretta's trigger. He pumped one 9 mm hollowpoint round through the temple of the ski mask, as much to put the guy out of his misery and slow dying, as he was motivated by desire and good sense to leave nothing to chance on his blindside.

Bolan stowed the Beretta back into its holster, listened to the silence. He had heard the Uzi stammer, but no bullets came flying his way, gouging divots in the wall or chomping up the door's edge. He wasn't sure what that meant, then, a quick peer around the edge, and he found the man named Marty stretched out, a pool of blood spreading beneath his form. There wasn't a second to indulge wondering over the dead or the dying. Four lives were counting on him to end this nightmare, see them safely on their way.

He was hauling in the assault rifle to beef up the firepower when the shooting resumed. Dropping back, lead chewed up the frame above his head. Bolan knew he had to end it within seconds. Instinct and experience warned him they were already on the move, set to come at him from converging points. He judged the direction he'd made out the chugging of the sound-suppressed Glock. Say roughly nine o'clock out in the dining room, the Uzi spray at twelve. Now, if either hardman stayed put out in the open long enough...

The Executioner went for it, the coughing rounds closing, the Uzi stutter going on, but both weapons went silent the next moment as he went for broke. Bolan had to presume it was tough, even suicidal for them to hold their ground in the wide open when he thrust the combat shotgun around the corner and began spraying the room with 12-gauge eruptions. He stayed low, hugging the cover of the wall, reaching the shotgun out while triggering the autoloader one-handed. The recoil seemed to hold in the vicinity of fifty percent less than any standard pump shotgun he'd ever used, but Bolan still knew less bucking or trick shooting wouldn't possibly nail down this final chore of butcher's work. He fired away, not hoping for an easy tag out of the gate. The idea was to make his adversaries think twice about closing the vise, the plan to see them rabbit for cover while he broke out with the AR-15, in search of an up-close and personal finish.

He was cutting loose the thunderous sweep, left to right, when the third blast rewarded the effort with a howl. Tracking on, blind, he pumped out another two rolling waves of 12-gauge death, the Uzi going silent. Staying put was never an option for Bolan when under enemy fire. He had to gamble giving up his body, and maybe his life, if he was going to nail them, confirm the kills.

It was a glimpse of a ski mask, Uzi darting for cover somewhere in the smoking section, but Bolan was driving onward, hauling in the AR-15, ready with the shotgun in the other hand. He came around the corner, rolling on and off to the right, staying low. He was momentarily shielded from Uzi fire by the low partition dividing the smoking section from the main dining area, when he spotted the hardman rising off the table to ten o'clock. The soldier saw the spray-and-pray had taken Glock down low, judging the gaping shredded red ruins around his groin. The Executioner glimpsed a set of white orbs blazing with hate and agony, the hand shaking as the gunner tried to line up a shot.

Bolan flayed the air with another 12-gauge burst, hitting his target with a bull's-eye charge in the chest. The body was flying back as the soldier veered on for the partition, blasted out another charge on his run for cover, and engineer the ploy. Downrange, wood exploded beside the bobbing masked face. Bolan chucked the spent riot gun away, directed a short burst of autofire toward the far end of the smoking section, the rounds chopping up the top edge of a cushioned booth. He waited until the last critical instant, making sure Uzi spotted him moving on the run down the short barrier leading for the opening to the room. The Uzi was chewing up the wall behind the soldier, as he stayed hidden, a few swift steps taking him back the other way. The way Uzi was hosing the low wall behind his backtrack, Bolan figured the gunner was quagmired in a personal twilight zone of fear. Pro that he was, the man had to be feeling his nerves at that point, alone, eyewitness to at least three of his shooters getting waxed.

The Executioner popped up, the muzzle of the AR-15 fixed on the startled flash as Uzi's eyes darted toward his position. Bolan didn't waste a millisecond to consider the primal fear in those eyes, Uzi aware of the deadly maneuver. Too late. The Executioner held back on the AR-15's trigger, blasting away a portion of the ski mask in dark meaty hunks, gravity next quickly hauling down the deadweight, dropping him out of Bolan's sight. Done.

The Executioner straightened, took in the carnage. It was a slaughterhouse, front and back. He searched the gun smoke, the fluttering bits and pieces of stuffing, satisfied it was over here, when the man named Marty came to life. He was sputtering around blood-flecked lips, when Bolan crouched beside him.

"Thank God...you... Can't feel my legs..."

He was gut-shot, bleeding out fast.

Paralysis from the waist down would be his last worry, the soldier knew, but a part of him still felt compelled to give the man hope. "Hold on," Bolan told him. "I'll get help."

"The others...the kids..."

"The four of them are still among us."

Bolan was about to lay a slew of hanging questions on the man, when he heard the engine gunning to life, pricking his ears from the distance, to the south, he judged. Weed, no doubt, running.

COLLINS COULDN'T SAY what had happened or why. Basic instinct for survival, not to mention an urge to stay free, took over. It was a twin force, it seemed, demanding his muscles move. The double burning combo told him in no uncertain terms he didn't need to know anything more than beating feet and hauling ass.

Run, vanish and don't look back.

His nerves felt like razors slicing him to the bone as he stamped on the gas, flooring it, sending the van lurching ahead, head thrown back with the sudden G-force. He was rolling, gathering momentum at light speed, a rocket ride skimming the earth, streaking him on and away, into the night. It didn't seem fast enough.

"Crazy bastards, I knew it," he cried, a bleating plea to the silent night around him, causing him to briefly wonder why it sounded as if he were imploring some angel to float down and assure him everything would be all right.

It was simply Nevada, he decided, an endless desolation that was home to Area 51, after all, whole towns gone crazy, no less, where the few humans dwelled. All those wild-eyed fanatics sure little gray men were deep-freezed in underground bunkers, claiming all over the place flying saucers jealously guarded by government assassins. All manner of weirdness cropping up, like poisonous fruit, since he'd been there. Messed-up folks, go figure, brains fried by too much sun and whiskey. Strange outside forces getting him mixed up with kooks and killers. Now he was talking to himself, on the edge of insanity, with hallucinations of ghosts and lights in the sky shoved against his will into his thoughts.

"Get a grip, you're going to be fine."

Reality check, realizing he really had no place to go except the commune with the UFO nuts. Food and shelter, at worst, a place to regroup, think out the immediate future. With any luck and a clever move or two, he could find the stash of guns and money he knew was there. One of the fools, showing off or implying it was simply destiny he had arrived among them, his end of line, that he was one of them—in search of the truth. Idiots, pigeons to be plucked, but there was money and guns to be found out there.

Escape first, since beyond this frantic moment nothing was guaranteed.

And, oh, but it wasn't his fault he was bolting, he told himself—the men in black had screwed up. How could he be held accountable for leaving them behind when they—or someone—had gone berserk? That wasn't part of the plan, gentlemen, forcing him to become a coconspirator to a death-row charge. This was their baggage, they had kept him in the dark all along, not the first clue they had in mind mass murder.

He didn't need to walk inside the place to know a bunch of dead bodies were strewed about. And hadn't he held on as long as possible? While listening to all the shooting, the screams of someone in horrific pain adding to whatever horror show had unfolded.

Somebody else's mess. Time to fly.

His only concern was to get as far away from the scene of the crime as possible. Just drive, distance alone would take care of the predicament, steer him, unscathed, from the unknown. He might be a wanted skip, but life in hiding was better than no life at all.

He was flying past the restaurant, heard the startled cry tear from his throat when he looked at the shadow barging through the door. It couldn't be, but the face was framed in enough light...

The cop!

Just catching sight on the flying blur of the rifle in the shadow's hand, as the cop stepped farther into the light, framed in his side glass, and Collins thought the big guy might take a potshot. Evasive maneuvers were called for. It was risky, jerking the wheel an inch to the left then the right, the narrow road leading to the interstate, which was still miles away. The least error in judgment could see him careening off the road, tumbling out into the desert, crushed inside a flopping coffin. He almost lost it, the wheel threatening to wrench itself from his sweaty clutch as rubber squealed and grabbed at a running lip, some edge in the roadside like jagged teeth. It was luck, or maybe fate blessing

him with a second chance, that saw him bound back
onto a level stretch, straightening out the lightning
ride. A look to the side to be sure he was in the clear,
the mirrored image was fading quick. Only Collins
saw the muzzle-flash winking in the glass, the shadow
winging bullets his way. His heart jumped, pounding
with jackhammer fury as he braced for a round to
come blasting through the back window, drilling him
in the head. Another hundred yards somehow, and he
realized the choked sob in his ears for what it signaled.

Relief. He was still in one piece.

Far from clear and free, but Collins clung to the
hope he could vanish, lay low, sort out his next move.
He hit the lights, those twin beams like rays of salvation ahead, paving the way to freedom, and choice.

RATTLING AUTOFIRE echoed after the van, quickly
died as chasing lead whined off asphalt, swallowed up
by distant blackness. It would have been a lucky score
at any rate, blowing out a tire, then watching in grim
satisfaction of wrapping up the whole nightmare in
one tidy but bloody encore. As it stood, no crippled
forward momentum sent the vehicle slamming off the
road, with the wheelman waiting in the pulped metal
container for Bolan to step up.

Before he could try again, aware it would pan out
as nothing more than a waste of bullets, Bolan saw
the wheelman bring the rig out of its second whiplash.
Barreling on, the van gained rapid distance on a
screech of rubber, racing ahead, well out of any effec-
tive range of the assault rifle.

He hadn't seen the driver, with black-tinted windows concealing the face at the wheel, but he could sense desperation and adrenalized fear at the helm, the runner hell-bent on nothing but flight.

Weed, he was sure, saving himself.

It fit. What measure Bolan had taken of the guy's shady character earlier, and he could hazard the safe guess as to the invisible wheelman's identity. Well, Weed would keep, dangled on the back burner, even if he was lost to the waiting embrace of the night for the time being.

Beyond a fleeing coconspirator, Bolan knew he was looking at whole buffets of dark, unfinished business.

He let the AR-15 fall by his side as he checked the night, listening to the silence after the roar of Weed's getaway was finally eaten up by the dark.

Gone, the guy believing he was home-free.

Bolan walked, intent on giving the blackness around the perimeter of the slaughterhouse a thorough scoping for any armed stragglers. He didn't think he'd find a lurking threat left in the wake of Weed's dust, but he would check to cover his back. From there on, the only guarantee promised were X factors unknown.

Some horrific chain of events had erupted, a magnet of death cast his way by fate, perhaps meant to draw him here all along, to this very time and place. He couldn't say what was what or who was who, at least not yet. But he strongly suspected either black ops, acting on its own or with orders handed off from some rogue faction higher up in the food chain of some intelligence branch, was the lethal impetus behind the massacre inside.

The Executioner went in search of shadows. It took a good twenty minutes to make sure there was no threat to rise up from the night. Then he went through the screen door at the back of the Howling Coyote. As the hinges squeaked, he could feel the tension reaching him, out of sight, on the other side of the counter. He simply told the survivors, "It's me. Stay here. I'll be back."

And the Executioner walked on, in search of answers.

CHAPTER SEVEN

"We've hit a snag, I believe."

"So it would seem," he told the disembodied voice from the black box. "In our business, no news is *not* good news."

"We should know something in the next two minutes."

"You should have known something by now."

"What can I say? We're on it."

Grimacing, it was all he could do to choke off the gasp of pain. The heat, yet again, boiling from the fiery core deep in his brain, bringing on the hot flush in his face, the nausea welling up so quick and furious the cramps nearly doubled him over.

"Are you there?"

"A moment."

He took the bottle of pills, despising the very sight of the hairless skin on his hand, flesh so white it seemed to glow against the shadows of the monitor. Uncapping the bottle, he took one of the black pills and gulped it down with ice water.

What had they told him about his affliction? A leak in the seal of the damn thing, he thought, the element mass and radiation seeping out... Sorry about that. Just his bad luck. And how could something with no visible component parts, attachments, not the first nut or bolt, be called sealed up anyway?

Someone had lied to him; that much was certain. Well, their day was coming. It was his only reason to live anymore, he knew. Vengeance. If they thought they could simply put him out to pasture to rot away in a slow, agonizing death...

What he looked like burned him up with rage as he caught the stark image reflected on the monitor's screen. The accident had turned him into a freak show. Not even a whisker or the first stubble of hair anywhere on his body. Albino eyes, blinded by sunlight almost, unless he wore the wraparound visor glasses— that was if he ventured on rare occasion outside the mobile home.

And the sickness was getting worse. Not even the bitter taste of the sulfuric so-called wonder pill worked its magic anymore. No cure, no answers. He suffered from what they called symptoms of advanced radiation sickness. A second opinion from a civilian doctor and that genius didn't have a clue as to what his illness really was, but had wanted to run a battery of tests, just the same, which he had declined. He was dying, and no amount of poking and prodding would find a cure. And it certainly would never return to him the man he had once seen in the mirror.

Being terminated from the project, viewed, he could be sure, as both a liability and a ghoulish aberrant of anything that smacked of the human race, well, he was still chief of security, even if it was in an unofficial capacity. It might even work out better that way, he decided, with eyes and ears still tuned and pressed to the ground for him on the inside, irons in the fire, so to speak, helping him stoke the sort of heat he intended to burn them back with, bring the whole damn place down.

And take "it." The thing that had turned him into a monster that could glow in the dark.

A plan was in motion, two plans actually. He just needed some extra leverage, a little more time, groom the cannon fodder out in the desert.

A long overdue judgment day was just around the corner.

"Status?"

"A cleanup crew is en route."

"Our people?"

"Our screens," the voice said, referring to infrared and heat-seeking monitors on board both van and helicopter, "are showing one occupant in the vehicle. I'm having it tailed. I'm assuming it was your stooge, going rabbit when it got too hot in the kitchen."

Was that meant as a cheap shot, questioning his judgment to bring in a civilian sheep? An insolent tongue was the last thing he needed. He was ready to tell the man just such when he quickly filled in his report.

"Gunfire was called in to the sheriff," the floating voice said, but the name and number of the good citizen was already scrolled up on his monitor. "We are about to get a read on the inside, two minutes until my people are in place. Something went wrong—that much I can be certain of. I really don't want some delicate juggling act with the sheriff when we go in and if we find a bunch of dead civilians, which is my guess is what we'll be looking at.''

''The sheriff is your man. The sheriff, therefore, works for us. Handle it. Report back within the hour.''

The voice confirmed the order. There was nothing to do now, he knew, except wait. And, of course, hope the pill eased his suffering.

THE GUY WAS GONE, with just a bloody splotch where Bolan had left him, as if Marty had vanished into thin air. The moment felt strange to the soldier, all out of whack, even threatening in some bizarre way he couldn't define. He was certain the slaughter here had only left more armed shadows in the wings, ready to make a move, boil up out of the night to pounce on the place. Given the carnage strewed about, the myriad hanging questions, Bolan—if he was so inclined— would have felt it was almost a paranormal phenomenon, the way the body was missing. Such as a mother ship coming down and abducting the man. A lot of folks in these parts, he knew, were publicly sounding the alarm about UFOs, with alien invasion as close as tomorrow, little gray men floating through the roof to snap up humans as experiments for ominous reasons undisclosed, supposedly humankind being crossbred with alien hybrids, a new race meant to inherit the earth.

He was a grim realist, though, and his second search

turned up the answer. He was advancing toward the puddle of blood, when the soldier saw the streak of crimson, leading in broken smears to a point at the edge of the bar. A quick haul across the room, and the blood trail turned up the man behind the bar. The vacant stare told Bolan there was no need to check for a pulse. Before succumbing to mortal wounds, the man had crawled off in search of the disk Bolan now found clutched in his hand. A safe had been built into the floor, carefully constructed to blend in with the wood. Feeling inside the narrow confines of the safe, Bolan discovered it empty. One disk, a Pandora's box of some extortion angle maybe, or hidden knowledge about a classified black project perhaps? Naming names, events? The whole bloody ugly truth? All Bolan knew right then was that four now dead men had come here to take whatever truth Marty had jealously guarded, even if that meant sacrificing his own life and the lives of others. Which was exactly what had happened. Well, the Executioner intended to find whatever dark truth was spelled out on the disk.

He was closing the lid, settling back in place the floorboard, when the light descended over the restaurant, a penetrating white sheen, flooding the place, out of nowhere. The floor trembled around Bolan next, his gut churning as a thunderous blanket of rotor wash hit the roof. Braced for bad company, the Executioner plucked the disk from Marty's death grasp and slipped it in his pants pocket. It would be a start, assuming he could crack any access code built as a firewall to conceal the truth. If not, he would transfer its contents to

Stony Man Farm on the briefcase satlink in his rental vehicle. The Executioner intended to stick around this stretch of Nevada, at least until he learned why four men had gone on a murderous rampage. Clear enough they had come here to take the disk. But why? What was on it? Even if they were black operatives guarding a classified military project, it hardly gave them any right to threaten, much less execute, unarmed civilians. Truth was, in Bolan's mind it made them that much more accountable.

So much for vacation; Bolan was in for the long haul.

The truth was out there.

The light vanished, but Bolan saw the silhouettes of two vans lurching to a halt beyond the window, believed he could almost sense bodies hitting the ground around the perimeter, dropping from the chopper to surround the place and storm it.

The soldier was up and moving, the AR-15 aimed at the front door, ready to call out to the kitchen for the four of them to get to him right away, when two HK MP-5s were thrust his direction, and drawing a bead. Two hardmen in black had taken up positions on either side of the front door, their faces grim as death. Full body armor, balaclava helmets with com links, Bolan noted on the fly, securing cover at the edge of the retaining wall. He swung the AR-15 around the corner.

"Drop the weapon!"

"I'm a cop! Justice Department," Bolan shouted, heard next the scuffling from the kitchen, a cry of alarm sounding, telling him more classified SWAT-like goons were charging the rear, closing the net.

"I told you to drop the weapon!"

"Get those guns off me first," Bolan growled. "We'll talk about it."

Another voice flew at Bolan from the flickering shadows beyond the men in black. "This is Sheriff Walsh. Do what they say. No one's going to get hurt."

Bolan figured he might as well believe in the tooth fairy. "Let me see a badge."

The soldier swung his aim as another helmet and subgun materialized in the kitchen doorway off to his side. Bolan's voice of reason told him they would have already started shooting if they meant to kill him or the women and children, wrap up whatever mess had been created. Even still, given the horror show he had just waded through, he wasn't about to trust a simple demand to disarm himself, official G-men or not.

"We're with the United States government," the hardman rasped from the edge of the doorway. "This is official government business. Drop the weapon."

"I'm thinking the four guys who just came here, with all the love of a saint in their hearts, were like-wise official."

"I'm Walsh! Here's my badge!"

Bolan kept the assault rifle pointed at the hardman's face, turned his head and saw the stocky figure in brown with matching Stetson hat stepping through the door. There was a star pinned to his chest, the guy holding out an ID wallet, Mr. Officialdom holding his ground.

"Okay," the man said. "Shown you mine, how about letting me see yours."

"In my coat, on the floor in smoking. The women and kids?" the soldier barked at the hardman hunkered beside him.

"We have them. They're fine. Just drop the weapon."

The Executioner knew it was pointless to drag out the standoff. Hemmed in, front to back, there was nothing to do but wait and see what happened. Bolan was standing as the sheriff rifled through his windbreaker, felt the angry looks drilling into him, the gunners edgy as he held on to the assault rifle.

"It's okay," Walsh called out. "He's with the Justice Department."

IT WAS A MESS worse than imagined. Venture a guess, and Thomas Thornton figured to be staring down a potential fiasco that could expose the project, not to mention some hard truths that would land him and a few others for a long vacation in Leavenworth. Unless, of course, some quick moves were initiated, all manner of smoke screens erected, a plethora of lies and half truths cast about in some official capacity.

In short, though, he was faced with a nightmare of the fifth-dimension variety.

To call the immediate future a whopping migraine while performing a balancing act on a high wire a thousand feet up with no net, he thought, was the alltime classic understatement. This was sphincterpucker hell.

The slaughterhouse he found told Thornton it would be a definite stretch to clean up this one without Washington getting into the act. If he was lucky, he might keep the rumor mill from spinning out of control, pointing fingers toward the classified base just south of this massacre. Immediate answers, beyond blustering about his status as an operative for the National Security Agency, escaped him. Four civilians and one badge from the Justice Department were still walking around to sing his potential swan song. Talk about a future in peril...

For one thing, the sheriff and deputies, he knew, weren't even elected officials. That alone might raise the red flags—hell, it would be a civilian nuclear blast seen and heard all the way from Eureka Springs to the steps of Capitol Hill if word leaked out about this slaughter circus. The "official" badges had been brought on board by the NSA specifically to keep tabs on local civilians, those wandering curious who hankered to find out just what was going on out in the desert, might even be prone to bring in the media before they were paid a call by one of his security people. Men in black, marched out to convince them a tongue flapping wild rumors in the breeze might not be in their best interest.

But, he feared, no amount of dire warning could hold the lid down on this one. People talked, loved, even nurtured their conspiracy theories, especially when it involved the government, the military or the fantastic and every shade of phenomena between. It was human nature to spread gossip. They could lurk around the Fifth Ring at the Pentagon, keeping all manner of jealous knowledge to themselves under threat of imprisonment or worse, but this was Nevada. Simple folks. The unwashed. Be that as it may, ignorance and speculation spreading like some virus to infect all corners of the state, at last count the next four towns beyond this abattoir down the road had gone UFO bonkers. How in the hell, he wondered, would they cover this up?

Nine corpses. Fortunately, four of them, at least, could be explained away, since Braxton and his crew didn't even officially exist. Not on paper, or as a number in cyberspace. No immediate family, not even a driver's license or a social security number between them, which was SOP for anyone trained or recruited for special ops by the Department of Defense, its Special Security division. So, there would be no official report filed in triplicate on the sheriff's end; that went without saying. But the man would have to tap-dance around some minefields, and in the public eye, go through the motions of an investigation. Notify next of kin, spinning out the lies, like that. And hope.

No matter how deep it was eventually buried, Thornton started having visions of a congressional hearing, elected officials going berserk, demanding to know the truth. He told himself it was best to rein in the paranoia, deal with the moment.

There was a wild card waiting outside. And he thought if the big guy IDed as Michael Belasko of the Justice Department was a G-man, then he was one of those little gray—

Thornton was snapped out of his anxiety as the sheriff walked up and commented how the place was a slaughterhouse, as if he needed reiteration of the facts. He didn't need to look at the man to read between the lines, either. Walsh was eating on his own nerves, worried about covering his own butt.

"You questioned them, I assume."

"Same story you got," the sheriff said.

And that bugged the hell out of Thornton even more. The Justice badge had cleaned up Braxton and crew. One guy, incredible. Gunning them down, if he could believe the first reports, as if these guys—his own men—were nothing more than a few street punks with a Saturday-night special. But this Belasko had some look, and Thornton was unable to pin it down. Still holding on to the assault rifle outside, looking around, no, through all of them, sizing them up, suspicious. No G-man he'd ever heard of could crank up killing heat to this kind of extreme, burn down four men he knew were professional assassins who had been selected particularly for their skills by the DOD and the NSA.

Some guardians of the truth they turned out to be.

"I read this Belasko as a problem."

Thornton damn near smirked at that, his gaze moving from body to body.

"The women confirmed it," Walsh said. "Your—"

Thornton pinned the man with a steely eye, cutting off the "people" bit. "Let me go talk to this guy. See if I can reason with the man."

"Good luck."

He looked away from the body off to the side as one of his men stripped off the ski mask. Burton. Laid out like a gutted fish across a table, a greasy strand of intestine hanging out from when he'd been on the wrong end of a shotgun blast. "Not sure I care for your tone, Sheriff."

"Not sure if I care that you do or you don't."

"While you're giving me attitude, I hope you're not forgetting who butters your bread, Sheriff."

"Not for one second. See, what I don't like, you can saunter off into the night, go back and hole up in spook city, with all your security clearances and high-tech gizmos to hide behind, keeping from us little folks whatever goes on down there in the name of national security, even if that means killing off a few locals, former colleagues of yours or a tourist like that poor schmuck over there with the Chicago rental. Me, I'm hung out here, on the front line. I've got families of victims to deal with, questions that'll need answering."

"Local media. I trust you'll see that's as far it goes."

"You're hoping."

"I understand your concerns. We'll talk some more later. First, I need to go make sure tonight's hero and me reach an understanding."

He was walking away, when Walsh couldn't resist a parting shot. "Yeah, you do that."

Thornton stopped, wheeled. "You got something to say, out with it."

"All I'm saying is if those women and kids were

getting zipped up in rubber, we'd all be in a world of hurt.''

Didn't he know it, Thornton thought, and marched off to have a word with the hero.

CHAPTER EIGHT

The Executioner waited by his Jeep Cherokee while the crew of gunners in black went marching about, conducting their business in grim silence. Which—if past experience with operatives who were the security or sanitizing arm of a black project panned out—was slapping together a cover story. He almost couldn't wait to hear the snow job they would dump in his lap, hoping, no doubt, he would swallow it, go blithely on his civil servant way. If they only knew. When they did finally deem a lowly agent of the U.S. Justice Department worthy of some explanation for what had happened this night, Bolan hoped they at least showed a little imagination. As for the soldier's own role in the murky scheme of things from that point on? It might be undefined in terms of concrete action, but he was sticking around, bent on making some noise. Figure part snoop to start with, but he intended to make himself a major pain in someone's tail as soon as possible. If armed shadows started popping up, demanding he leave town by sundown or else…

In that case the gloves would come off, no more Mr. Nice Guy.

Bolan watched as three black ops hardmen tore through the Toyota rental, the sheriff having already liberated some paperwork from the glove box. One of the men produced a briefcase from the trunk, took a thin metallic instrument from a pocket in his armor and jimmied open the latches. From his obscured point of view, Bolan couldn't see what was inside, but the man gave the contents a little more than passing curiosity. Briefcase and the man in black disappeared into the restaurant.

Another classified SWAT clone was rifling through the biker's saddlebags, Bolan making out the form of a stubby submachine gun, which looked like an outdated Army subgun from where he stood. Bolan was poised to sound off a word to the wise, but found it wasn't necessary, as they stayed well clear from his rental. And whatever craft he'd heard—a black helicopter, most likely—was now nowhere to be seen or heard. Again, experience had showed him it happened that way. Chopper swooping down, he imagined, the shock troops disembarking, then gone in one thrust of turbos.

So far, it was playing out true to shadow form in the soldier's experienced eye. These people operated with all the silent efficiency of a haunting ghost, or with the ruthless hunger of a wolf pack on the prowl. Spook stuff, but deadly, make no mistake.

Bolan looked through the restaurant window, watching the sheriff and the man in black who had just grilled him, the women and even the children, huddled together. He had seen the sheriff take a wallet from the pants pockets of the businessman. The first round of identifying victims, notifying next of kin? Or the beginning of an elaborate charade? First impression of the head gunner was basic and simple. Bad news, believing himself above the law. If Bolan had the time to pull off a ski mask or two from the dead shooters, Bolan believed the man in black now running the show—or at least the gruesome cleanup detail—would have been a carbon copy, from lean frame to chiseled features to crew cut. Bolan couldn't say yet about the county sheriff, but he had a suspicion he was on the payroll. It happened, and it would fit, if that was the case.

Whoever the nine dead people really were, well, Bolan figured at best, it would be need-to-know, if that. At worst, it was basic denial from there on, he knew. He could play that game, too. And he had the disk.

"Mister?"

Bolan found the two women standing at the rear of the Chevy pickup, the boys sitting in the cab. He laid the assault rifle up against the SUV. They had been through way too much already. The danger had passed, but only for the moment, unless some fluke of fate in the coming hours proved him wrong. Doubtful. No point at any rate, he figured, to keep lugging around a reminder of the violence they'd lived through, barely escaped. It was the children Bolan felt worst about. He could only hope the memories faded in time for them, no permanent mental scarring, bolting awake in the middle of the night, chased by the ghosts of the slaughter here.

Moving to the driver's window, Bolan looked in on the boys. "You guys hanging in there?" They nodded, keeping it together, Bolan sensed, even as the terror was holding on just below the surface. "A few more minutes, you'll be going home with your mom."

The downcast look the younger one gave Bolan tugged at a deep pain of his own the soldier thought he'd long since buried. "I don't think we have a home, mister. Our daddy left...."

"Tommy, the man doesn't need to hear our problems."

"You guys hang in there, you hear?" Bolan quietly said, then went to the women.

"I regret what happened, I'm sorry they had to see it. There was no choice."

"We, uh, I think, speaking for myself, are grateful you were here," the boys' mother told Bolan.

Betty was working on a cigarette, nerves still snapping at her. "Yeah, I mean, if if wasn't for you... God, I feel sick what happened. But..."

"You're alive. That's all that counts right now. You've got each other."

"What next?" the mother asked. "We have to hang around, get asked a bunch more questions? We already told them what happened. Self-defense, what you had to do. I'll never be sure, and I thank God for that— and you—but I can't help but thinking they would have..."

"They would have. It's over. Try and forget about it."

"So, we can go?" Betty asked.

"Let them go through the drill. Routine," Bolan said, but knew that was way off base from even a scintilla of truth. "I won't go into detail, and I'm not trying to alarm you, but do either of you have some-place out of this county you can go and stay for a few days? Do you have a man?" the soldier asked Betty.

"No. Husband passed away little over two years ago. Tina here, her..." She stopped, throwing an em-barrassed glance at Tina in the shadows. "Sorry, Tina. My big mouth."

"No harm. He made his choice."

"Everyone has a situation," Bolan told them. "But you need to think about yourselves."

"I have a sister in Reno," Betty said. "Why? You don't think..."

"I'm not sure what to think. I just feel it might be better for the four of you if you left the area for a little while." He paused, studied their pensive faces, wish-ing he could do more. "I guess you're both now out of work." They glanced at each other, not sure where Bolan was headed. He gathered the mother had a sit-uation involving a missing husband. Two kids to raise. No job, no father. Hanging in there, hoping another door opened up.

"Wait here," Bolan told them, and went to fetch the war bag inside the SUV. He zipped it open and dug out the wad of cash. Five thousand and change in walking-around war funds. He peeled off two grand.

They figured it out, since Tina said, "No, no. I couldn't. Please, you've done enough, mister."

"Call it a loan, until you get back on your feet. Thousand for each of you. All I'm asking for is a number I can reach you both to make sure you're okay. Take it—for the boys. Fair enough?"

They had pride, but they knew Bolan spoke from the heart. And sometimes all that could be done, he knew, was to survive, go on with it. Reluctantly, they took his money.

"Belasko! When you're done socializing over there?"

A SECOND LOOK at the man, scrutinizing his big shadow for a longer stretch this time around, and it didn't do much at all to put any fears to rest. In fact, Thornton sensed the guy building a fresh head of steam. Ready to fire off the questions maybe? More determined than ever to kick the feces through the fan, until some of it stuck?

However it was sliced or flung, the Justice guy was a definite problem, he considered, especially after taking in the end result of a display of lethal martial talent he now nearly found—what? Beyond belief, to a point where it almost struck him as supernatural?

Absurd notion? Or was it?

Chewing on his nerves, Thornton waited for the Justice agent to tear himself away from what he read as consoling the women. Edging away from the front door, he stepped out into the dancing shadows of the neon sign, again ready to bark for Belasko to get it in gear, but restrained the urge. They were over there, the Justice man telling them to write down two phone numbers, made sure he had them before they left. Now, what the hell did that mean? he wondered, but his knotted gut told him Mr. Justice wasn't going back east anytime soon. Not good.

Damn it!

When Belasko was finally on the move, taking his sweet time, slowly cutting the gap, Thornton took another look into those eyes as the face closed. Considering the slaughter he'd dished out, taking down four of his best men, Thornton decided if this was a G-man he was a priest. This was where, he knew, it got tricky. A subtle warning needed to be issued.

"Didn't mean to interrupt."

Was that a wry grin, flashed his way from the shadows? "No problem. I can see you're too busy to concern yourself over a few jumpy nerves."

"Right." Smart-ass now. "Anyway, I've talked it over with the sheriff. We're going to buy your version of events."

Those eyes peered through him again, as cold as a grave. "That's that?"

"Pretty much. This is official government business from here on. Classified."

"I see."

"Out with it, Belasko. I don't have time for games. What exactly is it you think you see?"

Those eyes, weighing something, glancing toward the restaurant. Had the guy seen, he wondered, what was in the civilian's briefcase? And that was yet another worry, compounding the migraine, Thornton knew.

"Let's just say I'm catching a bad whiff."

"Of what?"

"If I find out, I'll let you know."

"Meaning?"

"I don't really know."

"Just what made you stop in here anyway?"

"Would you believe I was on vacation?"

"Well, now you can go on and enjoy the rest of it, Belasko."

"But do it somewhere else?"

Thornton bristled, the guy putting out his own challenge if he read the tone right. "The Justice Department has no jurisdiction, not the first ounce of clout where this problem is concerned."

"Classified, eyes-only stuff."

"Exactly. So we are clear on that much?"

"Yeah."

"So, how come I'm not convinced."

"If you're having some emotional problem where I'm concerned, I'm not your shrink. Are the five of us dismissed?"

"Hold on a second before I cut you loose," Thornton growled, the guy starting to turn away. "The way you and the others described what happened, it fits my first walk-through of the scene. The thing I was curious about was the owner, the one I found behind the bar. If he was gut-shot in the middle of the room, like you said, well, why would he bother to crawl all that way to die?"

"He was in a lot of pain, I gather."

Thornton sensed a little dancing, the guy covering something. "Meaning?"

"Maybe he was looking to fix himself a farewell drink."

"You think that's funny?"

"You see me laughing?"

Thornton tried to get a read on where the guy was coming from, but all he found were those graveyard eyes staring back. He was holding something back, and Thornton's antenna was up, flaring. "You and the others are free to go."

"That's that."

"You keep saying that like there's supposed to be something else."

The shadow held his ground, a new depth of grim hardness in his voice as he said, "A bunch of people died here tonight. I'm thinking you know who marched in there and what they were after. I'm thinking they went for something and were ordered to not leave behind a single witness. I've had some experience with your kind."

"And what kind might that be?"

"The kind who thinks he doesn't have to answer for something like what happened inside. That you can wrap yourself up in some holy shroud of national security, even if that means killing innocent folks you think are in the way."

"Is that some kind of threat, Belasko?"

"Just an observation."

Good enough, Thornton decided. The challenge was

made, out in the open. He knew where things stood. Mr. Justice wanted to play hardball.

"Enjoy your vacation, Belasko."

He lingered with those eyes working around the hardmen, then walked on, silent, still measuring something. Thornton felt the hammering then of his heart in his ears, watching as Belasko went back to the women. Another powwow ensued by the pickup. Some final words he couldn't make out, but meant to once more comfort the ladies, he guessed, and Thornton found himself grateful when the guy was finally in the SUV, cranking over the engine. It looked like a plan, he suspected, the guy waiting until the Chevy and the Ford Galaxy with the lone female occupant backed out, then he fell in behind. Trailing them up 305 for the interstate, it looked as if the Justice man meant to ride their rear, maybe make sure they got home safe.

Thornton suspected his troubles had only just started.

The next chore, he knew, might prove just as unpleasant as gnawing on anxiety about what Belasko would or wouldn't do.

THE MAP HAD TOLD Bolan Interstate 80 ran parallel with U.S. 50 to the south, roughly four hundred miles east to west, from the California to Utah borders. Both might be tagged the loneliests roads in America, he thought, but his mental radar was alerting him he wasn't about to be alone for long.

The soldier watched the two vehicles swing to his

left as he eased out onto the interstate, the women leaning out an arm to wave goodbye in the fleeting wash of his headlights. They proceeded west, quickly lost to the night and the distance. They were going home to pack up for Reno. Bolan figured the four of them would be safer if he wasn't along for the ride, guarding the roost, even though he had briefly considered doing just that. They should be fine, if they all left for Reno by morning. He couldn't one hundred percent say they were in danger, but he wasn't going to put the enemy's paranoia to the test where they were concerned. If there was any lingering doubt or grim and potentially lethal interest in any of the survivors from the Howling Coyote, Bolan knew he would become the one singled out for a visit.

When asking about lodging, the women had told him there was a motel a few miles down the road, in the opposite direction to where they were going. A polite reference was made to him to consider staying the night at one of their homes, but he declined. He told them he'd touch base as soon as he was settled at the motel.

The soldier checked the pitch blackness behind and on either side of the desert as he motored along. By day he recalled low croppings of black granite hills, with vast sweeping mud or salt flats stretching in between barren rock stubble. All of it had shimmered in a white glare so burning, as the desolation baked under the sun, it felt as if more than a passing stare could singe the eyeballs out of a man's skull. It was hard, unforgiving country out here, could kill a man or a stranded motorist without water within hours.

Deadly terrain. Perfect for hunting, to stalk and kill the human animal. Where an adversary could boil up out of the night without a sound, or appear by day as nothing more than a mirage until the fatal blow was delivered. No one would be the wiser except the dead and the killer, since Mother Nature and a host of scavengers would quickly consume the remains.

If the soldier was thinking along those lines, he could hazard a guess any blacksuited nemesis was likewise running down the same train of thought.

A mile or so after departing the women and children, Bolan's suspicions turned up in the side-view mirror. He couldn't see it clearly, but there was enough star- and moonlight to just barely drop a sheen, outline the dark bulk of the van. Having thought ahead before venturing away from the restaurant abattoir, the Executioner had settled the war bag on the shotgun seat. One hand on the wheel, he reached over, delved into the open bag and produced the HK MP-5 SD-3 subgun. He eased off the gas, saw the dark shape fall back some, then rested the SMG on top of the bag, within easy reach.

The soldier grew weary of the obvious tail, decided to force the issue. He pulled onto the shoulder of the road and waited as they rolled on. He took the SMG as the black shape grew in the side-view mirror. The lights flared on, a twin winking beacon hitting him in the eyes. Squinting, he braced for gunfire and thrust open the door. He held the subgun by his leg, hidden from their view. The windows were tinted black, all but hiding the faces of the occupants. Combat senses electrifying him to act with lightning speed, he held his ground. The van blew by, the soldier feeling watching eyes, as the slipstream kicked a gust of hot wind and exhaust in his face.

Blacksuits, checking up on him. So, he thought, watching the van quickly disappear into the night, let the games begin.

CHAPTER NINE

The IDs collected by the sheriff from the civilian casualties were simply more reminders of the coming land mines he'd have to dance around. At first look Thornton judged them to be another nuisance. The second perusal, however, sitting at the minicontrol console, alone inside the van that doubled as a rolling command post, and some idea wanted to kick in, assure him there was a way out. It was a flickering flame of hope, a vague shadow of a plan, at best, tossing restlessly around in his desperate quest to find solutions, like a distant rattling chain in his head. He was forced to give it up the next moment, since it didn't help being distracted by his surveillance detail, wanting to know their standing orders.

The Justice man, he'd been informed, had claimed a room, called, of all damn things, he thought, A-Lee-Inn. The Extraterrestrial Highway, Groom Lake, which was home to Area 51, and the bizarre tourist trap that was the town of Rachel…well, all of that might be far south, but the locals in all the surrounding counties seemed to have jumped on the paranormal bandwagon, he knew.

The UFO craze wasn't worth heaping on his plate of problems. Belasko, he knew, was the reality that had him tweaked, edged out there in a dimension of his own of paranoia and anxiety. And since the shack that passed for an office didn't have a computer, there was no way Thornton could tap in, clue himself as to how long the G-man planned on hanging around the county.

"Monitor the situation and keep me posted by the hour," Thornton snapped, then hit the end button on the secured cell relay.

Again, he scanned the driver's licenses. What was that voice telling him the answers were staring him in the face? Was it the voice of treachery urging him to go ahead, risk compounding his dilemma? Proceed slowly, there were pieces of the puzzle to sort through, he told himself. Little by little, one at a time.

First, he had to wonder why the victim IDed as Robert Barklin was toting around two hundred grand in brand-new hundreds, but with credit cards under various names out the wazoo. There was a plane ticket found in one of three sets of luggage, the man apparently en route to catch a flight scheduled the day after tomorrow from LAX to Honolulu before, of course, a wild bullet from the biker's .44 Magnum gun forever punched out the lights on any dreams of paradise on Earth. If Barklin was, in fact, running from the law or ditching a marriage turned hurricane or both, he wasn't real slick at covering his tracks.

Thornton had already run the man through cyberspace, pulling out the name of the accounting firm he worked for—or had. It was safe to say the late accountant had moonlighted as an embezzler, cash siphoned off behind the backs of unwitting clients over a period of time, tucked away in a waiting offshore account. For some nagging reason, the question begging Thornton was whom had he stolen from? It would take some more digging through cyberspace, a few phone calls back east to answer hanging questions that would uncover the man's other life.

Well, Thornton decided he hadn't spent ten years honing all his hacking and tracking skills as a special NSA op for COMINT—Communications Intelligence—to see them wasted at a critical juncture, not when they were needed the most to find solutions, put out the fires. A social security number, he knew, was all it took for him to unveil everything about the lives of the victims. Simple as that. The average American citizen didn't understand the ramifications, he thought, of being branded by a simple string of numbers. If they ran afoul of the law, creditors or anybody else with a computer and even marginal hacking skills, their lives could become an instant condensed story, the *Reader's Digest* version of any John or Jane Q. Citizen from cradle to grave.

How, though, did he proceed from there? Knowledge was only power when it was put to use, to gain an edge.

Some angle of a preemptive strike was calling out to him, a diversionary Plan B, he thought. Something to throw at the Justice man, keep him sidetracked if he was bent on making himself more than a walking hemorrhoid of questions and suspicion. All Thornton really suspected right then was that if he didn't get busy putting out the few fires already burning around him, the coming hours might see him consumed by a conflagration.

Next he pondered the biker. Nevada motorcycle license, an address in Reno declared as residence. Hard to say if the address was a smoke screen or not, since the biker lifestyle was somewhat transient. Still, no matter how far a man strayed beyond the edges of civilized society, Thornton knew someone would eventually wonder about the biker, just as much as anyone would notice a nine-to-five pillar of the community had up and vanished from home and office. Did that mean a pack of scooter trash was already tearing up the highway, wondering what had happened to their missing bro, creating yet another fire that needed dousing? And what had been his business with the woman? The initial cyberspace jaunt through NCIC had turned up a long criminal record on one Samuel Dean, with a five-year stint at San Quentin for aggravated assault on a police officer. His gut told him to keep digging, piece it together, the answers were out there in cyberspace.

Then there was a dead cook from Denver, a quick run through his IRS files turning up a wife and kids as dependents. No criminal record, nothing untoward whatsoever. How would he finesse the cover story where they were concerned? Grieving widow and kids, crying out for justice after the body was buried. Well, leave the locals to the sheriff, a song and dance about a robbery-massacre, ongoing investigation, like that. It happened all the time in the country nowadays, goons rolling in around closing, some senseless rage urging them not to be content to just take the money. They had to execute everybody in sight. Go figure the ills of a society spinning out of control, fueled by its own dark, runaway impulses, eaten up by its own greed and lust. He didn't have time to bother with little fish like a mere cook, much less bring on another headache pondering over the larger social issues.

It was Rhonda Jones who flared up the worst bout yet of paranoia and worry. Much to more dismay, Thornton discovered she was married to an aerospace physicist, and from Area 51, no less. That meant the guy was familiar with some of the drill when strange things started happening to loved ones. Maybe Mr. Jones's suspicions about his wife's violent demise would run amok, Thornton feared, as he came calling on the local badge for answers. Even still, maybe a simple word of warning…

He almost jumped, laughing, as it hit him in the eyes, a bolt of lightning. It would take more research, but he saw the first shred of an answer. No way was he waiting around to see if the G-man launched some investigation or a personal crusade. He could iron out any details that flew in the face of suspicion later, after he pulled it off.

Fingers flying over the keyboard, he scrolled up the first of two phone numbers he intended to call. They weren't the next of kin, but they were the next-best thing.

They were pawns.

THE SECOND LIGHTS-OUT drive-by sent Bolan to the window, the subgun leading the advance this time. He heard the soft crunch of tread over stones outside, could almost feel the black van rolling slowly by before he confirmed it. Again, no lights framed the curtain as the soldier cracked it open an inch or so, body hugging the wall on the blind side next to the door, the SMG up and poised to track any encroaching armed shadows. He had a full stem-to-stern viewing of the dark vehicle the first time around, but now he glimpsed nothing more than the tail end of the oversize van, skirting by, its bulk moving on in what appeared to be the direction of the interstate.

Bolan let the curtain fall back, listening as the invisible wheelman put some gas to the engine, revving it up. Heading out? Or perhaps, he thought, merely giving the appearance of a quick recon before vacating the premises. Reporting back, no doubt, that Agent Belasko didn't seem in any hurry to be on his way back east.

Sorry about that, fellas, the soldier thought, felt the grim twist at the corner of his mouth. Until he had some answers, at the very least, he was there to shatter whatever classified dreams that had reached out to snuff out the innocent—women and children—simply because they had been in the wrong place, wrong time.

Bolan wanted it to be a simple task for the gunners in black to keep tabs on his whereabouts and movements. There were plenty of hills surrounding the dive Bolan had chosen as his one-man command post, having paid for the room in cash for three days. One way or another, he didn't care if they staked him out. An enemy with something to hide and nerves exposed could be maneuvered into making mistakes. The plain hard truth was that Bolan counted on their paranoia to push them over the threshold of raw nerves, blow a firestorm his way.

If the shadow men guarding the dark secrets of their black project thought they'd already seen the worst tonight, Bolan determined he was only getting warmed up.

He held his position by the door, ears tuned to the night outside. The dump had all of ten rooms, Bolan noting only one Winnebago with Georgia tags, edged up to number 1 beside the office. Could there be an enemy plant or two now holed in the adjoining rooms? he wondered. Maybe a gunner dropped off in the hills behind the building, a sniper rifle in hand? If they wanted to crash the door, nothing more than a simple chain and dead bolt would hold back any pack of charging wolves. The room itself was basic to the point of primitive, with a single bed, chair, a wooden dresser with a TV that looked every bit as old the invention of television. A bathroom the size of a closet, with a window Bolan had made sure was latched, for whatever good that would do if they came storming into the room. He could have snapped on the air-conditioning unit hung from the front window, but he needed vigilance homed to any sound outside. A box humming out a chill just to cut away the stifling heat in this cracker box could see a threat at his door before he knew it. Discomfort he could live with—getting caught off guard and shot down was never an option. From there on, the soldier knew the only guarantee was the unknown, and the uncertain.

The Executioner let out a long breath, aware his own paranoia was working hard on his nerves. Understandable, just the same, given what he'd walked away from. He had been around a little too long to be shocked or disturbed by much at all, even though man's inhumanity to man never failed to stoke a belly full of righteous angry fire. But what he suspected had happened tonight had fanned a new flame of hot fury. Because of the women and children, to some degree it was personal.

Someone out there needed to be held accountable.

The single lamp on, shedding its gloomy ray, Bolan marched to his war bag, already deposited and open on the bed. If nothing else, he needed to touch base with Brognola, arrange to re-up the firepower. An airdrop, he figured, should do the trick. A military flight from Nellis Air Force Base, the big Fed pulling the strings on the logistics from his end. All personnel, military or civilian, Bolan knew, were cleared through Nellis before being choppered or bussed to any number of classified projects scattered around Nevada. He was counting on a few raised eyebrows Nellis way when Brognola had Stony Man Farm blacksuits drop in, armed with their own official clearance to proceed over protected airspace. Simply more gasoline thrown on the fire he intended to build, as hopefully someone put in the call to the gunners that they were under close and armed scrutiny.

A starting place, twisting the thumbscrews.

A mental list of what he needed to replenish the firepower already tallied, he put his call to Brognola on the back burner. Even with Stony Man's sophisticated intelligence-gathering expertise, it would take time—if they succeeded at all—to crack through all manner of firewalls denying access to data on black projects. The soldier decided to try his own luck first.

Grimly mindful of lurking shadows in the night, he first strapped on the .44 Magnum Desert Eagle, checked the load, one round up the snout. After stowing the big piece in leather, he hauled the aluminum briefcase from the war bag. Leaning the SMG against the end of the bed, an easy grab, Bolan punched in the codes that released the latches. He settled in a chair by the dresser, facing the door. He fired up the small monitor on the satlink and slipped in the disk. As expected, ''Access Code'' flashed on the screen. He wasn't sure why, but it was just a hunch, something tugging from deep inside, telling him to attempt the obvious. The soldier typed in ''Howling Coyote.'' The screen went blank. Bolan was sure some firewall had been built in to erase whatever was on file if the first attempt failed. He sat there, staring at nothing, frustrated, when the screen flashed back on.

''Hit Return.'' Bingo.

Bolan couldn't believe it, thinking it was almost too good to be true. In fact, it felt so easy it seemed spooky. The soldier scrolled up the file, began reading.

Not even two lines along, and the Executioner felt himself chilled to the bone by the initial revelation.

THORNTON KNEW he was procrastinating, but he needed more time to think his plan through before the inevitable callback. The man-thing was waiting for a report, hoping for good news Thornton knew wasn't about to come anytime soon. Not without sweat, worry and more bloodshed.

How could he tell the hairless, pale creature, which he barely thought of as human, they weren't about to see the light at the end of this dark tunnel anytime soon? How could he simply state, in no uncertain terms, they might be looking at the mother of all shit-storms? That, unless he did something and quick, took action on his own, the Justice Department could land a whole platoon in the project's backyard, with badges and guns jammed square up their collective butts?

Thornton shuddered in the soft glow of the monitor. It could have been the darkness, the silence inside the van disturbed only by the rotor wash whipping up the mental picture of the freakish thing who was unofficially in charge, freeze framing the ghoulish specter in his mind's eye. Small comfort, he knew, he could report the cleanup crew was loading the four bodies of their own onto the chopper. They were the easiest victims to dispose of, explain away to next of kin through official Pentagon channels. Combine the slaughter, the roving Justice man, the plan he was concocting, and for some reason he could almost feel the presence of the former chief of security beside him, white pig-

ments staring him down from behind the black wraparound visor. Despite the fact this failed gig was in
large part the man-thing's responsibility, he would demand solutions to the problem nonetheless, dropping
full and immediate resolution in his lap. Another in-
voluntary shiver hit Thornton, as an even more insidious consequence to any failure on his part spelled out
a bottom line. The power that man still commanded,
he thought, even after being ousted from the project,
was almost as unnerving as the sight of what the accident had created.

The first number had been tracked to its source. It
was a judgment call on his part, if he followed
through. Once he initiated the scheme, he knew there
was little he could do but sit back and hope for the
best. Cromman probably wouldn't care for him—

The rap of knuckles on metal broke off the worried
line of thought. As the side door slid open, Thornton
didn't like the expression that he saw on the blacksuited gunner's face. It looked like defeat.

"We've searched the inside and the perimeter, sir.
Thoroughly. We haven't been able to find it yet."

And there it was. The whole reason Cromman had
marched his men in there, guns blazing, and now the
damn diskette was nowhere in sight. That left a thorough search-and-tear of Lake's home to attend to,
which he intended to proceed with pronto. Then there
was Baldone's widow. The Baldone house would likewise have to be rifled through, top to bottom, visions
of an irate grieving wife and mother demanding to
know what the hell they were looking for burning up

his thoughts. If she couldn't be mollified with reason, she would have to be warned. Let it go, ma'am. Case closed.

Thornton growled, "Well, don't stand there, mister, keep looking for it. I don't care if it takes all night and half the day. Find it."

"Yes, sir. And, sir, the sheriff would like a word with you."

"Tell him I'm busy. I'll get to him when I get to him."

"Yes, sir."

Alone again, Thornton stared back at the phone number on his monitor. He made the decision. The Reno number had already been run down, through Ma Bell, then with red flags cropping up in cyberspace, leading him to the mainframes at the FBI field office in the second-string Vegas. If he somehow set the plan in motion it could well blow up in his face.

No choice, he decided, once he weighed the risks against the reward of stomping out at least one potential fire.

A possible firestorm called Belasko.

CHAPTER TEN

Bolan had scrolled through the text in five minutes. It took a two-minute stretch after that, though, for the soldier to choke down the bitter fruit of what he'd read. Somehow he managed to will away the cold ball coiled in his belly.

Righteous anger alone wouldn't get the job done here, he knew, much less steer him any closer to the guilty parties behind the truth. When his guts finally unknotted, the Executioner was left feeling the ghost of the dead author, as if the shot-up corpse left behind at the Howling Coyote was right there in the overheated, stuffy, murky light, nodding over his shoulder, muttering, yes, what he'd read was the whole truth and nothing but the horrible and the unbelievable truth.

Uncle Sam's ugliest were, Bolan concluded, out here playing God. The soldier was already a believer in that much; it was the new light shed, revealing a dark and murderous monster in human form, that had Bolan as disturbed as he could remember.

It took another minute of sitting utterly still and listening to the silent night beyond his window before the soldier shrugged off a weight that made him feel he was the last man on a planet gone mad. There was way too much power, he concluded, in the wrong hands, and he could well guess where he could look first. Animal Man was alive and well and savaging the innocent in the desert wastes of Nevada. This, he thought, would soon prove a total war with faceless enemies who believed they were cloaked by the Stars and the Stripes, with the secret clout of special access programs and the front line legal muscle of four congressmen backing up anything they did, no matter what. And all the way to the doorstep of the Oval Office if it came down to that. Men, Bolan thought, who placed themselves above the law simply because they had a security clearance to guard the vaults of future supertechnology, some of which, granted, might even border the paranormal.

Bolan saw no need to dispute the facts as presented to him in the text. The knowledge from this particular poison tree was the reason, after all, why nine people were dead. It had also been the safety valve, he determined, meant to keep Marty and Angelo breathing. Well, apparently someone got tired of watching two loose cannons roll around the black project's deck, ready to expose the project and its wet work for public hue and cry if they believed their lives were in danger.

The problem now was yet more questions than answers were hovering in a dark limbo. Whatever truth was left hanging, before long, the Executioner would start applying maximum heat in all the right—or wrong—places. When he did turn on the burners, the jackals surely would come hunting. Only they couldn't possibly know they were stalking a lion who was the master of a domain that declared only the last survivor the winner.

Briefly he ran back what he'd read, more determined than ever to stay put, ride it out, flush out the purveyors of this dark truth, not to mention rooting out the killers of the innocent from their classified lairs.

The first eight pages were a running diary. Names, places, dates and events were laid out in sixteen separate assassinations of both military and civilian employees contracted for something called the Orion Project. Several incidents were listed "accidental." An electrocution, three heart attacks, two cars wrapped around telephone poles, and one incident where an aerospace engineer stumbled down a flight of steps and broke his neck in two places. Bolan could almost hear the ghost of Marty snickering at his own choice of the "a" word.

It was the first chronicled killing that stirred Bolan's wrath the most. Apparently, a former NSA black operative named Cromman, who headed up something called Special Security, had given the nod for two civilians to be marched out into the desert, shot in the head and buried in shallow graves. It seemed the two "college boys," their names not disclosed by the late scribe, had filmed a laser-pulsating floating device one night, the thing described only as a hovering metallic disk. The man Bolan recalled as Marty had been an eyewitness to the executions. It seemed Marty had absconded with the victims' IDs when the cleanup crew had gone to work sanitizing both bodies and vehicle. The young men had pleaded for their lives to be spared, that they'd hand over the film, keep their mouths shut, but Cromman felt only one sort of permanent closure could make his perceived problem go away.

In case the reader had any doubts these government-paid assassins could make its own citizens vanish off the face of the earth, Marty mapped out the route leading to the bodies. More incidents of threats and intimidation of locals who trooped out there in the desert, "sightseeing" the light show, were listed. More names and addresses spelled out for future verification by, Bolan assumed, anyone who read the contents of the disk and cared to make the effort to check the facts, put any lingering questions to the test. There was a three-page reference to a massive underground accident involving the antigravity device. Fifteen employees had been exposed to "leaking toxic matter of an unknown origin." Four died from a mysterious illness within days of exposure. No amount of decontamination scrubbed them clean, and ten out of the remaining survivors were executed, a cover story concocted for the next of kin. This Cromman had likewise somehow been exposed, but to a lesser degree. Reasons weren't disclosed why he was allowed to live, with an underscored reference that he was permitted "voluntary retirement." Following the accident and executions, an underground five-kiloton detonation buried the site, which was reconstructed in another location—mapped out for eyes viewing the text—within a month. Back to business as usual. Two pages then of numbers and passwords, stated as priority access codes for various files relating to not only the Orion Project but other classified work in this neck of the woods.

There was more, but the soldier knew enough. And Bolan knew he was looking at the mother lode, a who's who and what's what on everything from the Nellis Nuclear Test Range to Area 51 and beyond.

He stared at the seven-digit number with "EN" typed before it. Emergency Number? Assuming it was a local number, he believed it was a contact, a way for whoever got their hands on this poison fruit to reach out and ask for assistance. Or was it a trap? Dial up the number, and an army of men in black came rushing out of the dark, guns poised?

Only one way to find out, he figured. He could have switched his secured cell phone to landline, but he opted for the old rotary phone on the dresser. It was highly doubtful even the shadow men could break in and trace his secured line, but if they were hooked in to all local lines, he wanted to make it easy for them to eavesdrop when he put in the call. He dialed nine to get out, then let his finger roll through the digits. Five rings, then a voice, male and gravelly, sounding a little on the suspicious side, said, "Yes?"

Bolan decided to play it straight. "There's been a problem."

"The fact you're calling I would gather as much."

"You a friend of Marty or Angelo?"

"Who's asking?"

"The guy who saw them get killed by men I believe

were their former colleagues looking to get their hands on what I just read.''

"What do you want?''

"How about we meet?''

"How do I know you're not one of them?'' the voice asked.

"I could ask you the same thing.''

The voice went silent, the entity on the other end hashing it over. "Okay. I'll risk it. If you're an outsider, you have no idea what you're up against.''

"I'll need a friend—is that what you're saying?''

A grunt on the other side, then he started to lay out directions for a rendezvous when Bolan cut him off. "No.''

"No?''

"Do you know where I am?''

"How would I know that?''

"Caller ID,'' Bolan said, and listened to the hard pause on the other end.

"I know where you are.''

Bolan checked his watch. He needed to reach Brognola before he went any further. "How soon can you be here?''

"Sixty minutes, give or take.''

"Make it ninety, not one second sooner or later. Come to the door. Come alone.''

"And likewise unarmed, I suppose.''

"Your call, if you're the nervous kind.''

"Ninety minutes sharp. I'll set my watch.''

He thought the click had some anger, or maybe fear

behind it, as Bolan listened to the dial tone buzzing through the heavy silence surrounding him.

WILLY TUGGELL THOUGHT he was seeing red-eyed demons with hair like Medusa everywhere he looked, then realized it was only his reflection in the mirror, staring him back from behind the bar. He almost balked at the skeletal image on his third run down the bar, the cell phone trembling in a hand that felt more attached to an exposed electrical line than flesh and bone. For the briefest moment he was shocked at the ghoul staring him back. Eyes bugged out, the size of softballs, with red orbs flaming at him, little more than two points of fire. What little strands of blond hair left on a balding pate were greasy spikes, sticking out and up, as if he were juiced on a thousand volts.

Frigging Electro Man, he looked like.

And his heart? Man, it felt like a runaway train, derailing, shooting past one lung then back across the other, a ricocheting Ping-Pong ball in his chest. Three days' flying around the stratosphere on meth, no sleep, no food, his paranoia was understandable, and really nothing new. The problem he was having at the moment, he decided, had little to do with his brain cooked on crank and Jack. No, it was the voice on the other end of the cell phone, sounding way too damn official for his tenuous grasp on any remaining shred of peace of mind or reality.

He knew that type of voice, had heard it many times before, in fact, even in bad dreams sometimes. He'd heard it at last count four times from just beyond front doors before they charged in, guns and fists leading the way, Miranda who? Said you have constitutional rights, scumbag? He'd heard it in squad cars, cuffed and gagging on pepper spray. In police precincts, courtrooms from San Francisco to Seattle. Now this guy, whoever he was, some nightmare from the past. Was he lurking that very moment, calling from just outside, nearby in the desert, scoping the clubhouse? Was the voice chuckling in his ear, the implication being the Trojans' collective ass was grass and the biggest lawnmower he'd ever seen in his wildest hallucination was ready to bust through the door?

Oh, man, but he started seeing whole armies of armored pigs with submachine guns next, creeping up on the doors, battering rams poised to launch the raid minus Miranda. He practically flew to the curtain, landed, stumbling on a few feet before he cracked it back no more than inch. Shadows seemed to be dancing all over the desert, but he knew scudding clouds could play tricks on the eyes. What the hell was that behind the Joshua tree? The shape of a head poked out, then a canine figure materialized, scampered across the desert.

This wasn't good. Roving shadows. A disembodied voice in his ear. Heart like an endless barrage of grenades going off against his ribs.

Trouble on the way. But where? Who? How many?

For one thing, the clubhouse number was unlisted. Not even his old lady or lower-level dealers had the number. If it turned out Ma Bell had been duped somehow, she'd find herself gangbanged, a squealing porcupine, before he put the phone down. The biggest worry, though, was that if the cops were on the prowl, well, the clubhouse was both a small armory and a drug factory, with enough meth and coke to feed every addict west of the Rockies until New Year's Eve of the next century. An exaggeration, of course, but there was enough stuff under the roof to send him back to the penitentiary for a stretch that gave him nightmares just to consider. No mistake, he would go down, shot to hell, suicide by cop, before he went back to the joint.

"Who the hell is this?" Tuggell shouted into the phone.

The stereo, blaring out heavy metal rock, something about a welcome to the jungle, wasn't helping soothe his nerves any, nor did it make it any easier to hear the voice on the other end.

"Let's just say I'm a concerned citizen. Your boy Sam? He's dead."

"What did you just—? What the—?"

He wasn't sure he'd heard right, as his heart hit another speed bump. And how the hell could he hear? Why couldn't Barbell or Sasquatch get their faces out of the blow long enough, see he was on the horn and turn the racket down. Tuggell snapped his fingers, castanets in his ears, but the human vacuums were too involved. It was more than he could take. He snapped, bellowing a string of MF this and MF that, the 9 mm Browning Hi-Power out and barking. They were howling from the couch, old ladies with tits like pancakes out and flopping as they squealed at the gun blast, powder flying, hands swiping at white noses. He pumped two more through the compact disc player, reduced it to sparking ruins, just to let them know he was serious.

The bald giant that was Sasquatch was rising, grumbling.

"All of you, shut your holes! Wildman's dead!" Tuggell roared.

"I suppose you're ready to listen, Willy?"

"How you know my name? How you get this number? Who the—?"

"Listen real careful, asshole, I'm only going to say this once. This is a one-time offer for you to make Dean's killing right."

"I'm listening!"

Between the jackhammer pulsing of the runaway train in his ears, he managed to make out the words with some degree of clarity. When the voice was finished delivering the bad news, all Tuggell could think to say was, "How do I know you're straight? How do I know this ain't a setup?"

"You don't. And it isn't."

Just like that, supposed to trust the guy. He ran it back. A big, dark Justice man in a Jeep Cherokee shot down Wildman while he was conducting business with Rhonda. Seemed the bastard took out his old squeeze, too. The big pig was holed up at the A-Lee-Inn. It was too much to comprehend, how the whole deal had blown up, something Wildman had done dozens of times in the past. Wildman was too good, always skipping on, not a trace of evidence left behind, beating the heat. Or had his number simply been yanked? Fate, destiny, whatever, maybe it was just the wrong place, wrong time for that bro. How did it really go down? Something didn't feel right. He was about to rattle off a string of questions when the voice told him if he wanted Wildman's body to meet him at the abandoned Esso station west of 305. Did he have a pen and paper? Like he was an idiot.

"I know where it is!"

"If you leave right away, you should make it before sunup."

"I smell bullshit, friend!"

"Then you're smelling yourself. I'll wait with the body no longer than seven. If you're not there, I'll leave Sam for the birds and the dogs. What you decide to do about the big Justice cop is all on you. Whatever you decide to do about the guy, when I see you, I strongly suggest you don't decide to try and shoot the messenger."

"Hey, wait a second!"

The dial tone seemed to shriek like a swarm of angry locusts in his ears. While his brothers barked and rasped a bunch of questions, Tuggell stomped around, cursing. He knew there was only one course of action. Cop or not, no one killed a brother Trojan. It was the ultimate insult, especially since Wildman had gone to do him something of a personal favor.

All questions, any facts were on hold. It was real simple from there on. Vengeance would guide the coming morning hours. Whatever had happened, whoever the man behind the voice, this was a call to arms.

Honor was at stake, nothing more, nothing less. When he slowed down long enough in his furious pacing, it occurred to him Wildman had been prez of the Reno Trojans. He was next in line, not that claiming the crown really mattered. A fellow brother was dead and his blood cried out for retribution.

Simple.

"Some cop gunned down Wildman!" he shouted at his gathered Trojans. "Everyone 'cept Boner and ET I want saddled up and ready to ride!"

IT WAS PROGRESS, but Thornton was grimly aware very little, if anything, was guaranteed, now that wild cards had been dumped into the picture. The Trojans were on the way, riding in the wind, or whatever the scooter trash called it, as he sat there, contemplating how clever he was. If he read the scene, judged the temper tantrum on the other end correctly, the first chess pieces were fueled on a demonic mix of meth and rage over the killing of one of their own. Coming, he could be sure, to head-hunt for one big Justice badge.

Progress, but a long way from perfection.

One call was down, one maneuver in the works. It was time to plunge another iron into the fire, just in case the Trojans didn't come through.

He was racing through cyberspace at light speed, hacking into every bank Barklin's accounting firm did business with. He had already narrowed the list of clients all the way down to one name—a big name—the one he'd bet his future on who had seen missing chunks of laundered money walk off into Barklin's pink pudgy hands. Deposits and withdrawals from both Barklin and the client in question leaped all over the monitor, huge chunks, there yesterday, then gone. It took some work, dancing through bank records, but he traced the source of six million to three separate banks in the Caribbean, all of which were notorious for cleaning up money from the boys of Cali and Medellín. Six mil and change, rolling through Barklin's personal account in Chicago, socked away in offshore lairs. The numbers were right there for the client in question to see for himself if he had any doubts.

The second number stared him back, hanging alone on the monitor, urging him to do it despite any reservations. Thornton wasn't ready to smile yet, but he believed he was on the verge of seeing the light. Twenty-four hours tops, and the headache that was Belasko should be gone.

Call number two would take some finesse, but he already had the fabricated web woven, at least in his own mind. If he kept it short and to the point, didn't let himself get bogged down by questions from the other side, he could pull it off.

Again, it would boil down to a simple question of honor, whether the man in Chicago wanted to take personal action. What with his reputation as a pigeon to be plucked threatening to hit the mean streets and see rivals sharpening the blade, Thornton strongly suspected the man couldn't risk simply writing it off as the cost of business.

Two guns, or rather two armies, Thornton thought,

for the price of none and neither. Sweet. It was something like surgery by his own hand, he imagined. Only the cancer he was going to cut away was over six feet tall and packed a mean wallop.

It was a long shot one man could possibly stand up, much less take out a pack of drug-crazed, gun-toting rabid animals hungry for his blood. But Thornton needed the backup insurance if he would ever know anything close to peace of mind again.

If the Trojans couldn't take care of business, there was little doubt in his mind Belasko wouldn't walk away from the second team.

Vince Leanetti, Don of Chicago, had a lifelong reputation of making people on both sides of the law vanish without a trace.

CHAPTER ELEVEN

Bolan had given his old friend a condensed but thorough version of the horror show, from restaurant to disk. The follow-up silence on the other end was long and heavy.

Beyond the team at Stony Man Farm, especially Aaron Kurtzman and Barbara Price, Bolan considered Hal Brognola the next real thing to family. At this point along the journey of his own life, Bolan had come to think of himself and Brognola as inseparable.

It wasn't a stretch, he knew, to consider them that close.

The Executioner had known Hal Brognola for what seemed a hundred lifetimes, those million and one miles covered nearly together since the genesis, and down the bloody road of fate in his War Everlasting. Out of sight, almost three thousand miles to D.C., and Bolan could almost see the man's expression falling down in grim thought and worry. Yet another shadow of a ghost hanging in the heat and bad light, as the night and what he already knew weighed in, a thousand-pound gorilla on his shoulders.

The soldier allowed Brognola a few moments to collect his thoughts.

The big Fed had all the facts, so far as Bolan knew them. No sooner had Bolan roused Brognola from sleep, the man situated in his study at his suburban home, than the soldier had transcribed the disk's text to the big Fed's own satlink modem.

Brognola sighed heavily. "You know, Striker, I hear about this sort of thing once in a while through the grapevine. Black ops gone renegade, power mad, given the keys to the classified kingdom. Civilians disappearing off the face of the desert out there, seeing something the spooks think they shouldn't have seen. Strange lights at night. Civilians swearing, no, even catching on film cigar-shaped disks the size of three football fields, hovering one second, then streaking off, thousands of miles an hour in the blink of an eye, if one is so inclined to believe such stories. You know, all our state-of-the-art burglar high-tech, and we couldn't even tell you what really goes on out there."

Brognola paused, a grunt that sounded self-conscious, as if he knew he was getting sidetracked. His tone turned grim. "Anyway, I've already read some of what you sent along. It makes me sick to think a couple of kids were murdered by people supposedly on our side. Families left wondering what happened to them. I tell you what, you start eating your own like this, and for my money, that term 'national security' you always hear them use to cover their asses and their sins? That buzzword, their cure-all, fix-it, sweep-it-under-the-rug, just-leave-us-alone 'epiphany'?"

"I'm with you."

"No, you're there. Part of me could kick myself for insisting you hop off in L.A. and take a cruise of the Great American West. The larger part's telling me if it weren't for you, more innocent people would be dead and they, whoever 'they' really are, would have vanished into the night to carry on."

"It happened, Hal. For whatever reason, I was there. I'm here and I'm staying."

"I was almost afraid you'd say that."

"Don't worry, I'm already in my trust-no-one mode."

"Don't worry, you tell me. At any rate, there's a bottom line to what I and our people can do, as far as cracking these access codes, nailing down identities on any key players. If you try putting a name to any face anywhere along the food chain of a black project, you might as well try painting with smoke. We both know the kind of guys you waxed don't even have social security numbers."

"I know the drill."

"Hell, you can't even get a sat recon anymore since any passovers of areas where black projects are ongoing are monitored and guarded by both NORAD and the NSA. It's like they're holding the Holy Grail all to themselves."

"I didn't expect the usual intelligence miracle on your end."

"You need to beef up for the hunt. Tell me what you need."

Bolan laid it out, coordinating a drop site and a time

out in the desert where he intended to confirm two bodies.

"All right, figure two hours to pave the way and get our guys in the air. Nellis, huh? You want to talk about spook central. And a waiting chopper for our blacksuits once their jet touches down? I'm going to have to put a fire to somebody's tail out that way."

"I'm keeping the faith."

"Yeah? Well, every time I know the plan on your end is to make yourself a walking bull's-eye, my own armor starts to crack a little."

Brognola fell silent. Bolan understood his friend's concern and anxiety. The soldier didn't quite intend to put himself in some enemy gunner's shooting gallery, but the plan the way Brognola stated it was pretty much the working angle of attack. A venomous snake, he knew, tended to get nervous when cornered, and wanted to strike.

The soldier checked his watch. He still had time before the mystery guest arrived, but Bolan wanted to recon the layout around the building, find a dark roost where he could watch the front door to his room.

"I'll be in touch, Hal."

"Do that. And, Striker? Watch your six."

"I've already grown eyes in the back of my head."

THORNTON SAW the red light flashing on the black box beside his monitor. The man-thing, he knew, was calling, anxious for an update, the troll pacing around his mobile home black hole. Probably swallowing more of those horse pills, hating the very sight of his own flesh…

Thornton shoved the picture of the albino creature out of his mind. Back to business.

"You tell me now exactly why the interest in my personal business?" he heard the Don say. "Tell me why I shouldn't think you're just looking to remove this Belasko, so maybe you can skip off with the lion's share?"

It was nearly a wrap with pawn number two, moving the piece ever so closer to checkmate. But Thornton needed another minute to nail it down, push the man over the edge, make sure the gangster scrambled the troops for a trip west.

The voice from Chicago, though, was far more cautious than the biker. For one thing Leanetti was sober. Most important, though, he had an entire kingdom to lose if he came to Nevada, guns blazing, and it blew up in his face. It was definitely a harder sell this time around, but Thornton felt he was almost there.

Thornton felt he'd already passed a turning point, though, with the Don having fired off a battery of questions. The man's suspicions made perfect sense, Thornton had explained, and went on to field the inquiries with facts, figures and history. Like bank statements, with slews of missing cash, winding up in offshore accounts in the Caribbean. Like why did Barklin have a plane ticket for Hawaii, two hundred grand on his person? Then spinning out how the Don's personal AWOL accountant was gunned down in the shadows of the restaurant lot by Belasko. How Belasko—or so

Thornton had heard the man called by Barklin—appeared to be the man's partner. The way they'd hunched close in the dark, talking in what struck him as conspiratorial tones, well, he really wasn't trying to eavesdrop, but it was tough to miss the action when Barklin's ''partner in crime'' went ballistic. Hardly information that soothed the crime lord's nerves, but he had the man's undivided attention.

It wasn't difficult for Thornton to visualize the grim distress on the other end. Leanetti was, after all, a favorite whipping boy for the FBI and the Justice Department. He had beaten three indictments since the early nineties alone—extortion, murder and arson. The whole nine yards of RICO.

The usual.

But the Don, as Thornton deduced from the Justice files, came from the old school. He had risen through the ranks in the sixties, kicking ass all the way to the top. These days, he knew the aging gangster was a dinosaur in the new Mob, where college boys with law and business degrees from MIT and Harvard had replaced the soldiers and the button men; where they sipped French vanilla espresso and tooted a little coke; where a hummer from the mistress took priority over business; where they sold out their own for a book and movie deal and a cakewalk in the Witness Protection Program the first time a Fed knocked on the door to their condominium.

The Don had done it his way.

And it was just this sort of old-school rogue mentality Thornton counted on to see the man land on

Belasko's doorstep, soldiers in tow. Again, it wasn't that he didn't have faith in the scooter trash to see Belasko shot off into oblivion; it simply made good sense to make sure the dice were fully loaded. If the bikers took care of business first, Thornton could simply vanish from the scene, leave the Don and soldiers sweating out the whole fat mystery.

"Let's just say, Mr. Leanetti, that I simply don't like the man."

"Not good enough."

The moment called for some degree of honesty, so Thornton switched tactics.

"Then I'll spell it out. I work for the government."

"CIA?"

"Not quite. Classified work, however. Let's just say I'm an underpaid, underappreciated civil servant. I'm looking at the future, and I don't see my own beach-front property in Honolulu."

The man was chuckling. Now they were speaking in a language the Don understood and could respect.

"I'm listening."

"I have access to information, but hey, I live in the spook world."

"That's how you know so much about me and my business."

"Precisely. I just so happened to stumble into Barklin and Belasko when it hit the fan. Belasko put a stack of hundreds in my pocket to clean up his mess, look the other way. Hardly the kind of money to see me fat and happy through my golden years. So I did some cyberspace fishing into Barklin and Belasko. Barklin is a thief. Belasko turns out to be some con man with a few wants and warrants out your way. I traced their sticky fingers back to you. I figure there might be a pot of gold for me at the end of this rainbow if I came to you.''

"Simple as that?"

"Two and two still makes four the last time I looked. And it isn't love that makes the world go round."

The pause was so long that Thornton finally asked, "Are you there?"

"It's like this, Mr. Shadow Man. I haven't seen your face, and you don't even have the courtesy to give me a name. I do know how to use a computer. I'm seeing the numbers you laid on me match up with what's missing from the firm. Tells me I'm getting old and a little sloppy that some guy whose toughest day was sitting in a traffic jam could stick it to me like this."

Thornton was already tapping the keyboard, flying through the day's airline schedule from Chicago to Reno. "Sounds like we can make a deal."

"I'll come out there and have a look. Now, is this where I need to pass on a few choice words of wisdom to you if I get there and find I'm pulling a knife out of my back?"

"Your caution and your concern are under advisement."

"This isn't some game show, pal. I'll be a little more than just concerned."

"Understood." Thornton told the Don a flight was

leaving O'Hare for Reno in four hours. He gave the man a phone number at a diner in what passed as the closest town for any stretch from where Thornton sat. They agreed on a time when Thornton would field the call and give him directions for a rendezvous.

"How do you know this Belasko will even stay put long enough for me and my men to get there?"

"He told me. I guess you could say it was something of a threat. Said he was hanging around for a couple of days, make sure I lived up to my end. Maybe he's waiting to see that his back is clear of shadows before he heads out. I can't really say."

It made sense to the Don, if Thornton read the silence right. "Be there when I call."

Click.

Now to deal with the albino creature. A deep breath, wishing he still smoked, and Thornton hit the button on the black box. "Yes."

"You want to tell me why you've kept me waiting this long?"

There was a squeaky note in Cromman's voice, an edge of panic that walked some ice down Thornton's spine.

"Fires."

"I don't have time to figure out your riddles!"

"I've been busy putting out some fires." Thornton paused, then said, "There's been a little change in our plans."

"How come I don't like the sound of that, Thornton?"

"You'll probably like it even less when I tell you

what has to be done. It's unavoidable at this point, since you ordered my men to go in the place and shoot everything that moved.''

''You're laying their screwup on my head? Listen—''

''No, I'm done listening for the moment. I've taken a surgical step in what I feel is the right and only direction. Here's the deal....''

BOLAN'S MYSTERY guest arrived, almost ninety minutes on the dot. He wasn't about to give the man points for promptness, the soldier braced for the worst, as the dark Ford Bronco parked next to his SUV.

Thirty-some minutes earlier, the Executioner had reconned the motel, chosen an outcrop in the foothills of a granite chain, fifty yards or so south. If hardmen in black or the van were anywhere in the vicinity, not even his infrared binos and miniature heat-seeking monitor picked them up. He knew it didn't mean they weren't out there.

He clipped the binos to his belt, the minimonitor disappearing in his pants pocket. Time to move out.

A silent shadow melting into the night, Bolan was up and hauling out, cutting an angle, out of sight of the lone arrival. The SMG in hand, the soldier advanced up the rear of the building. Even with eyes already adjusted to the dark, ears tuned to any sound, it was still impossible to see much farther than a few feet beyond the motel. Around the office, a lone light shone over the vacated desk. Bolan whipped around the front corner, stepping away from the rear end of the Winnebago. The shadow was knocking on the door, looking over his shoulder, when Bolan aimed the subgun at the guy. Advancing, Bolan told him, "Grab some air."

Except for the curly flow of white hair reaching for his shoulders and the black bomber jacket, he looked just another classified clone.

"This isn't exactly inspiring my trust."

"Skip the speech," Bolan said. "Door's open. You first."

The lines on the shadow's face etched deeper as the scowl framed his chiseled features. One last search, but hearing and finding nothing but the silent night, and Bolan followed the man inside. He ordered him to step away, then shut the door, slipped the chain in place, then clicking the dead bolt shut with a twist.

"The piece," Bolan said, nodding at the lump under the man's jacket. "Dump it on the bed, then lay out on the floor."

"Hey, come on..."

"I've got this thing about having to repeat myself. Makes me nervous." He lifted the subgun, drew a bead on the man's chest. "Makes me think I'm being misunderstood by my fellow man."

"Yeah, I can already see how you open up lines of communication."

"The gun?"

A 9 mm Browning came out from shoulder rigging beneath the jacket. Weapon flipped on the bed, the soldier's mystery guest followed the second order. Two steps, and Bolan had the subgun's muzzle pressed in the man's spine. The guy was all scowls and grunts as Bolan gave him a rough patdown. No weapons or wires, but the Executioner liberated a silver flask, a black Zippo lighter with an engraved white death's head and a box of Marlboro cigarettes. He put the lighter and the man's medicine on the dresser.

"You know, you used a landline, right? If they were listening, they know you have it."

"I'm counting on that."

"You're crazy. Do you have any idea what and who these people are?"

"I'm thinking they're not volunteers for the Red Cross. Take a seat." Bolan stepped back as the man settled into the chair by the dresser. "You got a name?"

"Taggart. You?"

"Belasko. What are you?"

"Retired. NSA."

"Okay, Taggart, here's how it works. I ask the questions, you answer. I hear anything I even think smacks of a half truth…" The Executioner let it hang, as Taggart shot a grim smile at the subgun.

"And you can make life real miserable for me, that it?"

"All the booze in the world couldn't possible ease the pain," the soldier told Mr. NSA, retired.

"Well, in that case, do you mind if I have a nip and a smoke before we get started?"

"Whatever works. Knock yourself out."

CHAPTER TWELVE

Jason Nixon believed in a personal and preordained destiny, aware it was certainly contrary to the mantra of religious roots that had espoused man's free will. He had long since, however, shed the burden of some archaic belief system—since it wasn't his own—but one that had come full vicious circle, he had seen, all over America. The peasants, he thought, had been brainwashed, conned, in fact. From cable TV Holy Rollers, on through the political power structure to the New Age philosophers, the great unwashed had been duped into thinking they could do, be and achieve anything they wanted in life. They just had to believe in themselves, and God.

The only thing, divine or earthly, Jason Nixon believed in was the Others. And, of course, Jason Nixon.

Choices, he reflected, hitting the joint, savoring the harsh bite of the smoke as it flooded his lungs.

Ah, but human beings would always believe they were in charge of both their today and the tomorrow before them. Like lab rats on speed, he thought, humans would forever propel themselves along life's journey. They made a left turn here, a right turn there along the road, driven on primarily by their own desires, ultimately believing they could somehow determine the course and the outcome of their years.

Final destiny, he believed, was, of course, always waiting at the end of the road for every man. It was the sibling of Death.

Well, the trip out into the California desert that fateful night had seen the blinders removed for him, set him straight as far as any belief about free choice was concerned. Barring that experience, as a former psychiatrist, he had long before the first sighting seen what all that free will had done to every patient who dragged neurotic baggage into his office. Still, he had to admit he was grateful for all the rich and famous who came to him whining how empty their lives were. They had, after all, lined his pockets deep, allowing him to eventually cut loose from two alimony payments and go in search of his own destiny. At $175 an hour he had been all too willing to tell them what they wanted to hear, he recalled. Soothe them with fancy words and his Ph.D. theories. Pat them on the head even like the spoiled little children they were. Stroke their egos, which was all they really wanted anyway. Ship them off into a brave new world, all fixed up with Prozac or lithium, until next week's session.

What a sham, he thought. What a scam!

Back then he had hated himself for the patronizing mask he wore for all the beautiful people. And just for money, or whatever prestige he had believed might shine the spotlight his way for simply rubbing the right elbows. It had all been so pathetic it was laughable when he thought about it. Every time he had heard how miserable was the life of some coked-out executive from a movie studio who hadn't seen an erection in years, or how a magazine's yearly pick for sexiest man alive brooded how unappreciated he felt...

Well, not even deep in his heart he knew there was a bottom line to all their perceived and very much self-induced woes. They suffered from what he had privately tagged as the TM syndrome.

Too Much.

All the money and celebrity, all the drugs and sex in Tinseltown and beyond they could devour, and they couldn't even begin to fathom the first scintilla of how empty and shallow were their lives.

Go figure L.A.'s beautiful people, he thought. Not his problem anymore.

That was another life. The truth was, he had seen the blinding light, and on the way to Las Vegas. Transcended by the experience, he was now worlds apart from all the living dead, those bejeweled, perfumed garbage cans who used to be his patients. In more ways than just the physical, though, he had been transformed.

And the only knowledge he was sure of anymore was that some great calling was just around the corner, right over the next horizon.

Fate.

As he toked some more on the joint, he stared over the ridge, way off into the darkness where the stars hung and where his followers had marched off in hopes of seeing the hovering lights. He then looked toward the only light shining for any direction he could see, burning in the ranch-house window, a quarter mile or so east.

The place was his inheritance, clearly a gift from the gods, bestowed on him the day after the old widower had keeled over from a stroke. Apparently, the old guy had seen the light, too, many times, in fact. What little he'd known about the old man, Nixon figured it was more paranoia and fear of the unknown than any pure faith that had seen him collect enough weapons to arm the next three counties over. Before the old guy had grabbed his chest that day, Nixon now found he was grateful the desert rat had had foresight enough at least to store up food and water to keep a small community self-sufficient for two years, by his own reckoning. Nixon still figured the late and unlamented recluse for a deluded paranoid, or simply an alcoholic pushed over the edge by loneliness and Alzheimer's. That final personal analysis sure fit the way he had always raved how some phantom army of survivalists was just over the next hill and coming for his stash. Well, the only doomsday had panned out to be his own, and Nixon had simply buried the body out back, no frills, grateful to be free and alone at last.

Not long after the idea—born out of the light— beckoned him to chart the next course. With the computer he'd brought from L.A., he had gone online, setting up his own Website on the Internet. Not long after putting Otherworld.com out there, a handful of the faithful began responding. Naturally he weeded out the psychos, con artists and hard-core felons from instinct and experience. No, he was looking for true believers who shared the same experience, would abandon their former lives and ways to commit themselves to something greater than the human experience had ever known. And since he was going to meet destiny, prepare the way for the Others, he figured it couldn't hurt to have a few helping hands when they finally revealed themselves to the masses. Not to mention a few extra dollars to keep Otherworld online and spreading the word.

Everything had fallen, so far, into place. It seemed to be working out just the way the disembodied voice in the light in the desert had told him that night. Success, greatness and salvation were as close as tomorrow. The light had prophesied where one was gathered in the faith, more would follow.

Now, that was destiny. Not something as infantile in theory as following a certain alignment of the stars. That heavenly guidepost, opening the golden cosmic gates that the astrologists peddled off as the way to fame, fortune and earthly happiness, didn't fly with an educated man like himself. Nor, in his brief experience dabbling in the occult, would the future be exposed and mapped out by Ouija boards, crackpot fortune-tellers or a seance meant pretty much to clean out the pockets of the gullible who believed the spirits of the dead could be summoned forth for help in the here and now. Nothing born of man, he thought, could point the way to the truth and the light, much less reveal and assure a safe and nirvanic tomorrow.

The Others understood this, and they were coming to save humankind from itself. They were the truth and the way.

The wheezing noise jolted him, then he spotted the shadow traipsing down the trail. Before he realized it, the M-16 was up and aimed down the slope at the black shape. Nixon never cared much for guns of any kind, but there were enemies, assassins working for the government, no less, skulking all over the valley and desert beyond. The men in black were like vipers, he thought. They hid in the holes of top secret facilities, waiting to strike any prey that wandered too close or saw too much. Two of the blacksuited serpents had come to the house yesterday. Or so he had been informed, and only hours ago when he inquired on the whereabouts of Collins. Something to do about a job, he heard, the men taking the vagabond with them. He couldn't see the man's face, but he sensed the presence of panic. The drifter. He could smell the unwashed body, an odor of decaying flesh he knew belonged to only one individual under his roof.

Nixon stood, the joint dangling on his lip. The shadow was muttering something, but loud enough so he recognized the voice.

"Ernie! Up here!"

The skinny, dirt-grimed wretch had come to him, an outcast of some type, a while back. Nixon had allowed the drifter to stay on. It had been a show of compassion, a charade meant more to display a benevolent streak to his followers than some act of true charity. Even a god among men needed to show he wasn't above extending a helping hand to some poor soul.

To this minute, he still wasn't sure if the drifter could be converted, but he knew a con man when he saw one. Even still, he always found tolerance of the ignorant and the disenfranchised something of a challenge to his own character. Smelling the fear beyond the natural stink floating his way, he now wondered how wise was…his choice?

He waited as Collins blundered up the rise. The man was sucking wind in asthmatic spurts, throwing nervous swipes at the slick sheen on his face, looking over his shoulder the way he'd come. Another few moments advancing, and Collins stopped short, sniffing the air. Then Nixon saw the whites of his eyes as they fixed on the assault rifle.

"Brother, I've seen enough guns for one night."

"Do tell?" Nixon said, and held out the joint. "Take it. Looks like you need it a lot more than I do."

No twisting an arm there. Collins practically snatched the joint away.

Between tokes and bringing the hyperventilation under control, Collins wanted to know, "Anybody at the house?"

"Why do you ask?"

"We might have problems. I need a gun."

"Explain yourself."

And Collins related how the four men in black had either shot up the Howling Coyote or been gunned down themselves. How he'd taken off with their van when his nerves cracked, but quickly related he was smart enough to ditch the van a few miles away, in a gully. The fool, Nixon thought.

"Do you realize," Nixon said, "that you might have just brought serious, even potentially lethal trouble to my doorstep?"

"Hey, listen, I—"

Nixon waved a hand. "Enough. What's done is done." He was combing his thoughts, searching for some quick fix that might head off the problem of blacksuited wrath descending on the house, when the idea flashed into his thoughts. It was so strong and alive in his head it was nearly as powerful as that burst of light striking him in the eyes that night.

"Listen, we need to be ready, they'll be coming. They know who I am. These guys—"

"Silence. I have the answer if they do come here."

"You do?"

And Jason Nixon did, but decided to keep it to himself for the present.

"You feel like clueing me in, brother? How about that weapon?"

Nixon shook his head. "Not at this time."

Nixon found he was irritated by the fool's presence and ignorance. He walked away, heading for the house.

"Hey, where you going?"

"Enjoy your smoke."

He left the fool to his confusion. If the men in black came, Nixon thought, and they didn't go for his proposal, then it simply wasn't meant to be the unfurling way to fate. At least not for now. And if it turned out the fool had to be handed over to them? So be it. Even Pilate knew when to fold a losing hand. No, Nixon had no problem offering a sacrificial lamb if it meant saving Otherworld. Or the fool's head might prove an olive branch to the men in black.

All in the name of mutual cooperation, he hoped. In a joint search for the truth, an alliance to help pave the way for the Others. It couldn't hurt to ask.

THORNTON WAS confused when the brittle sound of distant laughter came through the box. After telling Cromman what he'd done, what he expected would happen when the Trojans and the Chicago Mob hit the county, he was steeled for a tirade. Instead it sounded as if the man-thing was chuckling his whole scheme off.

Of course, the punch line came next, but Thornton had already worked out six different replies and defensive stances in his head.

"You arrogant fool. Do you realize what you have done, Thornton? Are you aware you now have placed the plan in jeopardy? That my entire timetable for seizure and delivery could be thrown off with this little scheme?"

"Before you sit in judgment, hear me out. The way I see it, from the few bits of information you've fed me, it will fit your own diversionary ploy."

"How?"

"Belasko's not going anywhere. He could prove a

major fire raging out of control. It was my call. It's done.''

''One man! You're wetting your pants over one G-Man?''

''But, of course, you haven't seen this G-man's work. You haven't looked into his eyes. He's no standard government issue.''

''So you're saying.''

''So my experience and my gut is telling me. Listen, you want to move ahead right away, I want to make sure our backs are covered. No hounds barking at our collective rear ends when we go in and do the deed. When it goes down, the way you see it in your own mind, we'll need total chaos across the county. It will put the sister site on high alert. Any cold feet will come running right into my line of fire.''

''Or they'll go into lockdown! Or worse, send an SOS to Nellis!''

''Those are my men there, also. I told you. They will do as they are ordered, but to a man I can't be one hundred percent positive. We need the uncertain ones weeded out right off the bat.''

''You're in charge of security. It's your ball game to win or lose on the inside, granted. However, what worries me is some five-star windbag rolling in from Nellis to take over the project at both sites, and on the double.''

''Won't happen. If or when it does, it will be too late. We will be just a bad memory, a couple of ghosts haunting the Pentagon brass. I have the power and the authority to shut down all communications anyway.

Don't tell me you're feeling your nerves at this late date.''

"Of course not! We proceed as scheduled. I see you've left me no choice but to allow this diversionary plan B of yours to play out." A pause, then, "I don't know, perhaps...now that I think about it, I can see the benefits of anarchy and panic working to our further advantage. One, you seem unable to produce the disk. That leads to number-two problem. Since without securing certain truths for our eyes only, and with the sheriff's loyalty depending on how high the lid blows on what happened tonight...you see where I'm headed?''

"Time to get out of Dodge."

"And follow through with an arrangement that's been in the works.''

"Mind if I ask when, where and who?''

"In good time.''

"You don't trust me.''

"I don't trust anyone. Let me ask you something, since you seem to have all the answers.''

Thornton felt the invisible fist clutch his chest. He knew that tone. Cromman was getting himself jacked up to lash out the superheated criticism, rant and rave for some failure he hadn't anticipated.

When the voice sounded, Thornton was briefly surprised it was even, in control. Perhaps Cromman had the finer details he wasn't privy to already worked out.

"Since you have this one-man army under surveillance and seem to have all the answers for the both of us, did you stop and think that maybe he found the disk?''

''How would I know that?''

''Well, I'm showing a phone call from his room. It leads straight to the home of one of our former colleagues. Specifically Taggart.''

Thornton swore to himself. How the hell could Cromman expect him to be everywhere at once, know everything in the snap of fingers?

''What are you saying?''

''I'm saying yet another one of your fires, now mine, is building. I'm asking you in all your professional expertise if you have this Belasko's phone tapped.''

Thornton gnashed his teeth.

''I'll take your silence as a negative. Make sure your services are available to me in the morning. There's a lot to be done before we make our move.''

The voice vanished, but the parting words left the sting of the man's judgment echoing in Thornton's ears. He checked his watch, the anger like steam swelling in his head. A few more hours now, and he counted on seeing at least one fire trampled out. When that happened, he figured the old confidence would come roaring back.

It had to, if their plan to steal the alpha and the omega of all seven wonders of the world was going to succeed.

WHILE TAGGART COMPOSED himself with a nip and a smoke, Bolan went first. When the soldier was finished relating his lethal role at the restaurant, wrapping it up when telling the man what he thought he had shot his way into, Taggart sat, stunned.

Another belt and puff to ease his anxiety, and Taggart began, "It's happening. I know what Jim—Marty as you heard him called—put on that disk. Yes, it was meant to keep him and Baldone—Angelo—alive. I was there that day in the desert, right alongside both of them, when Cromman gave the order to kill those kids."

Bolan took a seat on the bed, one eye on the front door, the subgun canted across a knee. "Who pulled the trigger?"

"Guy named Braxton. Who knows? Maybe he was one of the four tonight you nailed."

"If he was, it sounds like justice to me."

"There is no justice in this, Belasko. There's only shadows and a chase to see who ends up with the most power. And these guys have the power to do whatever they want to keep the doors sealed on classified work out here. Any extreme measure necessary, read my lips. As far as Orion goes, not even the military wants to touch it. Special Security is in charge the whole way, it's their show, no questions. Spooks, recruited specifically for the project from a classified arm of the NSA. It's buried so deep only a few men know they even exist."

"Don't recite chapter and verse to me about the obvious. I'm thinking Marty, or whoever he was, left something out."

"He did. One of those access codes he listed was a

Website he set up, but with ten layers of firewalls. In it he lays out certain evidence he collected on Cromman. Cromman, as you read, was afflicted by the accident. The workforce that fell ill was given a lethal injection on his orders, thinking it was some cure for what they were told was radiation sickness. Again, that extreme measure. Cover up the debacle. Keep it from going public if the stricken-down brains behind the device went back to the suburbs looking like something straight out of the *X-Files*."

"Where is this Cromman now?"

"He's here in the county. Moves around in a mobile home he uses as a command center. I hear when he ventures out into the sun, he cruises around in a chauffeured boat with specially tinted glass. You want to go hunting for him, you won't need me to describe the guy. One look at him, and you'll think he just walked off the mother ship. The missing pieces you think Jim left out are this—foreign agents were contacted before the accident about the antigravity device."

"And Cromman was looking to put the thing on the auction block."

"Something like that. Only now, the scuttlebutt I've caught, this coming to me after Jim had his last encounter with the guy, is that Cromman wants a degree of revenge. You know, smear the feces all over certain faces behind the project, all the way to the Pentagon, carve out his pound of flesh, I gather. They forced him to quietly retire, keep his mouth shut. There you have Cromman left with his bone to pick, maybe because the shadow powers are unable or unwilling to restore the man he once saw in the mirror.''

"He managed to keep himself breathing.''

"Sure, he's alive. But I have to guess any man walking around looking like he does has to be a little ticked off about what happened to a face and body that might have once been plastered on the cover of *GQ*.''

"Who are the buyers?''

"Subcontractors, they call them.''

"Whatever you call them. I see traitors in the ranks of your former pals ready to sell out to enemies of this country.''

Taggart grunted around his smoke. "The usual suspects. I've heard Chinese, Iranians, North Koreans. Rumor is he has them all lined up, but he's narrowed down the shopping list. My guess is whoever comes up with the most cash. It would be his coup de grace, flying off into the sunset with the thing. Vengeance, and a gift to himself maybe to see him vanish somewhere, set up for the rest of his life. Retired. The golden twilight years. Maybe carry on, safely hidden overseas to bring public disgrace to the shadow powers. Maybe blackmail.''

"If he was bumped off the project, why am I thinking he's still in charge?''

"Friends in high places. Maybe the elite shadows in the Pentagon just want to keep him quiet, and hidden.''

"Why not just give him a taste of what he did to those kids?''

"It's not that easy. Just like Jim had some leverage to keep the wolves at bay, Cromman could have the same deal going. Guy named Thornton is officially in charge. He's probably the one put the evil eye on you at the cleanup." He pulled the smoke down to the filter, looked around the room for an ashtray that wasn't there. Taggart let the butt fall, ground it out in the carpet. "Am I scoring any points here, Belasko?"

Bolan stared into his eyes. On the surface the man seemed to play it straight, but the soldier had been down this road before. Nothing and no one appeared as it seemed. Absence of truth or lies, he knew, didn't mean the lies and the truth were absent. Bolan picked up the Browning and tossed it into Taggart's lap. "If you're asking to play Robin or Kato, the answer is no."

"I'm here if you need me. The only reason you're still breathing is two things. One, they've got too much of a mess already to clean up. Two, that family that came here in the Winnebago, sleeping like babies right now. Believe me, they're watching you. My guess is they've already put in motion a plan to drop a noose over your head. You've seen too much, and they may know you have the disk. Plus they're looking at a guy who shot four of their own off into the black hole of the next world. If nothing else, they need to save face, close up their own wounds. They'll pick the time and place. They'll wait until there are no more civilian witnesses to dispose of. You think you're smart enough or tough enough to take them on, mister, I wish you luck. Jim was a friend of mine. We went back to the old NSA days, did some things put me in the position I'd have to kill you if I told you about. But both me and Jim drew our own battle line when it came to murdering unarmed civs. All of a sudden you look like a man needs a drink.''

''I'll pass.''

''So, it's a wrap? I'm dismissed?''

''If I think of anything else, I'll call.''

Bolan watched the man as he stowed the flask and the Browning. He stood as Taggart went to let himself out. The man stopped, looked back over his shoulder at Bolan. Whatever parting words he appeared ready to say went with him as he silently left the room. Locked up again, the soldier waited until the engine fired up, and the rumble trailed Taggart into the night.

Beyond checking on the women, hoping they were on their way to Reno, Bolan knew he could do little until the morning. Daylight would hardly make it all any safer for him to move about, but at least he'd see himself beefed up to meet enemy fire by way of conflagration.

His watch told him he could try to catch about two hours of rest. Sleep, he knew, would prove impossible. And with blacksuited gunners potentially lurking around, he couldn't afford the luxury of dozing off.

And there was no reason, Bolan knew, to question the veracity of Taggart's warning about the blacksuited threat. The Executioner could almost picture them out there, wishing him nothing but the big sleep.

CHAPTER THIRTEEN

Laying out a solid course of action, especially with all manner of unknown factors hanging on the board, was definite uncharted territory for Willy Tuggell.

Sure, Willy the Terrible had blown away his bragging share of rival bikers or dealers in the past. And no problem at all when he had executed a couple of deadbeat citizens who had more craving for dope than they did cash or good sense to know when to quit and pay up the credit. But gunning down the opposition before now, he vaguely recalled, sifting through the crackling shadows of memory, was all impulse. It was one thing to do it on the spot, detonated by a rage and meth combo, plain going berserk to seize and fling the critical moment of shock and terror back in the other guy's face.

It was something else altogether to plan a strategy, cold and calm, then follow through. All anxiety and paranoia were driven closer still to the snake in his belly, since the target was, allegedly, a federal pig.

But a leader had to make decisions. And the prospect of calling a firm shot, at least for the moment, seemed a whopping chore for Willy the Terrible.

He watched as Barbell unzipped the black bag and took a few paces back so all the brothers could view the remains. Cursing, Tuggell crouched beside the body. Unbelievable. Wildman was really history. He tried to will away the shaking in his hands at the disturbing sight, aware the others were watching, waiting on their new prez to call the action.

He squeezed his shaking mitts together, popping knuckles. Unable to puzzle out Wildman's death or figure how to proceed next, he scowled over his shoulder at the man in black, as if that guy was the prime source of all mystery and his own growing ire.

For damn sure, something felt real wrong about the setup, Tuggell thought. The black oversize van, for one. No plates, no company insignia betraying origin of assembly line, but the armadillo on wheels bristling with antennae, parked near the rusted pump. The man in black, just standing there, a piece of rock, Bela Lugosi in a crew cut. All the expression of an undertaker on his face, but watching him through dark shades, and it wasn't even quite sunup. And what was that vehicle, like a scaled-down stretch limo, parked in the shadows next to the Esso sign all about? Backup? Impossible to tell how many occupants in either vehicle, since all the windows were as black as coal.

All wrong, and spooky.

Lifting the goggles off his eyes, he scoped the skeletal remains of the service station's abandoned cracker box. A voice came laughing from the electrified dark depths in his head. The voice warned someone might be hunkered down inside the black shell, gun pointed

at his head, itching for him to get froggy with the man
in black.

Surrounded by sixteen heavily armed and righ-
teously angered Trojans, he decided any edge belonged to them.

No sweat.

He let his raw eyeballs flicker back to Wildman's
corpse. Another disbelieving view, and Tuggell felt the
wrath boiling inside, but kept the lid on the rumbling
volcano. The old Willy would have blown up, but the
Rubicon was crossed with Wildman's death, the moment demanding the new Trojan leader show steely
take-charge control. Still, he wanted to lash out, found
he was even unable to begin to count the number of
ragged holes punched into Wildman's chest. Not that
it mattered. Dead was dead, whether it was one fatal
shot or twelve. It struck him next as something of an
insult the way in which no one had bothered to pull
Wildman's eyelids down. Was there a message in that?
he wondered.

Tuggell stood. Decision time. What would Wildman
do in his boots if that were him squeezed into a rubber
bag like some bloody slab of gored walrus meat?

No decision at all really, certainly not for a leader
of the Trojans.

"A cop did that? The brother's got more holes in
him than the Saint Valentine's Day Massacre."

"What can I say?" He watched the man in black
shrug it off, shit happened. "Maybe too much raw
meat in his diet."

Guy thought he was funny? Tuggell felt the shakes

reaching all the way to his toes. He heard the round of grumbling begin, the brothers stoked to kick ass.

"Before you boys get all in a big snit, last I heard, your man's still up the road. Probably sleeping right now. Sweet dreams how he put a righteous notch on his belt."

"Yeah, he's a big fucking hero!"

"Now, that motel is about—"

"I know where it is!"

"Then we're finished here."

"Hold on a second!" He took a step toward the man in black, annoyed the guy didn't show the first hint of nerves, much less any respect. "Why you handing the pig over?"

The man in black grinned. "Call it peace of mind."

"In case you're blinded by those shades, maybe you can't see none of us is in the mood for smart-ass routine."

"They say to be a smart-ass you first have to be smart."

Tuggell felt the raw anger flash the heat beneath his scowl. Any snappy comeback eluded him, so he asked, "How do I know this Belasko was even the one pumped our guy full of holes?"

Tuggell nearly screamed his rage when he thought the guy was about to ignore him, turning his back to angle for the passenger side of the van.

"Simple. Just ask him. And, believe me, when you see him, well, you can judge that no-shit look he has in his eyes for yourselves. That is, if you're any kind of judge of men at all."

Tuggell felt his head bobbing. Made sense. "Hey." The guy turned. Was that a condescending smirk on his face? "In case it looks like we're getting it broken off in our ass... You see what I'm saying?"

"I'll be around. What? You want my name, too?"

"Yeah, I'll take a shake with those fries."

The guy opened the door, grinning to himself. "Well, considering the gift of payback I'm putting under your trees...ask for Santa Claus."

Through the pounding thunder in his ears, Tuggell heard someone mutter, "Asshole."

Tuggell didn't wait for the black vehicles to leave. Pumped on crank and anger, he charged for his hawg and tore into the saddlebag. He produced an Ingram MAC-10, backup for the Browning in his waistband, then checked the load on the stubby subgun. Bolt cocked, he laid the piece back, butt angled up. As the van and limo kicked some dust in his face, Tuggell snapped out the strategy. One guy, he figured. No match for seventeen guns, but he didn't need all that iron and muscle when he rode up to the door. No, this had to be something of a solo act. A personal trophy to take back to the clubhouse would go a long way to establishing his stature as leader, no questions he was the right heir apparent. He told Barbell and Sasquatch they would ride with him to the pig's door. He ordered Saber Tooth and Thunderball to ride along, but fall behind and wait on the highway as backup. The rest of the pack grumbled bitter disappointment when he told them to go have a beer at the diner. He had to refresh a few meth-addled memories where it was.

Tuggell turned to Croc, the Trojan who had half his face burned to purple flakes and splotches when a meth lab had blown up on him. Croc and the rest would stand by, cell phone ready. Wait at the diner, the one they used to hit on a run to Utah, he told Croc. They didn't have to like it, just do it.

One last dive into the plastic bag, shoveling two fingers of powder up his nose, and Tuggell straddled his bike. The buzz fueled new confidence, the day looking bright despite the last hanging shroud of dawn. Tuggell was good to go skewer himself the pig who'd killed Wildman.

THE EXECUTIONER WAS under no illusions.

It was going to be a bad day.

The simple fact the night had passed without event already had Bolan on edge. At some point, between the three hours of a restless combat nap, he had placed a quick call to Tina Waylan, checking up. He was told the sister of the lady's friend couldn't be reached. It seemed they were forced to stick around Eureka Springs. Not good, the soldier had thought. Still, she had sounded strong enough on the surface, and Bolan decided there was nothing more he could do for any of them. Before hanging up, he had told her to try and find a place out of the county to stay for a few days, glossing over any basis for his concerns about their safety. She said she'd think about it, but her and the boys really had nowhere to go. No immediate family, both sets of the boys' grandparents long since passed away. She thanked him again for the loan, wanted an address where she could send along a money order at some point to square the tab. Bolan simply told her he'd be in touch.

Silently he wished them well, but he couldn't baby-sit. Unless he missed his guess, he would be hung out there, one hundred percent on his own, a hunted man. When the lethal stalk began, the last thing he needed was an innocent life tangled up in the cross fire.

The list of mental chores was already logged. First, a visit to the sheriff, light a fire under his seat. A few choice questions off the record, cast some doubt and suspicion Walsh's way, and Bolan figured the badge would sound an SOS to his paymaster once he left the man. The weapons drop was still hours away, but it would give Bolan time to make the site, exhume the bodies to confirm the first set of facts.

The grinding sound of a big engine sent him to the window. He figured it was the Winnebago, he needed eyeball confirmation of even the obvious. The big R and R rig backed out, Bolan finding the faces of a middle-aged man and woman framed behind the windshield.

Harmless enough by all outward appearance. Or was it?

One final preparation would lend him some minuscule sense of security his back was covered when he vacated the room. The cracker box would serve Bolan's twofold purpose until whatever lay ahead was faced, and finished, one way or another. That was assuming he had some answers, and, of course, he left in one piece at all. The sweatbox would double as both command post and central location if the blacksuited gunners came calling, for either a chitchat or anything else. If they popped in while he was gone, the miniature motion sensor he fixed to the rail under the bed would alert him to bad company. He checked the readout box, the small digital screen recording his own presence, filing it away in the number column as 1.

He was all set to go and put the branding iron to the sheriff, when faint rumbling thunder pricked his senses. War bag in hand, he was out the door when he spotted them in the distance. Two dropped back, halting on the shoulder of the interstate, while three more swung onto the dirt path leading to the motel. There was no mistaking what they were, but two questions leaped to mind. Why now? Why him? He was about to find out, but grimly decided they weren't flying his way to inquire about food and lodging. Instinct told him it was smart money they'd just come from a briefing about one Agent Belasko.

First problem of the day, and the sun had barely risen.

He took up position on the passenger side of the SUV, settled the war bag on the hood. The soldier then felt the adrenaline break a slow, fiery course in his blood, aware several sets of eyes were homed in on his stance, sizing him up, sharpening a mental blade of ill will. What had Taggart told him? Something about how the men in black would choose the time and place? Well, this was a new twist, he thought, but somehow it fit their style. He could only imagine the black magic con job either Thornton or perhaps Cromman had worked to get the bikers jacked up for the kill. Throw the live grenade of meth into the mix of rage and hunger for vengeance on the guy they'd been maybe duped into believing he had mowed down...

Here we go, Bolan thought, steeled inside, as he sidled away from the SUV, hoping to keep the vehicle and war bag out of any line of fire.

Only the Executioner didn't intend to let it go any further than his weapon speaking first and last.

The rolling thunder washed over Bolan as the Trojans braked their bikes, three tails of dust converging to suspend a grimy halo in their wake. Bolan felt his left leg slide out a few inches, hand slowly falling down toward the .44 Magnum Desert Eagle. They shut down their bikes, leaned them over on kickstands, reading him behind goggles. While the silence hung poised like a hammer over his head, the soldier weighed the moment and the men. One muscled behemoth, and one bald biker, the size of a battleship. A Trojan with little remaining hair like wet electrical wires sandwiched between, but eyes zooming. Clearly Wirehead was unable to focus on anything longer than a flat second, thanks to the wildfire of speed frying the brain circuitry. Two stainless-steel pistols, Bolan noted, were wedged in the front pantslines of Muscles and Battleship. And it looked like the stock of a subgun was sticking up in the saddlebag behind Wirehead from where Bolan stood.

Showdown.

Wirehead got it started. ''Understand you're the guy who wasted Wildman last night. Man tells me you went apeshit, blew away the brother and eighty-sixed an old squeeze of mine.''

Bolan decided to let their nerves get the better of them, let his silence speak his own grim intent. Wirehead was quickly losing it, he saw, slapping up the goggles, mouthing curses.

''How 'bout it?''

Bolan let it drag for a long moment as they fidgeted in the saddle, glancing at one another. ''How about what?''

''True what we heard?''

The soldier saw Wirehead twitching all over the seat, hand starting back toward the saddlebag, but holding the move for some reason. There was no point in stalling the inevitable, Bolan decided, and draped the tail of his windbreaker behind the butt of the Desert Eagle. Free access to the big cannon, but he knew it was hardly easy from then on.

Wirehead seemed to give something second consideration, as the pinballs of his eyes shot from Bolan's big piece to the buddies flanking him. He tried to brazen it out, but the Executioner heard his nerves cracking behind the chuckle as Wirehead told his boys, ''Look at this. We got Josey fucking Wales here.'' The eyes darted back to Bolan, and he growled, ''I asked you a question, Wyatt!''

''Sounds like you boys are going to believe what you want,'' Bolan said, letting his hand inch back.

''You tellin' me you didn't?''

''I'm telling you to think about that old saying.''

''Yeah! What's that, pig?''

"Something about barking up the wrong tree."

"Why, you—"

"I'm telling you to ride on."

Wirehead was cutting loose with the curses, his buddies snapping out their rage, but following the lead as they clawed for weapons. Bolan had the hand cannon up and out. As Wirehead fumbled to get the subgun free from the bag, Bolan blew Battleship out of the saddle. The monster biker was all arms flapping in the air when the warrior swung his aim, tapped the trigger and punched another pile-driving .44 hollowpoint round through Muscle's sternum, likewise launching him for the end of the ride.

Two gone into the wind of oblivion.

Wirehead nearly made it in the heartbeat it took Bolan to line him up. Panic at seeing he was suddenly all alone had to have spoiled Wirehead's aim. The brief stutter of lead slashed the air, yards to Bolan's left when he squeezed out the third gong of doom. The angle of the .44 round's penetration was slightly off the mark, as Wirehead ripped a roar of agony, the slug impacting high on the right side of his chest. Wirehead spun, soaring back out of the saddle.

Down but not out.

The stainless-steel cannon leading the way, Bolan glanced toward the highway. He saw the two dark lumps in that direction, frozen. He figured a new level of rage was probably working its way through the shock at seeing how quick and easy their fellow Trojans just got dumped.

Bolan moved on to give them the encore.

Wirehead was writhing on the ground as the Executioner rolled between the bikes. The biker was making strangled gagging sounds, his eyes unmoving, protruding cueballs in his skull. The slug had torn its exit, Bolan saw, out the shoulder, nearly amputating the arm.

The Executioner triggered a mercy round into Wirehead's forehead.

A new thunder sounded after the final peal faded over the desert. Bolan saw them cranking it up, bikes fishtailing around on smoking tread. He couldn't be sure, due to distance and bad light, but it looked as if one of them had a cell phone pressed to his face.

Marshaling the reserves, no doubt. Good enough.

He stowed the Desert Eagle, marching back for the SUV. Where they were going, and how many Trojans waited at the end of their ride Bolan didn't know, of course, and pretty much didn't care. He would give chase and run them down.

If he didn't stomp out this one nest of vipers…

First the Trojans.

As he moved behind the wheel, Bolan hoped a blacksuited gunner or two had caught the showdown. It would give them something to think about, nerves torqued up, pushing them closer to the edge to force them out of the shadows.

The Executioner almost couldn't wait to take the firestorm to the enemy. The truth might be out there, he reckoned, but it would take a flash flood of bloodletting before he spotted the light.

CHAPTER FOURTEEN

"Yes, I'm quite human."

Thornton was marching into the living room behind Cromman when he read the faces of the gathered cultists. They were studying Cromman, a bunch of zoo goers gawking at some endangered species, but a peering mass armed with assault rifles. Fearful wonder followed Cromman to the corner of the room, where he took up a somber post. To Thornton he looked more like a Sunday preacher set to rain fire and brimstone on the sinning crowd than one of the most feared power brokers the NSA's black ops womb ever spawned.

And the watchers kept gaping, looking to Thornton as if their rumors and speculation about ETs had just floated through the door, in the flesh. He wanted to sound off a grim chuckle, but kept it to himself, aware it was touch-and-go, with no telling how the cultists would respond to Cromman's proposal. But the way they kept staring at the man-thing, and he imagined this was what their faces looked like inside the bubbles of hazmat suits when they had performed that alleged "autopsy."

Only these were dangerous fanatics, perhaps even deluded to new limits of paranoia, he suspected. This moment was all too real, facing off with a lunatic fringe nearly parked in the backyard of the facility. A brittle, even an insane reality—most certainly not the smoke of those floating rumors about an alien body going under the knife.

Nearly to a man they were armed, and suspicious. M-16s, a few fixed with M-203 grenade launchers, were the main weapon of choice. Four of the more raggedy members of the cult they called Otherworld looked relegated to side arms and coffee. The wretch who was chosen as Braxton's puppet lackey, he noted, was hugging the wall that led to the kitchen. Collins looked set to break and run, maybe standing there, Thornton thought, wishing that beam of light would come down and take him away to a warm yellow unknown. Anyplace but here, in the face of two armed hardmen, and something that pushed the boundaries of rational human explanation.

Cromman, Thornton had to admit, would make anyone's nerves jump, perhaps even quiet down any giggling about little gray bodies in cryogenic cocoons. Cromman's special one-piece white jumpsuit was made of some revolutionary fabric designed by NASA, Thornton knew. The clothing was a state-of-the-art combination of foil, silk and rubbery material. First impression, and Cromman was the poster child for what future astronauts would look like. Then the wide-brimmed matching hat, thick black visors wrapped around a face as round and white as the moon itself. It was especially unnerving to Thornton how the subterranean accident seemed to have erased the man's features, as if the facial bones had been melted, smoothed out, the flesh like irradiated silver.

Cromman folded white-gloved hands at a point where the skintight suit should have molded genitals. Nothing there at all to suggest even a minor-league package. It made Thornton briefly wonder if the accident had performed some form of radioactive castration. If that was the case, with life as a paranormal eunuch, well, Thornton figured he could begin to appreciate some of the man-thing's rage.

Cromman addressed the wretch first. "You, Ernie Collins, car thief from Pennsylvania. Relax. I'm not concerned about your role in what happened last night. Nor," he told the assembled motley lot, "am I interested in your snooping around of our installations, whatever your former lives of broken families, substance abuse, your personal failures and sob stories. Nor am I interested in your suspicions, your sightings, your theories. Mr. Nixon, if you would disengage yourself from your star children, please."

Thornton followed the stare behind the visor. Except for the wretch, he was surprised none of them betrayed confusion or anxiety that Cromman seemed to know them by name. Collins had been nailed by a simple fingerprint when he'd first touched Braxton's van last night. The key to unlocking the secret vaults to other identities were vehicles that had carried the various cult members here in the beginning. They were scattered around the valley, tucked away in gorges. A few of the vehicles were draped in brown camou netting the late occupant—a former Korean War vet and State Department official who retired here for reasons unknown—had squirreled away in this squalid rathole. He couldn't be sure of the reason they hid their cars and trucks, but Thornton notched it up once again to rampant paranoia. So, it was easy enough to run down their former lives once Thornton was armed with a license-plate number. No man, he knew, could ever truly hope to escape the eyes of Big Brother.

Thornton watched as the leader of Otherworld stepped from the corner of the room where a bank of computers was housed. The shrink from L.A. Nixon didn't look like much more than a middle-aged suburbanite to Thornton. Sports shirt and slacks. Clean shaved, neatly trimmed salt-and-pepper hair swept back from a face that was borderline movie-star material. Certainly not a man who would pitch it all away to hole up in the middle of nowhere, and surround himself with a gaggle of star-watchers clamoring for the mother ship.

Nixon kept the M-16 in hand, angled across his chest. "We know you've been watching us for some time. We know you are covert agents in a government conspiracy to conceal the truth about stolen alien technology and the existence of extraterrestrials. We know there was a nuclear explosion, in fact, in your old facility, which you have since moved. Only now has the electromagnetic pulse faded enough where we can use—"

"Please, stifle yourself. I have no time to get sidetracked confirming or denying anything you think you know. I am here on a most urgent mission. I have a proposal, one whereby our side and yours can work together in a mutual effort. Let's call it a joining of hands, 'we are the world,' prepared to take up arms even against this ongoing government conspiracy you mentioned.''

"Really? Funny you should say that." Nixon almost smiled, the weapon lowering to a nonthreatening point, muzzle pointed toward the bare floor. "Only last night I was thinking along the same lines."

It was Cromman's turn to show suspicion. "Do tell."

"Perhaps there is something to be said how great minds think alike."

Or sick ones, Thornton thought, silently urging Cromman to get on with it. Belasko was out there, and the day was full of worry and trouble enough without getting stalled here, playing mind games.

Thornton listened as Cromman said, "Here is what I propose...."

THE NEEDLE WAS hovering around eighty when Bolan saw one of the Trojans drop back. When he'd hit the interstate, they hadn't shot away, but split off, one hawg to a lane, the bikers appearing to discuss something as they thundered on in the wind.

Roughly two football fields now, he figured, and closing, and some spur-of-the-moment tactic to end his charge up their rear was in motion down the highway. There was no accounting for any strategy on their part, fired as it might be by meth, blind panic or a lingering acid taste for revenge.

Or a murderous jagged-edge combo of all three.

The Executioner saw no point in debating the issue why the biker had fallen behind his comrade to circle the one-man wagon. All the soldier saw was the one-percenter sluicing onto the shoulder, then pulling up hard, and swinging the hawg around.

All he knew was a compact subgun was leaping out of a saddlebag, aimed his way.

If, somehow, a voice in the whacked-out circuits of the biker's head told him this was an optimum stretch—free of traffic and witnesses—to make his blazing stand, Bolan's own grim thoughts were clear, loud and decisive.

A death knell clanging, in fact, on the vacant ribbon to his twelve and six.

It looked like the runner popped a wheelie down the road, nearly losing it and flipping over before the front end bounced down, appearing to shimmy on the surge before the rider hauled it back and tore on.

Gone, but not forgotten.

One at a time, Bolan told himself.

Flame shot out from the subgun. Bolan gave the wheel a little twist, fists holding hard as the wheel fought the sudden lurch. Momentum and gravity almost got the better of Bolan's effort to evade the tracking fire, but he yanked back to the right, on-line again and roaring ahead. Two, maybe three rounds went skidding off the starboard side on the biker's second attempt, flying off to nowhere.

With range to impact lopped to a simple toss of a stick, Bolan saw the whites of the eyes, bugged and framed, like a hung portrait of doomsday's child, as he stomped on the gas pedal. Beyond the bulldozing it came down to controlling the rig, riding it out when he hit what appeared a fairly level stretch. He wasn't about to question some fateful blessing in disguise on the lay of the land beyond.

It was roll and ram.

The Executioner grasped the wheel in an iron grip, body tensed. The Trojan's final desperate two-step shuffle to the side loomed beyond the windshield as he plowed the starboard front edge through metal and flesh on a thud and a scream. A blur of the soaring package of man and machine in the corner of his eye, then he was shooting off the shoulder, jouncing over the hard soil, concentrating on the earth ahead.

Bolan tapped the brakes. Gently he turned the wheel, then let the vehicle roll out its own flight, riding out a dip or break in the desert hardpan while searching out the nearest stretch of smooth earth. A little gas then, and he cleared the blooming dust cloud on his rear. The soldier was giving the panorama of hills and desert a hard search, unable to detect any watching eyes, when he discovered the Trojan wasn't roadkill yet.

The bike was a twisted skeleton, thrown a good fifty yards from the point of impact. Close by, the Trojan was pulling himself along on his elbows, jaw slack, face screwed up in agony and aimed Bolan's way.

A few yards out from what was left of man and

machine, Bolan parked, hopped out and slid the
.44 Magnum Desert Eagle free. The Trojan was snarling out his anger and pain, a human snake wriggling
for his subgun, when Bolan spared him a send-off
round to the head.

THE WHOLE TEN MINUTES it took Cromman to lay it
out, Thornton resisted the impulse to check his watch,
the caller-ID monitor on the screen of his handheld
radio. He needed a report on the Belasko situation. He
was hoping no news was good news. All that was on
the plate, and he couldn't be sure of anything now,
one moment to the next. The day had only just started
and he already felt ten years older. When this was
done, after tonight, he decided a long vacation was in
order.

First business, and of the killing kind, he knew, before the sun rose again.

Nixon and his Otherworld stooges had listened in
grim silence, but their eyes slowly lit with rapture
when their part in Cromman's plan was filled in. Of
course, Cromman, he knew, had left out one important
detail.

Such as their own eventual doomsday.

"Well?" Cromman prodded into the lingering silence.

Thornton nearly groaned next when Nixon took
center stage and began the show-and-tell. The first exhibit was a burly backwoodsman type, who was told
to unbutton a red-and-black flannel shirt. That done,
and exhibit one displayed two vertical rows of perfect

red circles down the torso, which looked branded into his flesh.

"Idaho," Nixon said, pointing at the specimen's chest. "Those were the marks left when Harold encountered a grounded UFO. It glowed, gave off a tremendous heat, then took off, straight up into the air, hovered, then vanished after shooting off on a vertical line at speeds, he says, which covered hundreds of miles in seconds flat. These burn marks have branded him for life. Says they match the circles on the vents of the disk. Said he was not only sick for weeks, hardly able to get out of bed, but he claims he could practically see his flesh glow in the dark at night for some time after the encounter."

"I do not have the time for this nonsense," Cromman snapped.

"Indulge me. I am making a point."

"Make it and be quick about it!"

Exhibits two, three and four showed off tiny reddish marks just behind the left ear. Abductees, since birth, Nixon alleged. Tagged, he suspected, like game animals by the Others. A few more nuts he claimed to have put under extensive hypnoregression, the shrink having dredged up bits and pieces of encounters with the Others, little by little, filling in their missing time. Terrible memories were awakened by his professional mining of their brains. Needles slid up every orifice. Little gray men with grasshopper heads and black eyes floating above them while they were immobilized by some form of telekinesis, they believed. The shrink mercifully wrapping it up with a quick tale of his own three sightings in the California desert, but conveniently, Thornton thought, glossing over the specifics.

"Your point? No, your answer!"

Nixon stared at Cromman with a strange smile. "That was my point. That was my answer. You see, we consider you the enemy. The source of a jealously guarded truth you keep to yourselves. I believe you know we aren't alone in the universe. I believe you keep this knowledge to yourselves simply because it is your power to wield over the rest of us. Perhaps you consider us ignorant peasants, or children who might be so terrified by 'the' revelation of all human history they might take up arms against the conspiracy that is the United States government and its military shadow army of jackbooted goons and killers."

"Yes, or no."

"If I say no, do I hear an 'or else' hanging in the room?"

"What you'll hear is the sound of my vehicle leaving."

Nixon gave a thoughtful nod. "Let me understand what you want. We are to go into one of two installations, and help you steal a device that you have conveniently neglected to frankly state what it really is. I'm thinking you want this thing all for yourself, for reasons you didn't state."

"Why I want it is my concern."

"Indeed. You are asking me to risk my life and the lives of my people, taking classified government scientists and a civilian labor force as hostage while you abscond with the device. What is to guarantee our safe return here? What assurance do I get that we will be left in peace?"

"I'll speak in language you understand. The only thing that is certain is uncertainty."

"Indeed. Here it is—if you want our assistance, there is something I want in return."

"What?"

"Allow me to take my people into another room. Allow us five minutes to discuss it."

"The clock's ticking. One second more and I take the truth with me."

"I wouldn't want that."

Thornton heard himself groan now as he watched them troop down the hall, the wretch picking up the rear. He shook his head and looked at his watch.

"Problem?"

Thornton looked over at the man-thing. "Nothing that can't wait another five minutes."

Or so he found himself clinging to hope.

THE WOODEN SIGN READ: Shambala. Gas And Food. 1.5 Miles.

Bolan had left the roadkill 6.6 miles behind. From there on he really didn't care if a roving state trooper was alerted to the carnage by a concerned citizen, or just happened across the bodies. If necessary, he could phone Brognola to get any legal weight lifted off his shoulders.

Someone else had called the opening shot. And the Executioner was hell-bent on firing back, long and loud, until he saw the light on this one.

Bolan checked the highway, then scoped the chains of hills north on the desert floor beyond the slightly crumpled tin of the starboard hood. Two hunches. One, the Trojan runner had hit the dirt road leading to whatever abodes comprised Shambala. A closer search to the right, and he confirmed it, spying the series of one-wheeled grooves in the track. Hunch number two alerted him watching eyes were somewhere in the hills. Blacksuited gunners or bikers?

No matter.

He decided he'd take on both, if it came down to that. The hardware and reserve ammo was alreadymeasured, and good to go. Four clips for the HK MP-5 subgun, with one magazine in place, the SMG laid across the open war bag. Mini-Uzi, two clips altogether. The problem was guessing enemy numbers, and that's where the handheld HK 69 grenade launcher was factored into the scheme. Again, he was running low on rounds even for the big numbers cruncher. Three missiles remained for the launcher—one frag, incendiary and a buckshot round, all in 40 mm. With two more fragmentation hand grenades, he could only hope it was enough.

Nothing he could really do about it anyway, except work with what he had.

And once the Trojan pack learned the fate of at least three brother one-percenters...

Well, the soldier didn't need to be looking over his shoulder the whole time for any wild cards. The men in black would prove formidable enough in the coming hours without having to dodge a leadstorm thrown at his blind side by a meth-crazed Mongol horde on iron horses.

Now the tricky part, he knew, easing down on the gas and beginning the long roll down the track. The sun was free and clear of the sawtooth ridge of hills to the east. Maintaining a sharp eye, and he might be able to spot any light twinkling off a sniper's scope in the hills, assuming a blacksuited gunner might have him lined up for a long-distance tag.

The slow roll found Bolan going up a gradual incline, moving over the rise. The track leveled out, an arrow-straight run before the ground rose up again, maybe a quarter mile ahead.

He was scouring the nooks and gullies cut into the hills, which formed a horseshoe around the bowl he was easing into, when the sound touched his ears.

Thunder rolled his way in louder peals, followed by a dust wall lifting a dirty screen to signal their advance.

The Executioner angled the SUV across the trail, blocking off any exit past him, and watched as the horde rolled over the rise, before one of the bikers shouted something, throwing up an arm. The Trojans stopped, a couple of nervous hands cranking on the rumbling horsepower at the sight of the SUV blockade. There was a brief exchange among them, the words lost to Bolan, but the strategy became clear when the weapons came out.

They were fanning out in jerky motions, forming a skirmish line, when the Executioner took up arms.

CHAPTER FIFTEEN

"We want the pudding, but we'd rather not have to eat the meat."

"What?"

"We don't want no thought control, but we do want an education."

"What?"

"We refuse to be just another brick in your wall."

Five minutes and fifteen seconds, and Nixon had returned with his raggedy following. Cromman had nearly reached the door when the shrink got the head games launched again.

"I have certain conditions."

"No conditions. This is a nonnegotiable offer. I don't need you that bad," Cromman said.

"If that was true, you wouldn't have come here."

That little gem of a comeback, Thornton saw, pulled Cromman up short.

"Thirty seconds. What are they?"

"One, what is this 'thing' you are looking to steal?"

Cromman appeared to think about it, then nodded.

It was a small concession, no great mystery. "It is an antigravity device."

"And does what precisely?"

"It allows a craft to hover. It contains an element that, when powered up by a nuclear reactor, can propel a craft at hypersonic speed, or even faster—so I am told."

"Where did you get the technology?" Nixon asked. "Is it alien? Reverse engineering?"

"That, Mr. Nixon, is for me to know. However, should you fulfill your obligation to me, I am more than willing to share the truth."

Nixon practically beamed. "Our reward. The truth. Fair enough."

The handheld radio beeped on Thornton's hip. He left Cromman and Nixon to haggle over the details, stepping outside to take the call. He was hopeful, anticipating progress on the Belasko front, then heard Walsh's barking in his ear, "We've got problems. I suggest you get over to the motel right away."

BAILING OUT, a shoulder through the door, with sub-gun and grenade launcher ready, and Bolan weathered the first storm of lead. A few rounds tattooed the far passenger side, glass caving on the shotgun seat. For the moment the lightning surge over broken ground was spoiling most of their aim, but he knew if they made the SUV and started to circle in from both directions...

Bolan knew he couldn't let it get that far.

The soldier figured twelve, thirteen armed riders,

tops. They were triggering off subgun bursts, one-handed, cutting the gap quickly, in the neighborhood now of eighty yards and counting. The Trojans were hardly the sort of finely tuned, disciplined fighters they'd borrowed their club name from.

Their hard charge was meant to end it quick and messy, a casualty or two maybe anticipated on the way in. The fact they were bunched in a loose skirmish line only further aided Bolan's tactic. Their reckless surge gave the soldier all the edge he needed for the moment.

The HK 69 popped off a 40 mm frag bomb, Bolan dropping the thundering fireball in a tight group of three bikers at roughly ten o'clock. A few wild rounds skidded off the windshield, the warrior ducking to fill his stubby launcher with an incendiary missile.

The blast radiated shock waves and scorching heat to bowl down the fourth Trojan in line, and Bolan lurched up, didn't pull them up short to rethink the situation.

Four had their lights punched out, the only shining a dark one calling them to Hell. Too late they figured out that they were little more than a rolling shooting gallery, packed in at near arm's length to one another, making it easy to thin the herd to less than half in two shakes.

If they were shocked and angry before, they became downright horrified when the white wall of fire erupted on the other flank. Bands of flame torched up three more Trojans, human fireballs flying out of the saddle, dumped to the ground, writhing and shrieking their agony.

The fire might have washed away their troubles, but it sent them soaring to new heights of unearthly pain.

One Trojan, just the same, was bursting past the shooting tongue when his arm was lit up like a Roman candle. Meth and pure rage kept him medicated against the pain long enough for him to cut loose with a few rounds from his Ingram MAC-10.

Bolan sprayed the broken line, shuffling down behind the hood's port side, return fire thudding off metal, the soldier's HK MP-5 sweeping them flank to flank. Enemy fire rattled on for a brief moment, then the Trojans were taking to the air as the warrior hosed them down, bodies spinning out of the saddle, crazed eyes finally registering the pain of absorbing the one-man hellstorm. An unmanned Harley streaked away from the toppling riders, slammed into the shotgun door. Bolan ripped another stream of 9 mm Parabellum shockers, stitching the last rider up the torso before he was sailing to join the carnage.

A fresh 30-round magazine cracked home, and Bolan heard a moaner or two beyond his steel fort. The last of the flaming scarecrows was screamed out when the Executioner rolled into the slaughterbed. A Trojan, his arm bent an impossible angle, was rising in a stagger, a pistol in hand when Bolan tapped out a 3-round burst into his chest, pitching him to drape over the mangled heap of his Harley.

Advancing, the Executioner pinned Groaner Number Two, scrabbling for a discarded subgun, with another brief stitching up the back. Number Three came as something of a surprise, a bloody glimpse looming up from the dead in the corner of his eye. The Trojan made a double-fisted stand, a mini-Uzi stuttering in one shaky fist, a Colt .45 ACP booming once in the other bloody mitt. Pain had the better of the biker's aim, the rounds sailing past Bolan as he wheeled. Shooting from the hip, the soldier hit the biker in the chest. It took six rounds, the Trojan bellowing out a string of curses, before he toppled, still clutching his weapons in a death vise.

Shambala on the dark side.

His senses pinched by a mixed bag of noxious smells, the Executioner gave the deathbed a thorough walk-through. Nothing but vacant eyes, frozen in shock and horror, stared at the sky.

Thirteen confirmed kills.

Next the soldier gave the broken ridgeline around the arena a long scoping. If someone was watching, he was either too well buried, he decided, or had maybe beat a quick exit when the curtain here was dropped.

Either way, the men in black were playing games, he knew. Devious bastards, they had groomed the Trojans as lackeys, hoping they could wash their hands of a problem from the Justice Department.

Not this day.

The soldier knew the drop was still a few hours off. The desert could prove as lethal as any armed enemy, so he figured he needed to stock up on bottled water, some food.

As he retraced his steps to the SUV, he couldn't shake the feeling he was being watched. One last view of the empty panorama and the soldier gave his wheels a look. A few scars and dings, the passenger side mashed in where it took the Harley's ram. Cosmetic damage, nothing to hamper him from rolling out into the desert to the south.

He had to believe the three sets of messes he was leaving would bring the sheriff running after him. Good enough. If that happened, he had a plan to crank up a little more heat.

Brushing the glass crumbs off the seat, the soldier piled in behind the wheel. The last 40 mm hellbomb deposited into the launcher, a buckshot round, and Bolan settled the HK hardware on top of the war bag.

The Executioner put it in drive and set out to follow the road to Shambala.

NOT EVEN off the starting line, and Thornton was already seeing it all poised to unravel before the day was out. He toed the three bodies, grunting, as he felt the full force of both the sheriff's angry stare and the baking sun.

"And this is just some federal cop? Looks to me like your Belasko headache dropped these boys like they were nothing but paper targets in some carnival gallery."

Thornton ignored Walsh, looked past the scowling face toward the black Lincoln Towncar replica. From the Otherworld commune, Cromman had trailed him to the first sight of the Trojans' failure. Number two disaster was just down the road, Belasko apparently having used his SUV like a runaway bulldozer to mow down one biker who had, presumably, stopped and started to shoot. Report about the third debacle was just coming in. It was so incredible—no, belay that— it was unnerving, this latest mess slapping him in the face of his plans, that Thornton started to reevaluate the immediate future, its ever dimming prospects. He would let the gangsters arrive—that much would stand, the Chicago Mob on schedule for their impending face-off with Belasko. It was the end game, once they had the device in hand, that posed new and troubling questions for Thornton. What would keep Cromman, for instance, from removing him once he had the antigravity device in his possession? Until now it never occurred to him that Cromman might be unable or unwilling to meet his fee of two million. Since Cromman was essentially a government employee, he didn't have that kind of loose change readily available. The man's promise was a fat payday once he sold it to the subcontractor. Thornton decided at some point he needed to come up with a safety valve, just in case Cromman was reserving some fatal solution of his own if the asking price was too steep. He had a hunch where to look for a net to catch any sudden fall.

First another bunch of bodies to dispose of, courtesy of Special Agent Belasko.

And no doubt, Thornton knew, Cromman was sitting in the cool, dark confines of his rolling boat, itchy to start flinging the blame, casting the doubt, sounding the Klaxons of doom.

Thornton briefly returned the sheriff's dark scowl, adjusting his dark aviator shades a little. The two so-called deputies were giving the corpses a grim appraisal of their own from the far side of Walsh's SUV. They were Thornton's men actually, NSA men posing as county deputies. They were "legal" eyes and ears, inserted to stay attached to the side of their chosen sheriff from the beginning of the project. It was hard to read their faces, but Thornton had to believe they had some lingering questions of their own.

Which led to another problem hanging on the wire. When it went down, he could be sure a few of the operatives would balk at the heist of the device. In the hours to come, Thornton decided he would have to mentally weed out any remaining ops who might want to prove themselves a hero. He would discuss it some with Cromman, but his gut already told him where that guy stood on the not so little problem of questionable loyalties.

"Look at the holes your Belasko pal put in this biker trash. I'm looking at something out of the Wild West here, Thornton, showdown at the A-LEE-INN. I'm wondering how many more messes of yours I'm going to have to clean up. I'm thinking this whole county is set to blow. I'm thinking maybe you and that freak down there in his limo are cooking something up that might leave me high and dry to face the music."

"Anybody but the old geezer in the office see this?"

"No. Just the dead and Belasko."

"You have a gift for stating the obvious, Sheriff."

The bodies would be removed, of course, burned in the desert by his own cleanup crew. Beyond that, a few dollars would land in the geezer's hands, a subtle warning, the implication that if he didn't blind himself to what had happened here a mothership of a different sort would come calling to abduct him.

As Thornton took his handheld radio and patched back to Calley, he took a few paces to clear himself of the sheriff in case the man decided to keep issuing the rebuke in earshot. "Where is Belasko, now, Calley?"

"Just rolled into that tourist trap the Johnson brothers call Shambala. I have to tell you, sir, the way we saw him mow down those bikers, well, it strikes me the man's done this kind of thing before."

Walsh couldn't resist another dig. "Meaning he's far more than any Justice flunkie you thought he was."

Thirteen more bodies to dispose of. And God only knew who or how many pairs of eyes might have witnessed or stumbled across the slaughter by now.

Thornton saw Cromman's personal driver-bodyguard step outside the boat on wheels. Now what? he wondered.

"Keep watching. Keep me posted. A cleanup detail is on the way. Out."

The expression on Cromman's bodyguard was impossible to read as he stepped up, checking the dead Trojans from behind the cover of his dark sunglasses.

"Mr. Cromman says to send the sheriff and your deputies to try to talk some sense into Belasko."

"And do what?" Walsh rasped. "All's forgiven? No charges? Smooth it over, buy the man dinner and a few beers?"

"Simply convince the man it might be in his best interest to leave the area as quickly and quietly as possible."

"Oh, I'm sure he'll listen to reason now."

"Failing his departure," the man said to no one in particular, "you are to inform him that he may have an unfortunate accident by day's end."

"In other words, you want me to do your dirty work. You want me to threaten to kill the guy if he doesn't saddle up and head out."

"I couldn't have said it any better."

With that, the bodyguard marched past Walsh, the sheriff scowling, grunting, shaking his head.

"You heard the man, Sheriff. What are you waiting for?"

"I'll go do this, Thornton. Not because you people elected me as your spy and watchdog on the locals. Not because these two goons want to keep me on your tight leash. I want to see Belasko gone. The kind of heat he could bring from back east will only end up in my lap. I go down, I know I go alone. Not only that, but any more Wild West shows, and I don't think I'll be able to keep stalling what little media we have in these parts."

While Walsh lumbered off in a huff, banging his door shut and revving the engine, Thornton examined the dead once again. The numbers alone mind-boggling. Seventeen, no, twenty-one when he tallied up Braxton and company from the previous night. It staggered his imagination to even consider how one man could wipe out a small heavily armed army, biker trash or not. He couldn't be sure, but Thornton suspected he hadn't even begun to see the worst.

And despite Cromman marching the sheriff off to put a word to the wise to Belasko, Thornton knew damn good and well the man wasn't going anywhere. To pack it up, simply leave a bunch of questions suspended in the air, wash the blood off his hands and call it just another day at the office wasn't Belasko's style.

The man was a killer. And his nose was full of the scent of blood, mind buzzing, no doubt, with 101 questions he wanted answered. The Justice credentials were simply a smoke screen, he believed. Exactly who and what the man really was Thornton may never know.

Well, there was still Vince Leanetti about to step into the equation. According to his watch, the man was due to land in Reno anytime.

Thornton hoped the Don came more prepared than the Trojans. Meaning more guns, more heart, more skill. Given what he'd seen, he could be sure the Don would leave a few soldiers behind in the desert.

Fine.

As long as Belasko was among the buzzard meat.

CHAPTER SIXTEEN

An armed reception committee of three desert rats was waiting for him when Bolan rolled into Shambala.

And no light other than the frantic shining of paranoia hit the soldier in the face.

He eased off the gas, then the Executioner draped a hand over the HK MP-5, taking in the desolate sights. This poor man's tourist trap was planted in barren bowels, a devil's tumbleweed-choked dustbowl ringed by ominous black hills. The heat shimmer and shark's-teeth edges along the hills were a perfect combo, Mother Nature's gift, he noted, to conceal any snipers. The immediate weapons in question—a double-barreled shotgun, M-16 and a Colt .45—weren't aimed his way right off, so Bolan stole a cautious few seconds to further scope out his surroundings.

And stay braced for the next sudden eruption out of nowhere.

Welcome to Shambala.

Through the blasted-out window, Bolan felt his anxiety drop a notch when Shotgun called out from his porch stand, "It's okay, Rudy, Bobby! I seen him waste that biker scum left here owing me over a hundred bucks for beer!''

An olive branch, squaring the tab.

The day was already full of surprises. And how did the desert rat know about the slaughter on the other side of the hills, unless, of course, he'd seen it?

Shambala, Bolan noted, was made up of all of three structures. The narrow dirt track cut between two buildings. Aluminum prefab, glinting sunlight, made the disk-shaped rooftops glow, nearly a mirage that made the buildings appear set to lift off for the sky as they mirrored the burning eye above. To his left, braking the SUV, he saw the wooden poles holding up the awning over the wooden boardwalk were festooned with ET dummies. Ceramic, or carved from wood, it was hard to tell, but over twenty mannequins with large gray heads, black eyes and spindly limbs lined the porch front. Then there were coffee cups, beer mugs emblazoned with grinning little gray men, silver disks suspended from coat hangers, models of ET sitting up in the hatch. Black, white or gray undershirts were hanging in the hot stifling air. Logos ranged anywhere from The Truth Is Out There, to We Come In Peace, or We Need A Few Good Earthlings, then all the obligatory sayings in between about a government-military conspiracy to hide the facts that We Are Not Alone.

Shotgun held his post on the stoop to his store. Colt .45 was opposite, directly across the hard-packed dirt, in front of a plate-glass window painted Shambala Diner in bold black letters, with a floating ET dummy.

The single gas pump ahead, with silver structure number three just behind, and Bolan saw the desert rat lowering the M-16 in that direction.

Bolan leaned his head out the window. Shotgun was lanky, a mane of white hair flowing to bony shoulders. He had the sort of wild eyes that betrayed a mean distrust Bolan figured for paranoia to the deluded twilight zone of anyone outside this three-man band.

"If you watched me work, then you know I get nervous when people point guns at me."

"Not a problem, mister," Silver Head told Bolan. "Long as you're not with the government, we have no beef with you. Well, you with them?"

"Who's them?"

"The men in black."

"I'm with me."

"Good enough."

"I need gas, some food and bottled water."

"Step inside my humble spaceship. Fix you right up."

Bolan bailed out in the harsh sunlight, slipping on dark aviator shades.

"What's the subgun for?" Silver Head demanded when Bolan advanced toward him.

"Let's just say it's helping me build a bridge over troubled waters."

"What are you, a smart-ass!? You don't trust us?"

"Like the T-shirt says," Bolan told the man, nodding at Trust No One hanging nearest his face.

"Okay, so what you're saying is what we got guns for."

Bolan watched as the other two desert rats silently turned and melted into the shadows of the doorways to their respective disks.

"What's your name, stranger?"

Bolan followed the man through the door. Inside he found enough ET paraphernalia to cover a sci-fi convention.

"Belasko."

"I'm Jordan."

He offered a wrinkled, liver-spotted hand. Reluctant, infused by the man's paranoia, Bolan glanced over his shoulder, then accepted the handshake.

Jordan took a crate, marching for the coolers stocked with beverages. "How many bottles?"

"Ten."

"Nice round number."

The soldier took some candy bars, beef jerky sticks and set them on a counter where two four-foot ETs holding laser guns stood sentry.

"Maybe you think the three of us are paranoid or maybe crazy."

Bolan shot the man a fleeting grin. "Never crossed my mind."

"Patronizing me now, are you? Anybody ever tell you got an attitude problem?"

"I'm working on it."

"Well, if you were one of them, I figure you wouldn't have come alone anyway. You got a look of a killer about you, but it's not the same in the eyes they got. 'Sides, they never ride around the county 'less it's three or four of them. Got our phones bugged.

I see them all the time in the hills, watching us, like they can't wait for one of us to go out there where they keep them things so they can gun us down."

Bolan was almost afraid to ask, but the moment could prove a valuable fishing expedition. "What things?"

"Why, flying saucers, of course," he rasped, as if anyone with two eyes and half a brain should already know. "Usually it's Wednesday or Thursday night they go on maneuvers. Sometimes Sunday." Jordan came back, moving behind the counter, his eyes shining with some stolen knowledge as he settled the crate on the counter. "Been chased off fifteen times. Me and the boys, we seen it, filmed it even. Want a showing of a real flying saucer?"

"Some other time."

"Kind of hovers, red and white lights glowing, then goes off to the horizon, like a shooting star, but none I've ever seen move that fast, no, sir. Once in a while, one of us in the county turns up missing. Here yesterday, then gone. Ones who start talking about going to the media, mostly. Me, I keep my mouth shut. Not like I'll ever know the real facts anyway."

"How much I owe you?"

"It's on Mr. J.'s mother ship, friend." Jordan finally let the shotgun go, laying it over the counter, Bolan figuring he had passed inspection. "Those bikers nearly tapped out two kegs before they shot out of here, cussing me and threatening to shoot me down in my own place. Looked all doped up. Trash, but crazy, shoveling shit up their noses on the way out the door.

Gather one of them got some bad news. I'm thinking it had something to do with you. You wondering maybe how I know all this good stuff? This way, friend.''

Curious, Bolan followed Jordan toward the back of the store. A wooden bar front lined with stools ran from wall-to-wall, but it was the bank of camera monitors that grabbed Bolan's eye.

''Yup. Not even the men in black know I'm watching the desert. I got my own eyes buried in the hills, gives me a little peace of mind. They come, we're ready to square off. Me and the boys, a few others scattered about, we're the only sane folks you gonna find in these parts.''

Somehow Bolan kept a straight face.

''First, you got a sheriff who was never duly elected and who we know for a fact is one of them. Two deputies, look cut from the same cloth as the MIBs, their guys attached to Walsh's hip. That's partly why we act so edgy. I don't even sleep at night 'less that shotgun's by my side.''

''Curious. What's the rumor on how Walsh got his job?''

''Last sheriff up and retired, and Walsh just stepped right in, assumed his job.''

''Nobody questioned the passing of the baton?''

''Why bother? They do what they want. Find me a square mile out here Big Brother doesn't own. Government and military property staked out from corner to corner across this state, signs everywhere telling us common folk they're authorized to use deadly force.

Rumor is they have this spray they use, cover themselves with it, makes them near invisible in the night. I gather the stuff deflects light, or maybe absorbs it. Invisible killers, yes, sir, I hear they can come up on you out of the dark, you'd never know what hit you till you're up there, crying to God how such a sinful thing could've happened. 'Nother thing, they have something that's been killing folks off around here, something, I'm sure, has to do with that disk. Past two years folks are dropping like flies from cancer. One day healthy, people with no history of medical problems. Within a couple weeks, they can't even get out of bed. And let me ask you? When was the last time you heard of cattle dying from radiation sickness?'' He nodded, tossing in a grunt. ''Not only that, we've got to protect ourselves from armed riffraff, UFO cultists hunkered out in the desert, like the Apocalypse is as close as the next sunup. Look like one big house full of shady characters on the run from the law when I went out there and took a peek.''

Bolan thought of Weed and pressed Jordan about the cult.

Jordan told him if he wanted to take a look that bad, he could go check himself, and gave Bolan directions to the yard. An army of lunatics with guns, he thought, snooping around classified black projects, drawing their own fantastic conclusions. Armed and dangerous. But Bolan wasn't inclined to go hunting down a loose end, to some extent responsible for the slaughter that had happened the previous night. Weed was dumped on the backburner. If he popped up in Bolan's line of fire, he'd deal with the guy then.

It occurred to Bolan the man made no mention of any ominous rumble he might have caught about the Howling Coyote. For people who seemed to thrive on rumor and speculation, based on fact or conjured imaginings, it told Bolan the slaughter had been buried, swept away into the desert wastes. Chalk up another round won on deceit by the men in black. The soldier would even bet if he went back to the restaurant he wouldn't find the first spot of blood.

"Looks like we got company coming, friend."

Bolan saw the SUV framed by a camera. The light bar and county insignia warned Bolan the sheriff was on the way to pay him a visit. Two shadows appeared to be riding with him. More Thornton games en route for a face-off, he suspected. They stopped, and Bolan could almost read the grim faces, hear the worried thoughts as they inspected the graveyard of wreckage, the dead men strewed around them, a few of them charred to blackened human toast.

Bolan had plans to remove the thorny problem of the sheriff and the NSA deputies.

"You up for backing my play when they ride in?" Bolan asked Jordan.

Jordan's smile practically made his face shine like that disk he claimed to have seen. "How come I'm likin' the sound of that already?"

"Think hard before you answer. You could be putting yourself and your buddies in danger."

"Can't be any more dangerous than breathing the radioactive air out that door."

THE GATES to a grand destiny were about to open, allow them all to enter where the truth and the mystery would be revealed. They were about to cross a threshold, a Rubicon, in fact, poised for greatness to land on the other side, at the very foot of the tree of wisdom itself where the sinister government shadow powers jealously guarded a secret knowledge. And where one truth was hidden, there had to be more, waiting for their eyes to behold. The Others, indeed, worked in mysterious ways. Sometimes they even used the enemy to do their bidding so the forces of righteous seeking could prevail.

Or so Jason Nixon told his assembled following. With the exception of Collins, most of them looked convinced by his brief, impassioned speech. Voices of doubt, naturally, were raised here and there. What happened once they were inside the facilities? The government's assassins intended to split them up between two sites. Attempting to isolate them? Weaken them in numbers? A trap, duping them to do their bidding to help steal the device, then kill them?

"It's a bad idea, brother," Collins blurted into the chiming questions.

"No, it's destiny, my friend, Ernie," Nixon told the man.

It was time, he decided, to start separating the wheat from the chaff. Disbelievers had no place in the grand design of the Others.

"If they're so ready to let us play ball, why the armed guards outside?" Collins asked.

Nixon shrugged off the question. "Go ask them, if you need to know that badly."

Oh, but they were like such frightened little children, afraid to venture into the unknown, he thought. They needed a gentle shove, so Nixon decided to prey on their fears, hold their shortcomings up to the light of his own wisdom. He was an educated man, after all, and words were primarily his weapon of choice. To know the human heart had always put him one step closer to playing the puppet master.

"My fellow travelers, my fellow seekers of truth and knowledge, have you not yearned all of your lives to understand the mysteries of the universe, to have the unexplained explained? Have you not left behind dismal, tawdry lives to go in search of the truth of all ages? Finally you have shed the stigma and cloak of past failures, you have arrived at a moment in time, a turning point that could make you immortal. In your former lives you were aberrations of sorts in the eyes of your fellow humans. They called you freaks and quacks who shouted the sky was falling, but no one listened. Can you not see what is happening? You have had what those normal people call paranormal experiences, if they simply don't dismiss it with a smirk as hallucination, or tell you it was only a comet in the sky, or the Air Force dropping magnesium flares, or swamp gas. Listen to the voice of reason you know you have heard before! The Others, we know from personal experience, have telepathic powers beyond anything we can imagine. They are showing us the way. They have inserted their own will into the minds of the enemy, sent them here to enlist our services.''

''They say we might have to kill the workforce, civilians, just like us. That…albino thing hinted as much he may give the order to do just that.''

Nixon addressed Radkin, the hillbilly from Georgia. The man had come to him a wild-eyed drunk, fleeing marriage with children when his family mocked his sightings to the point he was a physical wreck, an emotional cripple who had only been brought back from the dead with several hypnoregression sessions. Now he was a stone-cold sober pillar of seeking.

Another Nixon success story.

Maybe the M-16 was spooking on the doubt and worry. Nixon rested the assault rifle against an armchair. He spread his arms, the prophet calling forth the faithful. ''Need I remind you they are pawns in the greatest conspiracy of all time? There are no innocents on the other side. Need I remind you they are likewise aiding and abetting the enemy, only they give their brains instead of muscle to create technology the military has stolen from the Others. Think back, my fellow seekers. Recall your own experiences. Think back even further to when you were children, and perhaps caught that fleeting glimpse of the future, that distant ship smoke on the horizon. A faraway voice in the smoke, warning you the path already laid for you before you were even born, that the road to greatness on the way back home would be full of trials and trouble, that your lives would appear difficult to the point of contemplating perhaps suicide. Suffering the ridicule and contempt of the unbelievers. No hope. No future. The trappings of this fleshly world were never meant for you. The way was shown you, because you were chosen. And you have now arrived. This is it! What we have journeyed our whole lives for! The coming hours are our united destiny, a coming majesty that will transcend and transform our very souls. You are on the verge of knowing what only the secret shadow government knows.''

Nixon stepped back. There was a bottom line coming, and he needed to know. ''Before the enemy returns here tonight, I need a show of hands. In or out. Hand up if you're coming with me tonight.''

One by one, the hands rose. As expected, Collins was last to join in the show of hands. As anticipated, it was something other than peer pressure when Nixon heard the man ask, ''Now do I get a gun?''

Nixon told him, ''Now that you appear willing, but of course.''

BOLAN WAS OUT the door, HK MP-5 poised when the first few heavy guitar riffs thundered the air out front of ET heaven. For whatever reason, Jordan was cranking out the song that was the tourist trap's namesake, a scratchy noise hitting the air, telling Bolan it was old forty-five vinyl going under the needle of an ancient phonograph. Whether it was to rattle Walsh and company or mute the sound of his own blind-side advance, Bolan couldn't say. Whatever, the marching anthem would certainly make normal conversation nearly impossible, but the soldier was going to let the subgun do the talking for him.

Bolan was moving toward the beat. Moments earlier, Jordan had pointed the way to the back door when he told Bolan the good sheriff was pulling up in front. The warrior had a general principle about shooting a lawman, even a tainted badge, but he wasn't opposed to winging Walsh if the man turned a gun on him. The blacksuit "deputies" were fair game.

All of sixty paces, and the Executioner came around the corner, crouched at the gleaming edge, and weighed his next move. Walsh and the two deputies were advancing toward Jordan, the trio throwing looks around at the armed desert rats.

"Turn that racket off!" Walsh shouted.

Jordan was grinning from his porch, cupping his ear. "What?"

The deputies were grumbling something lost to the song, but there was no mistaking the menacing intent as they dropped hands over hip-holstered pistols.

"Drop the weapons!" a deputy hollered.

"The hell you say!" Jordan barked.

"Where's the man came here in that vehicle!" Walsh demanded.

Show time.

Bolan stepped around the corner, glimpsed Jordan grinning his way, gesturing with the shotgun.

It might have been the heat, the music or the slaughter they'd just seen. Or it might have been a combination of all three, but Bolan saw the deputies tense, sensed the killer heat building their way. There was a moment of indecision, Walsh set to pull his own pistol when Jordan brought up the shotgun.

The deputies dug out the hardware, spinning, and went for broke.

CHAPTER SEVENTEEN

"Almost" would have maybe cut the mustard in some mythic nirvana where everyone was a winner, every soul lucky and blessed no matter how mediocre the talent or unwashed the sin brought to the golden gates. As it stood in the ugly reality of earth time, the deputies almost made it.

Only the Executioner's subgun blazed out their losing hand.

The NSA gunners had whipped around on their heels, their Browning pistols nearly on-line when Bolan chopped them up with a heavy sweep of 9 mm rounds, left to right and back. Meanwhile the sheriff was shooting his hands up, hopping away from the dancing dead men, screaming, "Don't!"

As if it were all a terrible misunderstanding and they had come in peace.

Before the black-op deputies took the final dive, Bolan saw other holes exploding fabric and carving off flesh. Rudy and Bobby had jumped into the act, pumping out overkill.

Unneeded and not necessary.

The deputies toppled in jerky spasms, guns and shades flying.

So much for nirvana.

"I'm not here for trouble, Belasko!" Walsh roared at Bolan, one eye on the twin barrels aimed from the porch.

Bolan advanced past his SUV. "On the ground, Sheriff."

Walsh was sputtering how he was simply a messenger for Thornton as he complied, stretching out in the dirt. Bolan relieved the man of his Browning, stuffed it inside his waistband. Binding the sheriff's hands behind his back with his own cuffs, Bolan hauled him to his feet. The soldier was grateful as the song faded, gone at last, then the scratch of a needle stuck on vinyl crackled through the metal speakers hung on wire from the porch.

"Last night."

"What about it?" Walsh said.

"Who gave the order?"

"I heard it was the freak, Cromman. They went in, probably like you might have suspected. Leave no witnesses. What I overheard, it was something those two had on disk Cromman wanted back."

"The idea they would murder women and children caused you a bad night's sleep?"

"Yeah, it damn sure did."

"You're telling me you've grown a conscience?"

"I'm telling you I want out."

"This big change of heart, before now or after?"

"What's it matter? This has gone way too far."

"It's only just begun, Sheriff."

"Going to get worse before it gets better, that it?"

"The storm's only building. You'd better pick a side."

"How 'bout the winning team?"

"Remains to be seen. It may look like I'm way ahead on points now, but you make some fair-weather call when the going gets real tough..."

"I'm with you, Belasko."

"We'll see."

Jordan was asking to be clued in, when autofire rattled the air. Wheeling, Bolan traced the source of the weapons fire to a point high up in the hills, past the diner. A black-clad figure was tumbling down the slope, an awkward flopping of loose limbs that signaled more buzzard meat.

"Check those monitors," Bolan told Jordan, then set off. He made for an easy target, he knew, in full view of a sniper's crosshairs, but instinct told the soldier some X factor had just covered his back. And was now gone. Who? Why? Another twist to Thornton's psy-war tactics? If so, why?

He was standing at the foothills, giving the ridgeline around the bowl a heard search when he heard Jordan shouting, "Nothing up there but another MIB. Behind the rocks! Wasted!"

Bolan turned away from the unmoving lump midway up the hill and backtracked to Walsh.

"Whoever our mystery shooter, he was gone by the time I looked," Jordan reported.

"So, what was the big message, Sheriff?"

"Actually, it was Cromman. Said for me to tell you to pack up and leave. Or else they'd come for you."

"What else?"

"They don't exactly fill me in on the particulars of their daily agenda."

Bolan decided it was time to bail Shambala, crank it up, keep building the fire on the nest of vipers.

"You don't mind if I leave those two laying out like that, do you, Belasko? Our way of showing them we're not just desert trash gonna roll over and get pushed around."

"It's your humble mother-ship center. I won't be the one who has to smell them."

"In the cooler with this one?" Jordan asked, nodding at Walsh.

Bolan nodded. "Sit on him until you hear from me. Give me a number I can call you. If this Thornton shows up here, give him a message. Tell him I have the disk."

"What are you going to do with me?"

Jordan reached out a skeletal hand and jerked Walsh toward the stoop. "Gonna get you cooled off, Sheriff. You look kinda hot and bothered. Deep-freeze you, so to speak, a specimen like those little gray men I hear about time to time."

A few more minutes here, fueling and stocking up, and the soldier would be on his way. He was now a moving target more than ever, four gunners tossed into the fire, but the Executioner was heated up to run and gun, bent on mowing down Thornton's goons wherever they showed up next.

Skip the palavering over any more Q and A.

From then on, the warrior determined to shoot first, from the hip. Any unresolved questions may or not get answered from the business end of flying bullets, when they were down and clinging to a last bloody breath.

Bolan wiped the sweat off his brow. Not even high noon, he thought, and already the day was hotter than hell, in more ways than one.

THE STINK OF DEATH in his nose, Thornton inspected the dripping metal on the bike's engine and frame. Solid metal had been warped all to hell, he noted, melted by superheated fire to nothing but running silver goo. And the flesh on the bodies of three Trojans had been eaten to the bone by what the late Calley had described as a ball of intense white fire. Even more than two hours after the Trojans had chomped down on the worm here, and he could still feel the heat smoldering from burned metal, catch the lingering whiff of cooked meat.

Since when, he thought, did the Justice Department start using white phosphorus?

The clank and grind of heavy machinery interrupted the train of brooding thought. More cleanup. He was nothing more than a glorified garbageman these days. It was time to change that, and quick, before it was too late.

He stood, a chill running through him as the sweat broke down his nape. He waved the dozer on, turned his back as the massive shovelhead scooped up the first few bodies and assorted wreckage. The black

dump truck was rumbling up the track, the first four
bodies and Harleys already picked up for waste dis-
posal. Rotor wash next filtered into his senses, as he
glanced toward the big sleek black chopper, the steel
winches used to haul the dozer from the facility trailing from its belly. The chopper was still hovering over
the hills, kicking up duststorms, the pilot having just
informed him of the latest situation.

Nothing left in that direction but more dead men.
His own.

Thornton was numb over the latest round of grim
news.

Walsh was nowhere to be found, but his vehicle was
abandoned in the rathole at the end of the trail. Worse,
four more operatives were down, two in the hills, the
sheriff's watchdogs laid out in the bizarre tourist trap,
rotting under the sun, shot to hell. At the rate he was
losing men, he would have to put in a call for a fresh
batch of reinforcements stationed in a classified retreat
to the east, near the Utah border. At least another fifteen guns were called for when this night's main event
went down.

If they even got it that far.

Belasko, he knew, was long gone from the scene,
heading south, in the direction of the two facilities.
Thornton had two units shadowing the man. Thornton
was considering having them go ahead and take their
chances against Belasko when Briggs patched through.

"Sir, the target's stopped. It looks like he's going
inside the restaurant."

For what purpose? Thornton wondered. To confirm

the cleanup or his own suspicions they were covering their tracks? Surely Belasko knew as much already. Or maybe the guy's pit stop was meant to lure his men inside.

It was time to make another judgment call. Thornton told Briggs and Marley to go in, leave the other team outside to watch their backs. And don't call back again unless they could make him proud. Even as he gave the order, signed off, Thornton knew he was most likely marching them straight to hell, into more Belasko meanness.

Thornton had things to do himself. And there was still the matter of his own safety net to unfurl.

First the next order of business.

He told his own team to supervise the cleanup there and wait for his return. He piled behind the wheel of the van, banging the door shut. The Don should be calling anytime.

And time, Thornton knew, was something he was running out of, quickly.

THE SOLDIER HAD THEM marked, about a half mile on his rear, when he returned to the scene of the original crime. Two black SUVs pulled up on the road, sat, baking under the sun, dark armored vehicles housing invisible killers. Thanks to the black-tinted windows, it was impossible to get a fix on how many hardmen had come calling.

So be it.

Bolan grabbed the HK MP-5, a fresh clip in place. He palmed a frag grenade, stowed it in the pocket of his windbreaker. There was no good reason to come back to where it had all started, except that it was in the general vicinity of his route to the makeshift gravesite and the drop.

It was also as good as any place to shave the enemy numbers some more, if they decided to come running and gunning. He figured Thornton knew his game plan was blowing up in his face, the man nothing but a walking static charge of raw nerves, and Bolan was working on a hunch the standing order was to shoot him on sight.

Good enough, if that was the case. At least everyone knew where things stood.

Bolan was out the door of his vehicle, rolling hard toward the Howling Coyote. No crime scene tape blocked the front entrance, of course, but the hung Closed sign nailed to the door was left behind in the wake of the cleanup. It might send a hungry traveler grumbling off to find another eatery down the road, but the memory of what happened here only hours ago was fresh in Bolan's recall, firing him up as he shouldered through the door. Inside the air was thick with the coppery bite of spilled blood, bowels and bladders emptied in the final microsecond of terror. The ghosts of the dead seemed to hang in his thoughts, and brief flashes of the shock and horror on the faces of the innocent slowed Bolan's strides even more. He made out the dark splotches on the floor. The fact they hadn't put out the extra effort with mop and bucket only reaffirmed Bolan's original notion these men believed only in themselves as the ultimate authority, gods among mere mortals.

They were nothing more than savages to the Executioner.

Outside he caught the sound of tread rolling slow and easy over the hardpan.

"EASY, FRIENDS."

Slowly Thornton stepped out into the glare and the guns, showing empty hands. He looked at the faces of each desert rat in turn. Raving paranoids, he knew it wouldn't take much to push them over the edge. He was their favorite whipping boy, after all, the armed tool of some government military conspiracy that fueled fantasies they openly displayed with their ET dummies.

Lunatics.

"You come in peace, that it?"

Thornton addressed the one with the shotgun. "I'm not here looking for a piece of you on account of what happened to my men."

"You're not the sentimental type? Oh, I forgot, these two were expendable. That how you people work? Deny everything?"

"Where's the sheriff?"

"The flunkie of your ongoing government conspiracy to hide the truth about extraterrestrials? The man said it was gonna be a little too hot out here today. He's cooling off inside."

Thornton knew he could have marshaled a team of ops and taken them down with a show of force. It would only serve to dump another mess in his lap. The moment urged some degree of diplomacy if he was going to make the deadline for the Don's call. Later, when the Belasko problem was laid to rest, he could come back here and settle up with these three tumbleweeds.

"All I want is to go into the diner, have a cold beer or two and wait for a phone call. None of what's happened is your problem."

"I'm supposed to take your word on that?"

"A beer and a phone call. That's all I want. Then I'm gone."

Thornton waited and sweated out the silence, while they looked at one another in some communion of the minds. Three nods followed the stretch of quiet.

Paranoids with telepathic powers, he thought.

"I see one of your kind comin' this way, I have your permission to shoot you dead?"

Thornton showed an easy smile he hardly felt. "I wouldn't expect anything less."

"Oh, by the way, almost forgot. Belasko, the badass eighty-sixin' anybody gettin' in his face? My new hero, the UFO hunter? Said to tell you he has the disk."

Thornton felt his heart lurch, but kept the jolt of nerves off his face. Even still, he heard the angry chuckle in his head. Why wasn't he surprised?

IF THE DROP WASN'T due soon, it would be a sorry expenditure of a frag grenade. Bolan saw no choice but to use it up on the two men in black heading for the front door.

Getting bogged down, trading fire…

No option at all.

A peek beyond the plate-glass window, and it appeared SUV Number Two was marking turf, waiting on the front-line shooters to clean it up, quick and neat.

The soldier's roost was at the far edge of the partition dividing the smoking section from the main dining area. He rose from a crouch and saw the shadows boiling beyond the doorway. They stopped, hunching, shaky nerves probably causing brief hesitation when Bolan pulled the pin, released and silently set down the spoon. The muzzle of a subgun prodded empty air, the two hardmen he'd seen move in still holding their ground as he counted off two seconds, then lobbed the lethal egg their way.

They finally made their charge, SWAT-like, coming in, one low, one high, weapons fanning the interior.

Wrong way, leading to a dead-end street.

The world blew up in their faces on a fiery thunderball of countless scything steel shrapnel. They were gone, out of play, and Bolan left them to ride the fireball.

The Executioner kicked it into high gear, subgun leading his surge toward the window. It was a bulldoze tactic, nothing more or less, as he caught full viewing of another gunner bailing out the passenger door. The man was frozen long enough at the sight of his comrades getting blown to smithereens for Bolan to cut loose with a long barrage of autofire. The first few rounds of the 9 mm storm blew out the window, then lead was searching out the flesh beyond the flying shards. Gunner Three was clawing for his side arm when he took the stitching line of bullets across the chest, the burst rising to tear out his throat. He was dropping hard and fast, bouncing off the van, when Bolan hit the vanishing window on the fly. Another hardman was on the move, rolling around from the driver's side, his subgun up and chattering in hopes of catching the blur in midflight leaping out of nowhere. Bolan counted on a split second of hesitation driven home by panic to spoil the gunman's aim.

Long experience in the face of enemy fire panned out for the soldier as the only expected rounds winged toward his charge flew high and wide. By the next heartbeat, it was over, the enemy gunner trying to bring his weapon to bear but Bolan emptied six or seven rounds up his torso.

Down and out.

Bolan listened to the silence. Sixth sense told him there was no one left in either van, but he checked, just the same, throwing back the door on each vehicle.

All clear.

The road behind was free of traffic.

But the Executioner felt the heat rising, outside and inside, as he reclaimed the wheel to his SUV.

Just because he couldn't see this particular enemy didn't mean the gunners weren't there. And he was making messes aplenty, shoving the growing problem of attrition in the ranks down Thornton's gullet. He could well guess the man had more guns on tap.

No problem.

The Executioner set off to pick up his special air delivery, a package that would help him carry on this shadow war game to whatever its bloody conclusion.

THORNTON SCOWLED into his beer. He was hoping a cold taste would smooth the edges of smoldering anger, that new, jagged flaring up of nerves shooting through his limbs. Unfortunately the beer wasn't providing the proper cure for what ailed him right then.

For one thing, his bartender never let go of the big Colt .45, or strayed too far from his perch. He was surprised they hadn't ask he shed the Beretta, but who could figure how the deluded mind of human tumbleweeds worked? There was no point really in pondering the issue of fanatics juiced around the clock by paranoid fantasies. The guy just stood, watching him, a dozen questions clearly dancing through his eyes. Unless Tumbleweed got antsy or aggressive, Thornton dismissed him as a viable threat.

No, Tumbleweed was as insignificant to him as any peasant who starved at the feet of a Third World dictator. The primary and only source of all visions of doom and the cause of the smoking rage in his head was out there in the desert, still at large.

And he had the disk. In his experience, the worst kind of enemy was a man who thought he was armed with a righteous truth, and an even more righteous anger.

Thornton checked his watch. The call was late.

He wanted to feel grateful for the time alone, away from the hassle of dealing with Cromman, the constant branding iron of Belasko on his neck. It was hard to sit still and enjoy the simple pleasure of a cold brew and a moment of silence when his world was falling apart.

"Is it true?"

Tumbleweed could speak. "Is what true, friend?"

"You people have a flying saucer out there? You got alien bodies in storage?"

"Do we know the truth? Is that what you're asking?"

"Well? You sitting there, drinking my beer, think you owe me the courtesy of some straight talk."

Thornton drained his beer, let Tumbleweed stew, believing he was ready to ignore the question. Briefly Thornton pondered how to answer. He could fire off a few half truths, mix a little fact with fiction. Sure, he'd heard the rumors himself, but not even he had the kind of security clearance that allowed him access to the kind of knowledge Tumbleweed wanted. From what he had heard, he didn't even want the kind of top-level pass only a few men in the country, hell, the whole world, had in hand. Rumor was they didn't live to see retirement, but that was just part of keeping it all buried. Dead men didn't tell stories.

Thornton felt a mean twist turn up one corner of his mouth. "I'm just a pawn in that ongoing government conspiracy your pal mentioned. A little guy. Bottom of the heap. I know as much as you do."

Tumbleweed bared a mouth with half his teeth missing. Then Thornton heard the expected ringing. He stood and walked to the pay phone mounted on the wall. He picked up it and said, "Yes."

"Shadow Man? I'm on the way."

"That's good. Your boy Belasko? He's gotten a little nervous, walking around with your money. He's going berserk all over the place."

"What the hell you talking about?"

"Trouble from the guy, that's what I'm talking about. The kind of trouble I'm saying you had better be ready and able to deal with."

"If he was helping Barklin stick it to me, his life is numbered in hours."

"That's encouraging—for you. Now, here's the story...."

CHAPTER EIGHTEEN

One moment's viewing of the skeletal remains, and the hole in the skull was all Bolan needed to confirm his worst suspicions. The heat of anger he felt swelling inside might have made a match in hell for the fury of the sun blazing at its noon zenith, beating down on the soldier's dark expression.

He kicked the small pile of dirt back in place. There was no point laboring to uncover the second mound with the tire iron. He'd seen more than enough.

Perhaps he had gone there simply hoping it couldn't be true what he'd learned on the disk, that two young people had their lives snuffed out on the twisted whim of a man he kept hearing referred to as a walking freak show. Whoever the dead had been in life, it would take some work by the Justice Department or the Farm, but with the information he had, their identities could be eventually run down. If nothing else, their next of kin deserved to know what had happened to their loved ones. Bolan offered them up a silent prayer that a far kinder and gentler other side had taken them home to eternity.

Suddenly the Executioner felt weary and stained

with a dark and perplexing cynical anger. It was different, in some cleaner way, he supposed, to wage war against a clearly defined enemy overseas or a raving armed menace to society in his country's own yard. The frothy-mouthed terrorist, for instance, or this week's crime lord, armed subversives or foreign spies. It was something else entirely, something dirty and bitterly distasteful, when he found himself pitted against rogue factions who were supposedly on the home team.

Traitors.

It could have been easy to stand there and let the righteous fury steam out the pores with the free-running sweat, rail at the injustice of it all, shake his head over man's inhumanity to his fellow man. Bolan knew better than to get sidetracked or spurred on by runaway anger, a red tunnel vision that would blind him at the worst critical juncture to a roving threat.

In all walks of life, he knew, a few snakes always slithered the underbrush of daily routine, striking down the prey out of personal greed and lust gone amok. Usually time and a few good men or women rooted out the human vipers for a much needed trampling.

Sometimes it took harsher means than a mere boot to the neck.

No, it didn't matter really if it was the neighborhood drug thugs, or the next Hitler on the horizon. It didn't matter if it was that nice quiet guy next door who went berserk at a fast-food restaurant and took out a couple dozen innocents before committing suicide by cop.

Or a covert NSA agent, Bolan summarized, believing he was backed by the law of the land to do whatever he damn well pleased in the bullshit guise of national security.

Evil was still evil in any man's name.

And the Executioner was in the business of slaying monsters and dragons in human skin. For Bolan it was always more than a mission. It was a calling.

The gods of war and his own skill permitting, whoever the dead buried at his feet would be avenged in due course.

He was walking back to the SUV, alternately checking his watch and the burning stark lay of the land. The drop was late. There could be any number or reasons why the chopper hadn't yet shown in the skies. And all of them were bad. Some human shadow bomb perhaps planted at Nellis, throwing out the smoke screen. "Sudden" and unexplained mechanical failure sending the borrowed blacksuit chopper plunging to earth in a fireball.

He shelved the line of doomsday thought. He'd give it another thirty minutes, then raise Brognola.

Right then he sensed he was once more being watched and marked. Where the broken hardpan ended to the north, a vast salt flat stretched toward a low hump of black hills. Before the task of uncovering the body, he'd spotted a distant dust spool, to the east, there then gone.

Blacksuited NSA eyes, no doubt.

As he strained to scour the unearthly panorama, he made out the sound he longed to hear. Turning his head, he saw the shape of the chopper, cutting an arrow-straight line, seven hundred feet or so above, and bearing down. As planned, the blacksuit pilot raised him on his secured cell line.

"Special Delivery to Striker. Come in, Striker."

Bolan punched on his handheld radio. "Striker here."

"Apologies for the late arrival, Striker. The spook show at Nellis gave us a song and dance about mechanical problems on the mail truck we requested. It took us a little longer than we liked to go through our own preflight checklist."

"No sweat, Special Delivery. I'm not surprised. Just watch yourselves going back."

"Roger that, sir. I left one of our people with our ride home, just in case we were left suddenly wondering why our engines might be stalling out twenty thousand feet over Nebraska."

"Stay frosty and eyes peeled on your six."

"Likewise, sir. And good luck. Special Delivery over and out."

Reaching the SUV, Bolan dumped the tire iron over the back seat. He took his bottled water, uncapped it and slowly drank. The subgun in hand next, he walked away from the SUV, as the Bell JetRanger's hatch opened and the package was sent falling, before the chute blossomed. Even with the dark shades, Bolan found he had to squint some against the harsh sunlight.

The package landed. The chopper veered to starboard, then began its short run back to Nellis.

As he scoped the salt flat and closed on the war

bag, Bolan spotted the black bulk of a vehicle in the distance. It was long and low, and there was no mistaking that rolling boat Taggart had mentioned. The hybrid cross between a stretch limo and a Towncar ran a slow parallel course with the black wall of rock. Finally it swung around, then sat out there on the sea of white glass.

Grabbing up his war bag, the Executioner retraced his steps to the SUV. He decided it was time to pay the freak a visit.

VINCE LEANETTI wasn't used to doing things the other guy's way. It had been some time since he'd jumped through hoops, pretty much at the beck and call of another man. Particularly an individual he'd never seen, much less didn't know the first damn thing about, other than the guy was some sort of government spook. If he had doubts, then the Don was sure his crew had more than a few questions stewing in their heads. They were smart enough, though, to keep any reservations to themselves. They were paid to follow orders, keep their mouths shut.

Still, he couldn't help but feel the charged static of nerves around him in the Lincoln as Gino Buono kept them rolling east on I-80, clipping along down the endless black arrow at around seventy. With the passenger seat all to himself, Donnie, Marino and Chubby Stanelli squeezed in back, Leanetti felt a sudden impulse to check on the second Lincoln in the side glass. Good, it was there, he saw, with five more soldiers from Chicago sticking on their rear.

Why wouldn't it be? he wondered, then chalked up his razor's edge of nerves to a couple of nagging factors. The Shadow Man for one thing, spinning out the yarn about some wildass, Belasko, out here, running around with his money and shooting up the desert. Barklin's pilfering, though, had been confirmed, thanks to the wonders of modern technology, and some old school muscle when he'd sent a few of the boys to the guy's associates, rousing them out of bed last night, tearing through their books, the terrified worms on a hook confirming this missing set of numbers and that unexplained vanished half-mil. And, oh, yes, Mr. Barklin was all of a sudden missing, and for two days at least, no rhyme or reason they could see for the disappearing act. They didn't know the guy was stealing.

Well, when he returned to Chicago, Leanetti had plans for the guy's partners. It had been some time anyway since he'd indulged a personal hand to feed the fishes.

And if he could raise Barklin from the dead and put the little thieving shitbag under a chain saw for a couple hours in a meat locker…

Then there was this godforsaken state working on his nerves. Nothing but burning desert, scrub, cactus and black hills that looked transplanted from the surface of the moon for as far as he could see in any direction. How the hell could anything human live out here? On a main roadway, well into the afternoon and not more than a few passing vehicles, mostly semis, going west. They might as well have landed, he thought, on another planet.

And they certainly hadn't come dressed for the occasion. To a soldier, ten shooters, including himself, decked out in sport or Aloha shirts, silk slacks, Italian or alligator-skin loafers. Dark shades, a few jackets and windbreakers concealing the side arms. Say a cop stopped them, wondered about the rolling NRA convention? Well, to a man they were all licensed private investigators, gun permits for both the state of Illinois and Nevada, as luck would have it, since Leanetti often did business in Vegas or Reno, or hit the slopes of Tahoe for some R and R with the snow bunnies. He had earlier acknowledged due respect and gratitude to an associate out here who had seen fit to aid him in his time of trouble, stuffing both trunks with automatic weapons. Not even the Don of Chicago could walk through an airport with six or seven oversize duffel bags stuffed to the gills with enough hardware to take down a small city without raising an eyebrow from customs or the lurking DEA or Justice staff. Power might have its privileges, granted, but the Don was feeling anything but in control of the moment.

Buono was looking all around, fidgeting.

"What is it, Gino?"

"You told me the spook said it was just past that sign that said Shambala. I'm looking for that black chopper you said was supposed to meet us."

Now the more adventurous began expressing some doubt. Chubby was the first to gather up enough courage, clearing his throat first, but sounding more as if he was choking on last night's stuffed veal. "I don't know, boss..."

"What don't you know?"

"I mean, all due respect, boss, but who is this guy we're supposed to meet, for one thing? How do we know this isn't some kind of setup?"

"We don't. That's why we're here. I'll know soon enough whether I'm getting jerked off. What I do know is he knows about Barklin and I know the little shit fled with six million of my hard-earned dollars."

He caught Chubby making a face, about to fire off more doubt when Buono pointed and said, "There! The chopper."

Buono hit the wheel, slowed but not enough as he took the shoulder hard, bouncing next onto the desert.

"Damn it, Gino, easy," Leanetti growled, head smacking off the window.

"Sorry, boss."

Leanetti watched as the black chopper set down in a storm of whipping dust.

"Pull it up, away from all that dust cloud, though," Leanetti told his wheelman. "I didn't come here to eat any more dirt than I already have."

He gritted his teeth, riding out the next series of bumps. Buono let off the gas, veering away from the rotor wash, well beyond the flying storm.

"Park it, Gino. Out, boys. I smell a problem, you'll hear 'Up yours,' and then we start blasting. Marino, you fall back and pass the word to the others."

"Got it, boss."

Leanetti stepped out into the heat. Not two seconds

under the sun and he was breaking a sweat, catching a whiff of the previous night's whiskey and cigar fumes leaking out to paste flesh to clothing. He was too old for this shit, he thought, but he wasn't old enough yet to be put out to pasture by some pink-faced suit who'd jammed a knife in his back. Or some wild-ass alleged to be in cahoots with Barklin. Leanetti rolled his shoulders, snugging up the weight of the shoulder-holstered 9 mm Browning under his silk suit jacket. Whoever the spook was, he took his sweet time before he came hopping out of the chopper. He was a lean, mean type, bullet head framed in dark shades, no expression as he marched out of the dust storm. A look around, and the Don saw his crew falling in.

"You Shadow Man?"

"Mr. Leanetti, pleased you could make it."

"What the fuck you smilin' about?"

Shadow Man pulled up short of the gathered soldiers.

Leanetti ran a closer look over the man, who was wearing some kind of skintight blacksuit, one-piece, like a spaceman's underwear, a pistol hung in shoulder leather.

"Forgive me, no disrespect intended, Mr. Leanetti. I've been under a lot of stress."

"Tell me about it."

"When we spoke earlier I told you your man is hiding out in the desert. You can't miss him. Big guy, armed to the teeth. I understand there's some damage to the right front side of his SUV. There's also the briefcase of money I saw him take from Barklin after he gunned the man down.''

''I'm thinking I need a little more convincing.''

Leanetti watched the spook nod, then grab a hand-held radio, snapping, ''Bring it out.''

Leanetti felt the tension knot his shoulders, another man in black leaping through the open maw of the chopper. He landed in the storm, reached inside, then hauled out a rubber body bag. It hit the earth with the unmistakable thud of a heavy corpse, then the man in black dragged the body bag out of the dust wall. Leanetti waited, the man in black dumping the bag nearly at his feet. Shadow Man's gopher zipped it open. Barklin, he saw, with a big black hole in his forehead, the frozen death mask distorted by the ferocious impact from the killing shot.

Shadow Man jerked a nod over his shoulder, and the gopher zipped up the face and began dragging the weight back to the chopper.

A piece of paper was held out, and Leanetti took it. ''What's this?''

''Directions. I've mapped out and marked off clear and precise territories where you can find your man.''

''And that's that?''

''Should you need to reach me, there's a number I wrote down. I apologize, but I have urgent business of my own to attend to. And like I mentioned, Mr. Leanetti, I figured my time and effort on this matter was worth a little something to help me get settled in my golden years.''

Leanetti didn't know quite what to make of the man

or the moment. Still, he didn't see any other course of action but to follow up. It might be good, after all, to rediscover the old street tough that had earned him his bones in his distant twenties. What the hell, he figured. He hadn't come all this way to kick a gift horse in the teeth.

"How much sweetening we talkin' about?"

Shadow Man shrugged. "Well, I'm not a greedy man, Mr. Leanetti. Let's call it a nice round figure of two hundred grand. Figure chump change, if you can make your man give back what he and his pal took from you."

"So, you figure. Where you going to be?"

"I'll be around. I'm sure you'll be in touch."

"Count on it."

"Good luck, Mr. Leanetti."

Just like that, he was moving, the Don watching as the spook spun and marched away, bounding next into the chopper.

Leanetti figured there was only one way to really find out what the hell was going on. As the chopper lifted off, taking the mystery man away to the south, he told his crew, "Let's go."

As he retook his seat, grateful at least for the blasting bands of chilly air in his face, Vince Leanetti's old animal instincts wanted to rise out of the closet, dust themselves off. It was a fleeting shadow of gut warning, but it was there just the same. Something didn't feel right where the spook was concerned. Something was missing. It all seemed too damn easy, too pat, even contrived somehow.

There was only one course of action he knew of, though, to see him dig up any hidden truth from the vast desert.

In short order, he'd find Belasko. One guy, ten shooters. How tough a chore could it be? Figure he'd be in Vegas by nightfall, telling war stories over whiskey, buoyed in the face of associates by radiating self-confidence earned by blood on his hands. Take my money, will you?

And if it took some sweat and rising blood pressure to track the guy down, so much the better. It never hurt to be motivated by a little discomfort, see it through, just in time to catch the next party. And, no mistake, he wasn't opposed to getting the truth out of the guy the old-fashioned way if that's what it took to get the blood pressure down, and retrieve his pilfered money. Not by a long shot. Maybe, he decided, Shadow Man was playing it straight. He was a government employee, after all, looking toward the future, wanting some good times to roll his way. That much made sense...

"Let's go find us a wildass who took my money," the Don said to no one in particular, feeling alive and in charge for the first time since he'd hit Nevada.

The old juices were flowing again, and Leanetti allowed the grim smile to touch his lips. The old lion was about to come roaring back to life.

THORNTON WAS chuckling to himself, but the sound was hollow and bitter in his ears, flung away by the chopper's rotor wash, empty of any mirth or promise of some future pat on the back. And he damn well suspected why the moment suddenly looked dark as midnight, felt cold as a whore's touch.

"Take us back to One Base Alpha," Thornton barked through the open cockpit doorway, then moved back into the flickering shadows of the monitors in the belly of the aircraft.

For some reason, he was weighted down with more doubt than when he'd played the Trojans and sent them roaring off to do battle with Belasko. He couldn't believe what he'd just left behind. One old white-haired man, paunchy and puffy from years of self-indulgence, now softened up like some perfumed calf for the slaughter. The Don was congealed human jelly, he thought, from having sat fat and sure of his tomorrows, too long all alone on the gilded throne for years on end, sticking the middle finger in everybody's eye from rivals to Feds to judges. Right, all that living off past glory, his reputation as the king of crime kings to be reckoned with, seeing him through, never dreaming the sun could, in fact, set.

It felt like the worst call he'd made yet. Hell, they had come here in silk threads, their aftershave and stink of booze and heavy red meat oozing out their sweat still in his nose. And these were the mighty gangsters from back east? They looked more like a bunch of overweight, punch-drunk former contenders shuffling through a Vegas casino than the lean, mean-eyed pack of shooters he had envisioned. When they did eventually track down Belasko—assuming now someone back there had an IQ anywhere close to three digits, and they could read the specific directions he'd mapped out...

Unbelievable. Thornton could almost see the badass dying of laughter instead of getting his lights doused by any amount of lead they could fling his way.

Thornton shook his head. Nothing he could do, except, of course, loosen the safety valve once he landed at the facility. Cromman had radioed moments after he'd hung up the phone on the Don at the diner. More flak, more blame dumped on his head. Maybe it was pure spite, but Thornton had passed on the word Belasko had the cherished disk in his possession, informed Cromman the guy was now traipsing all over the desert in the general direction of the facilities.

Cromman was on his own for the moment, doing whatever he was doing.

Screw him.

Thornton suddenly felt as if he were alone on a ship punched full of holes in a raging storm far out to sea.

SOS.

It was time to start thinking about number one. And he had on tap exactly what he needed to reach out and grab hold of his own lifeboat. Sure, he intended to see Cromman grab the device for himself. No problem there, the freak could have it, and Thornton fully intended to make the run with the man to wherever and whoever was lined up in the shopping market.

But if Cromman turned against him, the freak would find himself gone to the next world in such a way...

Well, if it came down to that, the man-thing would never know, Thornton thought, what hit him.

A nuclear blast, even one in the four-kiloton range, tended to get the other guy's attention.

CHAPTER NINETEEN

The blacksuited hardman rose out of the driver's door, gathered a head of steam in a few paces forward to cut off Bolan's advance from his SUV. Rolling toward the human barricade, the soldier was mentally tuned in to snipers, perched and hidden in the sheer black walls behind the customized limo.

"Lose the subgun."

Bolan slowed his strides but held on to the HK MP-5. He gave the clone a hard once-over. The crew cut, the dark shades, the holstered 9 mm Beretta and the one-piece combat suit might be standard insignia of their trade, but the warrior sensed a new level of menace in the op's stance and tone.

"You first."

The gunner made no move to empty his holster.

"Then I guess it's settled."

The man pointed toward the passenger end of the vehicle. "Down the side. Stand there. I'll be watching you."

As if Bolan needed to be told the obvious.

The Executioner stopped at a midway point on the unmarked limo. No plates, no insignia, but two antennae pointed up from the rear. He caught his grim expression mirrored in the black glass, which lowered on an electronic touch. A blast of air, cold enough to keep a meat house refrigerated, washed over Bolan, chilling sweat-slick flesh to the bone. At first look he thought the well was empty, then a step back, peering inside, and he found the shadow sitting on the other side of some tinted partition.

The freak.

It was hard to clearly make out the face on the other side, but Bolan saw the outline of a hat, some kind of Jimmy Buffett beach job, then noted the visor wrapped around the shadow of a face that had no visible features.

"So, we meet at last, Special Agent Belasko of the Justice Department," the shadow said. "Or whoever you really are or work for."

Bolan skipped past the friendly preamble, a hard edge in his voice as he said, "I have the disk, Cromman. I know all about this marvel of supertechnology you want to steal and sell to your so-called subcontractors. Since you've been watching me, and since you know I have the disk, then you know I know about those two kids you gave the order to murder."

"I hear a hostile tone."

"I didn't ride in to salute you."

"Of course. Excuse me."

"You're going out of business. How it gets done is up to you."

"The easy way or the hard way."

"Your choice. It will happen. Thornton's going

down. And this Project Orion is about to get scrapped into a toxic dung heap.''

''Ah, yes, more gunslinging to screw up my bowels, foil all my hopes and dreams.''

''You're out of hope from where I stand. And you're dreaming on stolen time.''

''What you don't know, Belasko, is a lot. I, for one, am sitting at the threshold of obtaining one of the greatest truths and discoveries of all time. Soon I will be holding the key to the future of humankind, at least as far as travel into deep space at light speed is concerned.''

''Telling me you're still in charge and I might as well spit into the wind if I take you on.''

''I would have used a word other than spit, but essentially, you're right.''

''I've made it this far.''

''You've gotten lucky.''

''I make my own luck.''

''So it would appear. A bunch of bikers, used to slapping around their women or gunning down unarmed men? Not much of a challenge.''

''Bring on the first-string talent.''

''In time. Consider yourself warned, Belasko. I will not allow you or the entire weight of even the U.S. military to keep me from taking what's left me less than, not even a full man, but a human being.''

''Cosmic justice.''

''What's that?''

''Those kids.''

''Insignificant peasants in the larger picture.''

Bolan choked down a sudden rising anger. "Which is what?"

"Why, my own immortality, of course. He who has the device could be capable of ruling the world. You're standing there, gawking at me as if I'm just someone with a huge chip on his shoulder."

"It's pretty much what I expected."

"From this point on, Mr. Belasko, nothing will be as you expect."

"Going to steamroller me," Bolan said, then looked at the blacksuited hardman marking his territory near the front end.

"It's you or me. The device will be taken, and tonight. There's nothing you can do to stop that from happening."

Bolan felt it in the air next, the shadow's lips moving behind his tinted shield, no sound, but giving the order. The soldier was bringing the subgun around, the hardman going for it, hand digging out the Beretta when Bolan shot from the hip, nailed him with a burst to the chest. The blacksuit was flying back, crimson history, hammering the ground, when Bolan swung the subgun toward the shadow.

"This glass is bulletproof!"

There was a high-pitched note of fear now rifling through the well.

"Not a problem," Bolan said. "I have a few grenades I could dump inside."

"You—"

"What? I wouldn't? Maybe I'll just burn you out

from behind your shield, rip off that visor. I understand your eyes are real sensitive to light.''

''You're a cold bastard.''

''That's me, Mr. Insensitive. Looks like you'll have to drive yourself for a change.''

''Unless you're available?''

Bolan chuckled at that, reading between the lines. ''No sale.''

''I had to try.''

''Have a nice life.''

''While I still have some?''

''There is a bottom line.''

''And there will be an answer?''

''Just like the old classic says. Only I can't imagine Mother Mary will be there to greet you on the other side.''

The pissing contest over, boundaries clearly marked on both sides, Bolan turned and walked past the body, heading for his SUV. The extreme limits some men would go to for power never failed to amaze, disturb and anger the Executioner.

It was time to go have a look at the site where it was all going to happen, where the marvel of all time was housed and ready to be sold to enemies of...

Well, national security.

Behind the wheel and rolling next across the salt flat, Bolan gave the limo one last look. It was still sitting there, a black shimmer in the burning mist, fading rapidly from the soldier's sight as he motored on. Apparently Cromman was too good to chauffeur

himself. Then again, Bolan thought, that was something he would relegate to a peasant.

THORNTON COULDN'T decide if the wonder device of
the ages looked like a giant kid's top or the funnel of
a tornado. Sitting at the console in the shadowy lair
of his personal control room, he stared at the object
of all Cromman's desire on the far monitor. The next
two or three hours, getting the device prepared the way
he wanted, would prove the tricky part. Worst case,
he'd put on a spacesuit himself and power it up. If it
came down to that, it would mean none of the science
crew was willing to pump the thing up with radioactive juice. It would also mean they were all very much
dead, a bullet each behind the ear.

The small nuclear reactor was housed in a special
glass-reinforced bay beyond the shiny tornado funnel.
The device could remain standing, like now, supported
by steel cables, with clamps attached to the disk-
shaped head from the reactor. Another monitor
showed him the science crew was off in an adjoining
room, poring over mathematical and chemical data
that was light-years beyond him. Numbers and sym-
bols, he thought, that looked straight from an alien
alphabet. And who knew? he thought. Not even he
was privy to where the mystery element that powered
the thing came from or how it had fallen into their
hands.

He did, though, have the clout to engineer his safety
net, one of the perks that came as head of Special
Security. He took the disk out of the safe and slipped

it into his computer. Thornton punched in a series of codes and passwords only he, as head of Special Security, knew existed, and he was online. First order of business was to memorize the eight-digit numbers, forward and backward, since to initiate any countdown he had to run them through both ways. As a precaution to keep the thing from falling into the wrong hands, a miniature radio detonator had been built into the skin of the device. He had the numbers down, the black box in hand and stowed in his pocket, when his handheld beeped again.

Cromman. Calling back. He had ignored the man two times already, but knew a third silence on his end might scramble the freak to the back door of the facility sooner than he wanted.

Thornton punched on. "Yes."

A note of either anger or panic shrilled in Thornton's ear. "Where have you been?"

"I've been busy making the necessary preparations."

"I need a driver and now! I'm stuck out here on the salt flat. Even with the windows and my visor, the light is killing my eyes!"

"Slow down, Cromman. Fill me in on your situation."

And he did. Belasko again, shooting down his personal chauffeur and bodyguard, driving off and toward the facility, stranding him.

"I'll send somebody," Thornton promised, only intended to let the freak stew and curse the light for a little while before he dispatched a man. It never occurred to Cromman, of course, to simply rough it, endure a little more pain and climb in behind the wheel, drive himself.

"When?"

"Soon."

"Now."

"He'll be there. Anything else?"

"Get the chopper ready. When the sun goes down I want those cultists loaded up and given one last briefing. How many men on your end do you have a firm fix on who will aid us?"

"That was something else I was working on before I was interrupted."

"Lose the attitude, Thornton."

"Is that all?"

"For now."

And Thornton was grateful for the silence once more. A check of the time, and he knew the fifteen-man backup was already bussed and rolling toward the facility. They should arrive, he figured, in thirty minutes, give or take. He already had their briefing down, how the thing was going to be moved to another facility, that security here had been breached. Most of the ops he knew personally, and believed if the right amount of cash was promised they'd play ball. Four, maybe five ops now under the roof were the ones he needed a face-to-face with.

Thornton decided it was time to have a chat with the head scientist, an astronuclear physicist named Anderson. He punched a button beneath the bank of monitors. "Mr. Anderson."

A balding, slight figure in a white lab coat looked up from his work bay.

"Come to the control center."

"Now?"

"Right away."

He waited, watching while Anderson lingered another moment then walked out of his bay. Thornton stood, aware in the next few moments it was either the beginning of the end...

Or it was going to hit the fan, stop it all dead in the tracks before it even got off the ground.

He slid open the wall to his personal miniarmory, selected an HK MP-5 SD-3 subgun. The walls to his control center were reinforced steel, soundproof, but he unlimbered the Beretta 92-F and threaded a sound suppressor on the muzzle. Usually, he knew from past experience, when a guy found himself staring down the narrowed black eye of a sound-suppressed weapon, he tended to listen harder.

Thornton knew he could settle for nothing less than complete obedience to his demands in the coming hours. Failing that, he'd marched them into the room, one by one, and fill it to capacity with a couple dozen bodies, if necessary.

Then go juice up the wonder device his damn self.

SINCE THE LINE in the sand was drawn, Bolan didn't much care if they knew he had breached the perimeter or not. He was beefed up on firepower, though, just in case they came charging the hilltop roost where he spied the facilities. The trusty M-16 with attached

M-203 grenade launcher was resting beside the soldier's prone post, 30-round clip in place, with a 40 mm frag bomb up the launcher's snout. Lugging the war bag several hundred yards from where he'd ditched the SUV in a wash to the east was a grueling task, bringing on enough sweat to fill half a bathtub. Well, he didn't need to find the war bag liberated from his possession when he returned to the SUV, not after the Farm's blacksuits had gone through all the trouble to get him the necessary firepower to bring down the house. As soon as the sun began to set, Bolan intended to slip into his blacksuit, webbing and harness buckled up, weighted down with enough party favors to see him through a hellground he knew was in the wings.

A battle he intended to wage, on his terms, time and place.

Sipping from his bottled water, the soldier gave the lay of the land a search in all directions next, taking up the field glasses. It was broken ground, cut by gullies and washes, studded with cactus and littered with rocks and boulders. If there were high-tech surveillance devices in the vicinity, he hadn't spied them out. It didn't mean they weren't there. No posted signs authorizing use of deadly force, either.

Two facilities had been built into the hills down in the valley. The larger of the two was due north. It looked like a giant silver dome, constructed, it appeared, to be part of the hill chain. Only one way in and out that he could see, straight through the dome. There was a conspicuous lack of activity in that direction, despite the grounded black chopper and five vans near the dome. Were they inside, watching him? Planning their next lethal riposte?

Let them come, he decided, the sooner the better. The more he took out of play before night, the merrier.

Panning on, he searched hills, framed shiny vents and fat smokestacks rising from the ridge. Air shafts for a ventilation system. No doubt a generator inside, probably a nuclear reactor below ground. That meant any number of levels of floors, a whole maze of interlocking halls.

The sister facility was a smaller dome, due west. One black van, again no sign of life.

He gave Cromman a brief moment of consideration. It might have been a simple bloody task to have burned the creature out of his shield, chop him down in a hail of bullets, but Bolan figured where Cromman went next was where the action would unfold. He was saving the best, or in this instance, the worst for last. Assuming, naturally, one of those invisible killers Jordan mentioned didn't boil up out of the night and nail him before he got within spitting distance of the dome.

Lowering the binos, Bolan detected distant movement in the corner of his eye. He slid up, crouched, then moved deeper down the narrow cut in the hill for concealment. Adjusting the binos, he lined up two Towncars, several hundred yards off, and heading his direction. No tinted glass, Nevada plates, but it appeared five figures were packed into each luxury vehicle. From their slow run across the tabletop, he knew they could make out his SUV down in the wash. Now what? Bolan wondered.

M-16 leading the way, the soldier hauled up his war bag and set off down the slope.

CHAPTER TWENTY

"Do you understand what you are proposing? Do you even begin to comprehend the risk involved?"

Thornton felt himself coiling up, a cobra rearing in his gut, as he leaned back in his swivel chair to a groaning spring. He felt a muscle in his arm twitch next, the Beretta so close, with Anderson standing a few feet away, staring at him as if he were insane to even contemplate such a recipe for disaster.

"Let me understand this," Anderson said, pacing next, rubbing his hands together. "You want to power it up to a level-ten readiness?"

"For full maneuvers," Thornton said. "The mother of all test flights, if you will."

"And by 2200 hours?"

"Those are my orders from back east. Now passed on to you." He pointed to the red phone, the hot line to their man at the Pentagon. "You want to make the call yourself to confirm it, or do I simply relieve you of duty now? Your choice."

"For one thing, it's stretching our resources alone simply to see that's it up to level ten within the time frame we are allotted."

"Then you're wasting precious time pacing around here, fretting like some old hag."

"Please, spare me the rhetoric. Try to understand the element is of a very and most unstable nature, my friend. Try to understand our position, which is our very lives are in grave danger if we go as far as you want. Once the element infuses with radiation and it is pumped into the device, well, we don't know exactly what could happen, say, if it decides to take off on its own, perhaps reaching superhypersonic speed in seconds, then hovering over in the skies as far away as Maine! The core of element-fused-nuclei acts as its own regenerating and self-sustaining source of power by, we believe, an ongoing splitting of atoms we still don't understand. In other words, it acts as a continual but self-contained nuclear implosion. Constant critical mass, how should I say, only appeased it would seem, by the element itself, which somehow keeps it from detonating into…an explosion of unfathomed power, combining both, I fear, a nuclear blast and the spread of the element in a wind of radioactive fire. And if that happens, not even we can predict the outcome. Not to mention I'm concerned about a repeat disaster such as the tragic incident which befell my now dead colleagues."

Thornton ignored the undercurrent of accusation. "We've fixed that problem."

"Yes. Added a few monitors to tell us if the element is leaking. Only by then it would once more be too late. Not only that, but since the element is stored in the other facility, it has to be carefully shipped here to even begin—''

''You're wasting time! Are you going to do it or not?''

Anderson hesitated, shaking his head. ''I'm the only one with the sufficient expertise to pull it off.''

''That's a yes, then?''

''Yes.''

''You're dismissed, but remember, I'll be watching you.''

Anderson peered, and Thornton saw a new look of doubt and suspicion in the eyes behind the glasses.

''What?''

''I should confirm this with General—''

Thornton grabbed up the phone.

Anderson held his ground, thinking about, then shook his head. ''Let it be on record I am opposed to this.''

''Duly noted. Something goes wrong it's my ass they fry back at the Pentagon.'' Anderson held his ground, a knowing smirk on his face, Thornton almost reading the thought, *If there's anything left to even fry.*

But it was only a start. Thornton took the small remote, hit a button and released the lock on the steel door. Sighing, Anderson left, looking to Thornton as if he just aged another ten years.

The first snow job was dumped. Now to start finding out who was with him and who was against him among his own ranks. Thornton slid the Beretta free, resting it on the console for easy access.

BOLAN FOLLOWED the wheezing and the huffing coming up out of the wash to a point where he found
himself on the lip, looking down on their rear, roughly
a hundred paces out. The Executioner dropped behind
a boulder, then brought the M-16 around the edge. He
counted ten of them, wandering around his SUV,
peeking inside, inspecting the front-end damage.

"Well, this is his SUV."

"No shit, Gino."

"Banged up like the spook said."

"So, where the hell is he?"

"How should I know, Donnie? Let's spread out and
go find him. Big guy, big guns."

"So the spook said. What if it's more than one
guy?"

"What if it is? There's ten of us."

"Right."

A feeble response, at best. Nerves were on edge
down there, twisting up the works, guys uncertain
what to do now, much less how to proceed. A none
too gentle shove, with a swift 40 mm kick in the rear,
was all it would take, Bolan figured, to start nailing
down this second NSA sideshow. And the Executioner
was gearing up to drop the hammer, pulling out two
more rounds from his war bag, another frag bomb and
a buckshot round for the M-203.

"So, now what, boss? We go traipsing all over the
desert, looking for some guy we've never seen?"

"Hey, we'll do whatever it takes."

Enough. Bolan had the gist of it. He couldn't pin

down the accents, but they sounded midwest. Probably Chicago. And Bolan knew Mob when he saw it.

Clearly they were city boys, perhaps accustomed to rolling out of bed probably at the crack of noon. Figure three squares a day complete with all the high-calorie trimmings, all the fine wine and good times they could consume from noon to midnight, clubbing it into the vampire hours with well-heeled ladies, schmoozing about town with cronies.

Gone soft.

Calves fattened for the slaughter.

Not even two minutes under the broiling sun, tromping around in their dandy threads, reeking of cologne and alcohol, and they sounded to Bolan ready to cut and run back for the chilled safety of their luxury cocoons. That they now dragged around puffy carcasses from years of excess and having their way out of sheer reputation landed a definite edge in Bolan's favor. Even still, they had broken out the heavier hardware from opened trunks, and he could bet they hadn't come all this way to pack it up at the first sign the going would get tough. Subguns and assault rifles, even wielded by subpar talent, could find his flesh with a lucky wild burst. To a fancy shirt they had an automatic weapon, with side arms either openly displayed or bulging under silk jackets.

Once again, Bolan figured Thornton had reached out and pulled in a wild-card factor to do his dirty work.

One more guy, like Cromman, riding along on stolen time, but with his shooting star rapidly flaming out.

Now this circus act to bog down his own play.

The Executioner knew his ancient war against the Mafia hadn't, of course, completely wiped the scourge of organized crime off the American landscape. Most of the old dinosaurs were pretty much, however, extinct by now. A few ancient Dons were still creaking around, barely holding on against the conniving rat packs under their own roofs, with Feds planted on their doorsteps around the clock, and the new breed of up-and-comers who were pretty much all show and little go skulking around the palace, itching for the old men to finally croak. Yes, Bolan had blazed through their ranks long ago, kicked enough ass to send them into bloody disarray. But, he thought, they said cockroaches would be the only survivors of a full-scale nuclear holocaust. These days, and that analogy in mind, a new breed of roach had crawled up out of the ashes of the Bolan conflagration to skitter into the gaping wounds left in the wake of his blitz against the Mafia. Most of them were armed with college degrees, erected legitimate business fronts, assimilated themselves into various offshoots of other rising criminal groups.

Then there were those rats scurrying all over the remaining Mafia houses, guys who wilted under the glare of the first FBI agent who came armed with wiretaps and threats of snatching up all their ill-gotten material goodies if they didn't start squealing on the rest of the pack. It had always been a dirty business, but the demonic allure of narcotics as the mother lode of all cash crops had plunged the old crime game to new depths of ugliness and treachery. They had no qualms these days about eating their own. In the old days, they talked about honor. Nowadays they didn't even pay that notion of principle lip service. The snakes, at least, used to have backbone.

The good old days.

The paunchy white-haired man they appeared deferential toward didn't strike Bolan as a new breed of gangster. He was out there, on the front lines, after something, and Bolan could only venture a guess as to why he was there to sweat it out, a million miles away from his own kingdom, ready to do battle.

Stony Man Farm had complete and thorough files on all known and suspected crime lords, homegrown and overseas. When there was time, Bolan would pore over the crime files, boning up on the who's who and what was what, in the Mafia world and beyond. He thought he should be able to place the beefy one's face in those files. Maybe when he got closer...

"Second thought, let's go take a ride around these hills, boys."

The Executioner slipped his finger through the trigger of the M-203. The pack was splitting up, huffing and puffing back for the vehicles. He folded back into cover of the boulder, in case of couple pairs of nervous eyes darted his way before he was ready to unload.

A few more seconds, riding out the wait, and Bolan would introduce himself.

THE OLD INSTINCTS WARNED Leanetti they were being watched. The HK 33 assault rifle was up and fanning the ridgelines on both sides of the wash. Nothing he could see up top, the sun hammering down and dropping a shimmering curtain in his eyes. Forget hearing any movement, such as a shoe scuffling rock or a sharp intake of breath, since his soldiers were babbling now among themselves, huffing about like old women.

It didn't make sense to Leanetti. He pulled up short of the lead Towncar, looking around. Why would the guy just abandon his SUV? Unless he knew he was being followed, spotting them on his tail earlier, on foot now obviously. Circling in from behind?

"Gino, Petie, Costanza, hold up."

"What is it, boss?"

"Keep your voices down."

Leanetti was sure he'd just seen movement, up there, along the top edge of the rock wall, at some point off to the rear of the second Towncar. It was a blur, maybe the sun and the heat playing tricks on his eyes, but he'd swear a figure had just melted to cover behind a fat rock above them.

"Okay, this is what we're going to—"

And then his grim suspicion became a horrifying reality. The figure popped up over the rock, like something in a carnival, a massive weapon in his fists, a rocket popping off and flaming toward them. The old instincts told Leanetti to hit the deck, but the legs wouldn't respond to the warning cry in his head. He thought it was like one of those bad dreams where the Feds were chasing him but he was paralyzed. Then he got some much unwanted help in the next instant as the explosion tore through a few of his soldiers near the second Towncar. The shock wave reached out, a giant fist, hurling metal and wet pieces of flesh in his face. Leanetti squeezed his eyes shut out of instinct, his ears full of thunder and the screams of his men carved up by flying shrapnel. Before he knew it, he was on his back.

But he was still breathing. And now he was angry. Clearly Shadow Man had been right all along. The guy, Belasko, was up there, ready to stick it to him again.

CROMMAN CURSED everything and everyone under the sun, especially the sunlight. He had no more pills, no water at any rate to swallow one even if he did. He figured if he stayed low in the well, back pressed against the door, eyes screwed shut, he could keep the blaze from knifing into his brain.

It didn't work.

And where the hell was Thornton's rescue? Oh, but he intended to see Thornton pay for this humiliation. Leaving him stranded like this, imagining the bastard was safe and smug, cooling off at the facility, even chuckling over his predicament.

Cromman would fix him in due course. He had planned to anyway, once the backup unit from the east was on hand tonight. Thornton didn't know it yet, but Cromman had been sending along an envelope with cash and note, unsigned, that simply stated for them to be prepared when they were called to act. Thornton would think they were more NSA black ops, arriving at the site to beef up depleted guns, bona fide help simply attached to the project, rotated in to relieve the standing team.

Thornton was in for the last and the mother of all rude awakenings.

First Cromman had to get out of there.

Panic set in next when he heard the engine clunk, grind, the chassis shuddering like some ancient behemoth wheezing out its final breath. And steam, he saw, was hissing from under the hood. The air-conditioning died next, and Cromman cried out in horror.

He would have to get out now, or fry, suffocate. He would have to walk, but he feared he would die the first few steps he ventured across the salt flat, the sun burning up his eyes, shafts like branding irons digging into his brain.

He was growling, cursing, visions of shooting down Thornton—and Belasko—stoking his rage and terror. He was shaking, balled up against the door, curling up into a fetal position when he made out the sound of a fist banging on the window.

''Mr. Cromman!''

One of Thornton's men. Could he see inside through the tinted glass? See him blubbering, the great man with the plan? No, of course not.

Cromman realized he was hyperventilating, unable to respond as the man kept hitting the window, calling his name.

Thornton was a dead man, he decided. But first the device, once he had that in his hands...

Somehow he found his voice, but detested the

squeaky note as he said, "Pull your van up alongside the door."

He would have to step out into the light, no matter what.

"Yes, sir."

"Hurry! This side, the driver's side!"

He tried to steel himself, pull it together. He had to appear strong, in control once the door was opened. He heard the van rumble up, its shadow falling over the well. He sucked in a long breath, felt some composure returning, the shaking in his limbs fading a little.

Escape, relief was coming. First he needed to fight his way through the light.

THORNTON HIT the button on the metal box that would carry his voice to the intercom beside the door outside in the hall.

"It's open, Benson."

He kept his back turned as the man entered. "Sir, we have a situation in the east quadrant."

"Close the door, Benson."

Thornton knew all about the situation. Belasko was kicking ass again, only this time in living color on a monitor to his right. That wasn't the work of any Justice Department issue, the guy winging down a grenade into the pack of mobsters, bowling down three right off the bat. But Thornton already knew the guy was far more than he claimed.

"Sir, security is being violated. The manual states we must initiate immediate and decisive action in the event of an armed intruder. Also, sir, myself and a few others have questions about procedure the past two days.''

"Names."

"Sir?"

"Who is doing all this squawking?"

"Why...I wouldn't quite call it that, but...well, Matthews, Thomas and Corley, sir. We have some questions.''

"You're dismissed, Benson."

"Sir?"

Thornton pushed himself around the swivel chair, the Beretta up and spitting a quiet 9 mm round, punching out the light of shock and confusion in the man's eyes. Before the body even came bouncing off the door to topple, Thornton was up and dragging the corpse to the corner of the room.

CHAPTER TWENTY-ONE

Three were down, blown around in screaming flight, when the Executioner cranked up the slaughter machine another scorching notch. The second 40 mm frag projectile dumped into the M-203's black hole, and Bolan rose over the boulder, sweeping them with a long burst of chattering autofire. The Aloha-shirt convention was gathering some speed when the first line of 5.56 mm lead hosed a slab of human flesh, too beefy and too slow to ever have a hope in hell of beating the warrior's tracking line of fire. They were finally getting their act together in spurts and darts for cover behind the front ends of their respective luxury rigs, subguns spraying and praying to cover their flight.

A fresh clip cracked home, a few heads popping up over the front ends and shaky hands winging off more wild rounds from subguns, and Bolan went back to work with the M-16 rain of doom. They came close, three or four rounds snapping the air around Bolan, when he turned both Towncars to ventilated scrap. The wall of Bolan's flying lead raked the luxury vehicles, stem to stern. Message—they could run and hide, but no one was leaving the wash. Unless, of course, they were stretched out as the day's dinner special for the scavenger birds.

Glass took to the air in sheets and countless gleaming shrapnel bits, a howl or two of pain as he either clipped another shooter with lead or someone received a glass facial without benefit of anesthesia. Tires blew under the onslaught, a radiator erupting in a hissing white cloud. Before the rigs flattened out, Bolan pumped off another 40 mm round, dropping the projectile into the closest hunk of metal. The fireball belched out the doors, blew the roof into warped tin, and it appeared to the soldier they didn't know what to do next. They were like mannequins, frozen and gawking at the horror of it all, even as the world was blowing up in their faces. The thundering shock wave had kicked one shooter off to the side, the vehicle jumping up in the air, before it settled back on limp tread with a pounding crunch.

A fuel line had to have been punctured by either the blast or all the lead he'd poured over the vehicles, but a secondary explosion ignited. The shooter launched clear of Bolan's 40 mm wrecking ball was scrambling back for the relative safety of the Towncar when the slick firewall roared in his face, bathing him in flames.

Bolan tapped the trigger, spared the shrieking devil a mercy burst.

He took a moment to get his bearings, the lay of the land down the top edge of the wash. It rose in broken humps and jags, perfect to shield his move toward their rear. The way they'd suddenly gone silent and still, hugging cover, told the soldier he'd have to go down there now and root them out anyway.

Four fancy shirts left.

He could have burned up another 40 mm round or two, but figured the quickest road to their hell would only pan out at eyeball level.

Good enough.

He was never opposed to doing things the hard way, if it came down to that.

Bolan crouched, advancing the few steps up the narrow gully cut into the near vertical face. He risked leaving the war bag behind, simply to lighten his load, opting instead for speed to wrap this up ASAP. On his way out he spotted the eye of the camera, buried in the ground. He couldn't be sure, but he hoped Thornton was catching the show.

Either way, the Executioner threw a mock salute to the camera, then set off to wrap up the Mob convention.

THE BIG BADASS had some pair on him—Thornton had to give the guy that much.

"Yeah, back at you, soldier," Thornton growled at the monitor, returning the salute before the bastard vanished off the screen.

If the Don was dead, Thornton couldn't tell. And what did it matter anyway? The camera showed the flaming heap, the smoking body that had been torched up and dropped after Belasko showed the poor slob a little compassion for his plight. At last count, he knew six of Chicago's meanest were out of the picture. Meanest? It was a joke. He might as well have marched out there, he thought, with a bunch of soccer moms. While whoever was left standing—or hiding, which was more likely the case—Thornton figured Belasko was moving out to come in on their rear. Tie up the whole bloody package, up close and personal, maybe some grilling of one of the goons.

Not that it mattered if one of the Chicago hitters filled Belasko in on the scheme.

Thornton knew he was next on the bastard's shopping list.

At least, he saw the science detail was decked out in hazmat suits, starting the process of pumping the radiation laced with the element into the device. Another lead bin of the element was now being slowly driven from the sister site.

Garner was patching through. He was one of the few ops on-site that Thornton could trust to help him seize the device. Even in the spook world, Thornton knew money talked. It was something of a plus that more than a few of the ops now on the way to beef up the numbers were either former NSA assassins or had sold their services around the world as soldiers of fortune. They would, he knew, prove themselves loyal, in the end, to the hand that fed. Whether their cut came out of his pocket, or Cromman had to cough up a few dollars more...

"Sir, what about the situation in the east quad?"

"Let it be."

"Sir?"

"Let it be," he rasped. "I want you in the briefing room in twenty minutes."

He heard Corley's voice over the speaker next, announcing their arrival. Thornton let them in. The trio marched into the room, Thornton telling Corley to close the door. It was Matthews who sensed what was about to happen next, the man sniffing the air, tinged with the coppery taint of spilled blood.

By the time Matthews spotted the heap of his fallen comrade in the far corner, Thornton had the subgun up and blasting away.

"WHERE IS he, boss?"

"How the hell would I know?"

Truth was, Vince Leanetti didn't know much at all, right then, except they were—all four of them—in a world of hurt. For the first time he could remember he was, in fact, clueless. And very much afraid of dying.

And one bastard had done all this?

The stink of Marino's toasted skin was swelling up the nausea in the Don's belly as he fisted the sweat out of his eyes, risking a look over the Towncar's hood, scanning the empty lip of the wash. Nothing. The guy was gone, like a ghost vanishing into thin air. Likewise, it was hard to make out any sound beyond their hiding point, the flames eating up the Towncar, Frotelli, Donnie, and Botalico sucking wind.

Statues of fear.

It was unbelieveable, he thought, Marino's shrieking, as he was lit up like a Roman candle on the Fourth, still loud enough to seem to hang in the air, the wailing of the damned. It had been a long time since Leanetti had pulled the trigger, granted, but he couldn't have lost this much edge over the span of a few short years.

Or could he? A vivid but brief recollection of all the guys he'd wasted over the years seemed to dance some collage of faces through his head. Rivals, witnesses, snitches, even a cop who couldn't be bought and that lawyer who had been more interested in scribbling memoirs than defending him against twenty life sentences. No, he wasn't opposed to taking down a man, armed or in cold blood. Sometimes they had been armed when he'd gone calling to put one between a mark's eyes. Sometimes, even a shot or two had been fired back at him in anger. But this? Rockets and his own men dropping like dominoes under precision autofire? This was more like something out of Bosnia or Beirut.

He had to make the effort just to remind himself they were in Nevada, the good old U.S. of A. And that, as far as he could tell, they were up against only one man.

Some feral rage, perhaps brought on by sheer panic, and Frotelli was baring his teeth, swinging up the MAC-10 to bear on the SUV.

"What are you doing?" Leanetti snapped, swatted the muzzle away. "You plan on walking all the way back to Reno?"

What was that look in Frotelli's eyes now? Guy sending out the telepathy, *We should end up being that lucky.* Smart-ass.

Leanetti grasped his HK 33 tighter, the assault rifle feeling unusually heavy, as if it wanted to slide right out of his sweaty palms. He checked the jagged slope, a narrow gully running up the side for the top east edge. A plan. No way would he sit there and wait for the bastard to come to them.

"Okay, we're going up top, that way," Leanetti said. "Gain the high ground, that's how the bastard took the edge in the first place." They didn't look convinced it was that simple. "Let's go."

Settled, the Don had spoken. Time to even it up.

And Leanetti was breaking cover, leading the charge for the high ground, when all hell broke loose again. He wasn't three steps toward the opening when the autofire rang out, and more screams of his own men in great pain were knifing the air.

And the horror show went on.

THE FLAMING PURPLE shirt with the MAC-10 had almost spotted him on the advance to their rear. It would have been a visual nailing of Bolan's rolling up on their rear, at best, if the boss hadn't stepped in, concerned about the only available ride out.

As if they even had someplace else planned to go after this.

The Executioner surged past his SUV, and jump-started round two. Holding back on the M-16's trigger, he nearly made it a clean sweep. They were breaking out in a sluggish staggered line, going for an opening, a way out of the wash. The wanna-be vandal went first, Bolan chopping the mobster to crimson shreds, then tracking on. Rolling ahead, another down, and three to go to victory, and the soldier was hitting them hard and ceaseless, the M-16 raking them stem to stern. Two subguns and one HK 33 were swinging around, a last-ditch gasp on their part to draw blood. Bolan showered them with lead, eating up the silk and perfumed sweat-tacky skin. Number eight was spinning on his heels, snarling out the venom but tumbling out of play, when Bolan adjusted his aim. Up close now, Bolan put a name on the face of the white-haired man.

Vince Leanetti had escaped the Executioner's brand of justice over the years, more out of luck and a conflict with Bolan's own busy schedule than anything else.

Funny how things happened, though, Bolan thought. Well, Nevada was as good as Chicago to sever one more tentacle of the Mafia hydra.

Whether it was pure accident or misguided sense of loyalty to protect the boss, but another shooter who'd seen one too many buffets shuffled into Bolan's line of fire. The Executioner beat a sidestep out of the blazing finger of lead, rounds slashing the air he just vacated. Shooting from the hip, Bolan stitched him crotch to sternum, blood, gore and the guy's last supper perhaps hitting the air in a slick kaleidoscope. He caught a lucky break, one step closer to nailing it, when Leanetti screamed, the soldier glimpsing a crimson puff in the air before the Don nosedived out of sight into a rocky minibowl.

The Executioner heard the Don throwing out vicious curses between ragged gasps. Bolan moved in behind the shield of fire, angling down the burning Towncar to bring the man into clear and easy death sights.

The Don started triggering wild bursts from cover, winging bullets down the wash. It was blind panic pretty much, but that didn't make the man any less dangerous.

Okay, Bolan decided. The hard way. So be it. A sudden lull in the shooting, the Don probably weighing his options.

Less than zero.

"Let's go, Vince. I don't have all day to play games."

LEANETTI FROZE, the HK assault rifle going silent, rounds echoing off beyond the bowl he'd dropped into. He nearly laughed out loud in bitter spite at those words. The bastard made it sound as if he had a busy day ahead of him, that this was just some poor man's skirmish, an irritating diversion against a few punks with guns. Made it sound that he should walk right out there and take it like a man. And how the hell did he know...

It couldn't be. Had the spook set him up? But, why?

He struggled onto a knee, the assault rifle up and ready again, his eyes burning from sweat but trying to focus on any movement beyond his perch. A piece of flesh was missing from his right arm, blood running free and fast. The heat, the stink of death, with a ripe odor of emptied bowels and bladders bringing on the sickness, but if he didn't get his act together quick a little pain and queasiness would be the least of his woes.

"Who the hell are you?"

If he got the guy talking again, there was a chance he could cap off a burst, nail the body where the voice sounded.

"You with Barklin?"

"I'm with me."

"The man said you took my money!"

Where was he?

"The man lied to you."

"You telling me I've been set up?"

"More like used to do his dirty work."

"He's got my money."

"There is no money, Vince. There's just you, me and a con job you fell into. The man sees you as disposable."

The mobster pinned the voice to the tall shadow, rising up out of nowhere. Leanetti was sweeping the assault rifle around as the guy appeared, as if by magic, on the other side of the fire devouring the Towncar. Before he even pulled back on the trigger, Leanetti knew it was over, the shimmering apparition already spitting out the lead.

THE DON WAS DEAD, but Bolan walked up, confirmed it was over with a nudge to the ribs. There was nothing in the eyes but some frozen rage the man had been cheated, duped, strung along.

Life was tough all over.

The question now was would the black ops agents use the time he'd burned up on the Mob convention to scramble the troops?

Slapping a fresh clip into his M-16, another 40 mm hellbomb down the M-203's chute, Bolan made swift progress out of the wash.

Topping out, he scanned the open ground around the two facilities beyond a rolling stretch of broken tableland.

All quiet, all still.

It felt all wrong. They had circled the wagons, hunkered down inside, sitting tight.

Waiting for the night's big show.

He moved down the lip, setting off to retrieve the war bag. Other than waiting for night to come, Bolan figured there wasn't much he could do but ride it out. If they came for him, fine.

If not...

The Executioner would go inside. One way or another he would be there when Cromman came to take the device. Whatever the plan, Bolan would trash it all to hell.

It was the only game left in town.

CHAPTER TWENTY-TWO

The curtain had dropped on the Mob slaughter show, the Don long since on his way to the other world. Now, what Thornton couldn't figure was what the hell Belasko was up to next. The guy was out there, taking a casual drive, then a stroll on foot around the far perimeters. Thornton could well figure the bastard was hardly ready to break out the picnic basket and champagne. No. That guy was a soldier, a killer, and he knew the drill, what it took to get the grim job done. He was out there looking for openings, any weakness in defenses, hoping to get a fix on the numbers of shooters inside. Well, there was only one way the bastard could get inside, and that was straight through the front door. Perhaps, he decided, that was exactly what Belasko intended. A full bulldoze charge, right up the gut, blasting his way in, shooting up the facility, all balls and fire.

Wherever he walked, Belasko was like some lightning rod of death and destruction. Thornton was nearly ashamed of himself for having so underestimated the man's martial talent, or placing too much faith in the hands of now clearly marginal skill. The Trojans and the Chicago gangsters never stood a snowball's chance.

Oh, well, he figured, shit happened, live and learn.

Cromman was bleating through the handheld radio once again. He had almost forgotten all about the freak, having ordered the operative he had dispatched to round him up to simply take him to his mobile home, sit on him. And what could he do about it? Since he deemed himself too good to drive his own car, and couldn't possibly walk around in the sun...

Thornton snapped up his handheld radio, went on-line, sniffing the air. The dead were starting to get a litte ripe.

"Yes."

"When this is finished, you and me are going to settle up. You, Thornton, aren't in charge of this. Do you hear me?"

"Aye, aye, loud and clear."

"Don't patronize me!"

"There's something you should know."

"Let me guess. You have Belasko perched on your doorstep."

That was exactly what Thornton saw on the monitor. The guy was parked on a ledge, in the neighborhood of a quarter mile south. Just standing by. Waiting for the night to come.

A lion ready to pounce.

"I scrambled the backup unit."

There was a pause on the other end. Thornton was surprised when the freak didn't fly off the handle, squeaky voice shooting up to castrated octaves.

"So, you're thinking ahead, and about what we must do. Good."

"For once, you mean to say."

"I didn't say that."

"I'd like some more details on how you wish to proceed."

"I'm keeping the shipping procedure to myself for the time being. Just have it ready at the gate to be choppered out. When our stooges go in and the shooting starts and with Belasko still lurking around, I have arranged an alternative to move the device. Oh, and Thornton, I expect to see that chopper in my yard as soon as the sun begins to go down. Roughly an hour from now. Don't force me to drive myself there."

"It's your show."

"Indeed it is."

Thornton stood in the silence of the dead. The idea was to use the cultists to round up, then mow down the science detail and the civilian labor force. Once they came here from Nellis to investigate, a fair amount of the blame could be laid on the cultists. That much made sense to Thornton. By the time the special investigative detail from Nellis sifted through the wreckage, IDed all the bodies, discovered the wonder toy of the ages was missing, Thornton would be well out of the country, with money in his pocket and a load of cash socked away in an overseas numbered account. There was a sweet and promising future to look forward to. Maybe he was born to be wild, after all. Tahiti sounded pretty good. Or Thailand. Someplace far away, where there were no Crommans or

Belaskos. Someplace where his only worry was where he'd get the day's first hummer from.

Garner patched through. "Sir, the backup team has just arrived."

About time, Thornton thought, moving for the door. The first string, the heavy hitters were finally pulling up to the gate.

THE BUS WAS a black Mariah, the sort of rig they used to haul convicted felons to their immediate end of the line. Bolan watched, curious, as the bus pulled up and Thornton stepped through a narrow slat in the dome to greet the new arrivals. The windows were, he noted, black tinted, so he could forget getting a clear head count on the number of new shooters off the bat.

M-16 in hand, the soldier strolled down along the ridge, cutting the gap until he could start counting heads at a closer angle as they disembarked. Two hundred and some yards shaved off, and he used the field glasses. One by one they stepped off the bus. He framed Thornton in the glasses, the guy actually looking his way, and Bolan half expected the middle-finger salute. The eyes may be hidden by dark shades, but there was no mistaking the new look of confidence radiating from Thornton's expression. A few heads among the blacksuited crew turned in Bolan's direction. These guys had hair, some beards and stubble, a mustache or two, an eye patch on one guy, dark shades all around. They looked more like felons on work release than the clean-cut black ops Bolan had seen up to then.

More like mercenaries.

Fifteen in all.

Stone-cold killers.

They lugged large black nylon bags, bulging with the heavy stuff Bolan could well guess they were anxious to use.

The Executioner considered dumping a 40 mm charge into the ranks, then passed.

Soon.

The sun was waning, shadows already reaching dark, skeletal fingers over the valley.

When darkness fell, the soldier intended to start pushing all manner of panic buttons.

And then he would walk down into the valley of death, find out who was who and what was what.

THORNTON FELT the smile coming straight from the heart, a beam of light, in fact, stretching his lips, swelling him with hope that these badass saviors would lead him out of the dark tunnel.

Carey, Jones, Barlowe and MacMurtrie piled out, falling in. It was good to see these men again, aware of the reputations that preceded them. They had done wet work, he knew, in places like Beirut, Damascus, Angola and Burma, just to name a few Third World hellholes where human life was less than cheap. These were the best guns Uncle Sam or some fat-cat diamond magnate, sticking it to colleagues or the poor man, could buy. They had also been used before, Thornton knew, in various black projects, as a last resort, when there were leaks and loose tongues and guys looking to squirm out of the bottom line on their contract with the government.

Emergency muscle. And the word *failure* wasn't in their manual.

Bags were dumped, a few cigarettes going up with the touch of a lighter. Thornton nearly felt like a proud papa.

Then the cleanup boss of bosses rolled off the bus last. He was muscled, a mop of shoulder-length white hair like a halo in the fading sunlight. Stubble on the chin, his face looked carved by a hatchet, sharp and angry, a couple of scars along the jaw where the mug had taken some shrapnel or flying lead.

And he was known in black op's circles as Mr. Seventy-One. The floating rumor was the man had, a few years back, engaged in a running bet with another operative. The game, Thornton had heard, was to see who could break the old record of the wet work body count—reportedly sixty-six confirmed kills. The scuttlebutt was the other op was ahead by two bodies, one kill from tying the old record, when he had a strange and sudden accident in the Sudan, something about a boating mishap on the Nile. Due to a few roving hungry crocodiles the body was never found, or so the story went. There was a definite no-shit look, a stance about the man that told Thornton the one thing he needed to know the most.

Mr. Seventy-One didn't play to lose.

"Gentlemen, glad you could make it," Thornton said as Seventy-One fired up an unfiltered cigarette, stepping down from the bus. "Trust a little R and R has got the batteries recharged?"

They were too busy watching the big shape of Belasko on the rise. No expression. One guy. No sweat.

Seventy-One blew smoke back at Thornton. "Is that the problem?"

"Let's just say he's not Mr. Sunshine."

The cigarette nearly disappeared in one massive intake of smoke. Seventy-One pitched the butt away, then reclaimed his bag. "Well, let's get this wrapped up so I can go talk to Dr. Seagrams."

THE ONSLAUGHT of twilight found the anticipated sudden activity. It looked low-key at first, but Bolan saw a few of them moving with a sense of urgency.

The Executioner had donned a blacksuit, and was harnessed and buckled, weighted down with enough grenades and spare clips to tackle the big numbers.

Ready to rock.

Thornton and the white-haired gargantuan came out of the dome. The rotors were spinning to life, but Thornton was waving two blacksuited gunners into the belly of the black chopper, the man staying behind to guard the lair. Why? And where was the bird headed? Winged pylons showed the soldier rockets were housed, and Bolan figured there was a machine gun or two in the nose turret.

The Executioner took up position on the far side of the SUV, lifting the M-16 M-203 combo. It wouldn't take much effort on the part of the flyboys to blow him off the hill, and if they started his way, nosedown, he'd have no choice but to fire off a 40 mm round. Figuring the black chopper was armor plated, he decided one well-placed round to the tail rotor should do the job nicely.

And there was still no sign of Cromman.

The bird lifted off, Thornton and the big guy holding their turf in front of the dome. Moments later, Bolan saw the chopper streaking over the desert, eastbound. Now what? Rounding up Cromman? Was Thornton hoping he'd follow the black chopper?

No. Best to stay put, he decided.

The curtain was about to come up.

Bolan dug in, just the same, alert for any movement around the compass, shadows headed his way. The darker it got, the closer to show time, he knew.

The Executioner was already geared up to take center stage, a command performance, in fact, that would leave no doubt who was playing master of ceremonies.

"I APPRECIATE the cash incentive we've been receiving. Money's always nice. It's what makes the world go round."

That revelation caught Thornton by surprise, but he kept the puzzled look off his face. So, someone had been sending along the so-called incentive on the sly. If not him...

Cromman. This latest maneuver by the freak, and behind his back, no less, started nagging Thornton with two realities, bringing on more doubt he was even meant to see his own payday at the end of the rainbow. One, Cromman had already reached out to the heavy hitters, greasing the skids, buying their loyalty, perhaps ready to make the announcement at a critical juncture he was their bank of Project Orion. Two, Cromman had to have already received a down payment for the device from the foreign subcontractors, holding back any cash advance all along for the man who had the power to launch his dream from the inside.

Sneaky freak bastard.

"You know what to do?"

"Hard to believe one guy has kicked all the ass you said he has," Seventy-One grunted.

"You saw the man's labor of love on the screen. Believe it. The guy's been a major pain in the ass."

"Mobsters and bikers. Used to having their way with a scowl and a threat. I don't scowl, I don't threaten. I deliver."

"Good to hear it."

"Okay. Soon as the chopper drops off half the riffraff at the sister site, believing they're free to take some of the element for themselves for future inspection, I'll send four of the boys out to say hello to our Mr. Sunshine. Sounds like we've got a busy night ahead of us. Last thing I want is some loose cannon rolling over my feet."

"This is Cromman's gig, for the most part. We follow orders, get the thing in the chopper. There's going to be shooting, chaos out the wazoo when we let the whackos in to hold down their part of the game plan."

"To take care of all nonessential personnel. I like it. Then what? You think Cromman's going to stand around and recite chapter and verse on the truth of all truths? Hand over all those classified NSA files on ETs and other UFO-related documents?'' He chuckled, adding, ''The NSA's cosmic Watergate. The common folks would skin us and eat us alive.''

''That's where you step in and fill in the blanks for the whackos here.''

''Sounds like you've got it all worked out. They'll be like lambs led to the slaughter.''

But who, Thornton had to wonder, was going to be the lamb when the dust started to settle? Seventy-One was all confidence....

He didn't want to even consider it, but he hoped to hell he wasn't looking at another puffed-up blowhard running out to Belasko, swollen on past victories, nothing but arrogance putting the iron in the backbone.

No, Seventy-One was the real thing, he decided. He better be, if the Belasko problem was going to get settled.

Failure couldn't be an option here. Failure meant he was dead and Cromman was skipping off to the wild unknown, the marvel of humankind in tow.

Thornton caught Seventy-One throwing him a glance. ''Lighten up. The party's just about to start.''

CHAPTER TWENTY-THREE

It was the sightings all over, but minus the tequila and the fat doobie that had only somehow, he believed, simply intensified the entire experience.

The gods were hard at work from the cosmos, mapping out his destiny in their mysterious ways. But what man born of woman, he thought, could possibly even begin to fathom eternal wisdom and knowledge? No earthbound prisoner of three-dimensional flesh, unless transformed, should even bother with a feeble attempt to reason out the why. Most men, he thought, were unworthy to dwell among the gods.

So Jason Nixon led the Otherworld following outside, held up the hand free of the M-16 to signal they should stop, allow him this moment alone. He stepped into the white beam, raised his face toward the epicenter of the light. It was a warm shroud, the light calling down to him with silent words of encouragement and approval, ready to uplift and transform his earthly flesh and take him away to immortality.

Soon he would know what the gods did.

It was only the expected chopper, of course, not the chariot of fire he remembered, but the experience was similar to the sightings he'd encountered in the California desert—a dark, silent mass floating down from the heavens, a blinding white light washing over his vehicle. Back then, he recalled, there was a static burst over the radio, a whine that pierced his senses like a swarm of hornets in his ears, then his Lexus had died suddenly, everything from radio to engine shutting down. Here and now, the grit slashing his face was an annoyance, nearly snatching away the grand moment, reducing him to mere mortal stature, but a man of the ages just the same, poised at the gates of knowledge itself. The loud whapping sound of man-made metal in his ears was also nothing like the silence of the gods he recalled, but this moment was surely the signal from the Others, the chopper coming down to scoop them up.

They were on their way. The gods were simply using the enemy like puppets to show him the mother of all truths.

"Take me away," he said to the light. "I am ready—I am your servant."

Then, just as it happened on those occasions, the light died, leaving him to wonder at the darkness and the silence, ponder over a few more sips of tequila and a couple deep tokes, exactly what he had seen. The man-made craft settled on its landing skids, all dirt and ungodly noise. The albino creature seemed a clumsy mass of useless flesh as he nearly stumbled out of the black hole, walking quickly up to his face.

"Let's go. I'm assuming you know how to use those weapons?"

"Ye of little faith."

"Spare me. Get your people inside."

Nixon turned and waved the assault rifle. One by one, his people boarded.

Time to go.

The albino thing seemed especially nervous as he snapped, "Do you and your people understand what it is you are supposed to do?"

"But of course. And you, sir, have made certain promises when we fulfill our obligation."

"And I intend to deliver. You'll get the truth."

"It is why we are prepared to do your bidding."

"Even if that means killing anybody you are ordered to?"

"Especially so. Evil walks at this place. Myself and my people are in agreement that the tools of the greatest government-military conspiracy of all time must become extinct if the truth is to be made known."

"Whatever."

THE BIG EVENT STARTED to go down as soon as the chopper landed at the smaller dome.

Bolan took a read of the flurry of activity at both sites. The blacksuited barbarians were at the gate at the main facility, armed with subguns, decked out in full battle regalia. One of the vans pulled out and began rolling away from the motor pool to cut a hard path on jouncing chassis through the valley. Full-blown night had settled over the facilities, but a cyclops beam of white shone just above the domes of main and secondary. The van appeared to be beating an intercept course to greet the black chopper's return. Bolan now saw where his bold stance was something of a double-edged sword.

Since the enemy knew exactly where he was, the chopper had veered far to the north before flying on for the sister facility. The flyboys, he had to believe, were under orders to stay well away from any projectile Bolan could fire to bring the works down.

The chopper, then. That was how they planned to move out the device.

Which meant moving in on foot, ramming all manner of blood and guts down their throats, eye-to-eye.

No problem. That was part of the soldier's plan to proceed anyway.

He had to figure Cromman was now on board the chopper, but who were the new players dropping into the fold? Ten or so armed shadows were leaping out of the chopper, into the rotor wash, charging the dome. A quick look through binos switched to infrared, and, strip them of assault rifles and subguns, the new batch looked more like civilians than soldiers or assassins.

Okay. The UFO bunch. But why would Cromman or Thornton bother fielding a ragtag army? More guns to throw into the mix? Stack the odds more on their side? Help move the device? He didn't know how big or heavy the supertech marvel was, but maybe Cromman and Thornton were looking at the UFO cultists as nothing more than cheap labor, the big shots unable to spare a little sweat except to pick up a weapon. Well, Cromman wouldn't stoop, Bolan knew, to thrusting himself into all-out battle. No, he would stay perched on the sidelines, pulling the strings, getting the device hauled out and loaded up.

And since Thornton never strayed more than a few feet beyond the dome, a small gathering of his new shooters by his side, Bolan strongly suspected the device was stashed in the main facility.

Game time.

The warrior would have to chance leaving behind the war bag. If what he was taking to the show wasn't enough to bring down the roof, he'd be dead anyway. The mini-Geiger counter fixed to his harness would aid his penetration of the facility, steering him clear of any hot zones. When the shooting started, however, it was a safe bet not too many folks would be concerned about a little radioactive dusting.

He almost missed the first shooter as he moved out to parallel the east side of the ridgeline and head north. It was incredible, nothing more than a snatch of a glimpse, one o'clock and rising fast. The figure was barely even a shadow in Bolan's eyes as it boiled up out of a gully spined down the east face. In fact, the blacksuited gunner was nearly invisible as he cut loose with autofire.

"I STAY with you!"

Nixon didn't have the time or inclination to bicker with the vagabond. He gave Collins a curt nod as he ordered the last of the chosen ten to jump off. He was beginning to wonder how smart it was to hand an

M-16 to the man, but there were other matters to be more concerned about.

Such as getting into the main facility, living up to their end of the deal and getting out in one piece.

"The van is on the way!"

The rotor wash pounded his senses, and Nixon had to strain to catch the albino's words. Supposedly the hatchway to the smaller facility was open to allow easy access to the lead-encased vat with the supernatural element that fueled the antigravity device. Supposedly this was part of their earlier agreement, a little something to take home, spoils from the fruit of the tree of eternal wisdom. With any luck, Nixon hoped to land himself a segment on the *Today Show,* trumpet to the whole world he was in sole possession of the truth of ages. Even the eternal wisdom of the gods, he decided, had to have a price tag.

"One man, that's all you get to take to question. The rest of the science detail and all nonessential workers will be executed on the order from my man. Agreed?"

Nixon nodded. "Yes. And when do you and I have our little chat?"

"When I have the device safely aboard this helicopter."

Nixon felt the electric charge of raw energy in the air. He had never fired a shot in anger in all of his life, but he was ready now to do what had to be done. Practicing on beer bottles and cardboard mock-ups, blasting unmoving objects all to hell, was one thing. They were going in to gun down earthbound prisoners.

And he had to remind himself the men—or women—
they would be asked to shoot down in cold blood were
enemies of the Others.

The chopper was lifting off.

A few more minutes now, Nixon told himself. And
they would be inside, closing down on the truth.

HAD BOLAN NOT MOVED out when he did, he would
have been tagged right out of the gate. As it stood, it
was close enough, the tracking line of steel-jacketed
hornets buzzing a hot path inches from his scalp. The
Executioner held back on the trigger of the M-16,
jacked on adrenaline. The invisible man dropped, the
HK subgun flying off into the night.

Bolan had earlier memorized the lay of the land
running to the main facility. It hardly made his swift
charge any easier, up and over broken ground, down
into a narrow spine, eyes scanning the darkness. He
heard the bleat of the rotors in the distance, but kept
combat senses tuned to another near invisible threat.
How had he missed the shooter leave the facility?

The glint of a stainless-steel tubular weapon, catching a wink from the cyclops beam, galvanized Bolan
into action. The multiround projectile launcher was
popping off two, maybe three rounds, when Bolan
nailed the shadow assassin in the chest. Launcher and
hardman shot up straight, then tumbled down the
slope. The projectiles sailed past Bolan, falling to earth
in the distant south in a crunching thunderclap.

Something warned the Executioner to hit the
ground. He dropped into a dark bowl as autofire

slashed the air. The expected rounds whining off rock never came. Instead the weapons fire died, a heavy crunch of deadweight at some point to his rear.

"Belasko! Don't shoot."

THORNTON HEARD the freak squawking out the orders in a feverish pitch.

"Bring it outside, five minutes and counting. Take our helpers down below and I want this done and wrapped in ten minutes!"

Thornton had taken up turf near the rear of the bus. With Belasko out there, no doubt on the killing march again, cover was the best idea he could come up with at the moment. Seventy-One, though, was rolling around beyond the bus, checking the ridgeline, the HK MP-5 SD-3 subgun held in one massive fist.

"Bring the chopper in, Cromman," Thornton barked into his handheld radio.

"No way. If Belasko wings my ride with a grenade—"

"The Belasko problem is being taken care of."

"I've heard that somewhere before."

The little freak wasn't about to get out of the chopper, Thornton saw, as the whackos bounded out of the fuselage, came running from a good hundred yards out.

The chopper was rising, Cromman bleating, "Call back when the device is outside. Hurry!"

"Where the hell is he?"

Thornton ignored Seventy-One for the moment,

raising Anderson. "You have five minutes to finish crating it up."

"We'll need some help bringing it out. Myself and the others have to decon first."

"Help is on the way."

Thornton severed the connection. A check of his watch, and everything was running right on schedule. He told three of Seventy-One's hitters, "Take these assholes down below and start bringing it out. But pick four of them, and leave them inside the hatch to stand guard. You know what to do."

And they did, his earlier briefing nailing it down, every move along the way mapped out.

Only he had pretty much glossed over the Belasko factor. No sense in pushing panic buttons—Seventy-One and company would think him a coward for messing his britches over one guy.

The trio of shooters marched away, he saw, intercepting the cultists. From there on, Thornton knew it would get dicey. There would be squawking and screaming aplenty once the labor force and the science crew began falling under the guns of murderous civilian radicals. There could be a mass stampede, a blind charge....

Deal with it.

And where the hell was Belasko? Seventy-One had dispatched four shooters to hit the ridgeline and clean up the Belasko mess. He had heard the shooting down there, two explosions rumbling in the distance like rolling thunder. Like very little else he had craved for in his life, Thornton wanted that guy dead and gone.

He was moving to the rear of the bus when Seventy-One obviously couldn't wait any longer for a report.

"Carey. Hanks. MacMurtrie. Stone. Report."

It might as well have been the voice of doom that patched through. Thornton nearly choked on some rising bile when he heard the familiar cold voice state, "They didn't make it."

"THEY CALL the stuff I-mox."

Bolan was a roving human compass, his M-16 sweeping the darkness, the slope leading down into the valley, muzzle fanning, twelve to six to twelve. He waited, heart thumping in his ears, as Taggart materialized out of the night. The man gave each of the two new kills a savage kick. Satisfied they wouldn't rise from the dead, Taggart took a few cautious steps closer to Bolan, the man smart enough to keep his HK 33 assault rifle aimed toward the valley.

"A little voice is telling me," Bolan said, tossing away the blacksuited gunner's radio, "this is more than just coincidence."

"What you lack in gratitude, friend, you more than make up for in the balls department."

"Well?"

"You're welcome, Belasko—again."

Bolan lifted the M-16, just enough to stop Taggart in his tracks.

"I followed you, okay," Taggart growled, and Bolan caught the whiskey fumes washing up in his face. "Instead of giving me attitude you should be thanking me. Those two had you dead to rights."

"Now you're a Monday-morning quarterback?"

"See how they smeared themselves with black war paint."

Bolan had.

"The stuff they spray on themselves is odorless, colorless, something like a few police departments now use, mostly SWAT, when they have to batter down a door and charge into a black hole. The stuff deflects light somehow. I had a heat-seeking sensor, but it just barely let me pick them up. Four down. No more on the way for the moment."

"And now you want to come to the party?"

"No agenda. I liked Jim."

"That simple."

"I know, if you even see my weapon twitch your way…"

"Then we understand each other."

With Taggart up close now, Bolan found the man weighted down with combat harness, complete with pouches stuffed with spare clips for the subgun and the holstered side arm. A dozen or so grenades hung on the harness, and Bolan figured he might need the extra help when he went into the main facility.

"So, we do this act together, Belasko?"

"Let's rock. Stick with me, by my side."

Taggart made a sound Bolan couldn't be sure was a grunt or a chuckle.

THORNTON WOULDN'T have believed it if he hadn't seen it in the flesh. The first flicker of doubt and fear dropped a shadow over Seventy-One's face.

''Those were four of my best hitters,'' Seventy-One growled. ''Who is this guy?''

''A bulldog. A scourge.''

''And he's on the rampage. Okay. I see what to do now. We leave the hatch open, let him come in. Chances are he won't even get past the front gate. Forget the desert trash, I'll put a couple of my guys just inside. Now, as I recall, there's a second-level hall leading up from the work area. We roll the thing out on a dolly, come up the emergency elevator. If this walking pain in the ass gets inside, he'll move ahead, come looking for us. By then we'll be rolling out past his rear, right out the front gate.''

Thornton liked it.

This was about to get real ugly, he thought, if it didn't completely unravel all to hell in the next few minutes. Cromman out there, calling the shots, the heavy hitters bought and paid for, in the freak's pocket. Then the UFO nuts, duped into thinking they were part of the team, marching down below to their own inevitable slaughter.

A mess.

Thornton took up his own HK subgun, then trailed Seventy-One toward the hatch, into the light. There was nothing left to do but keep pitching the dice and hope Belasko didn't crap them all out.

CHAPTER TWENTY-FOUR

Ernie Collins knew a scam when he saw one. Since confidence games normally involved a level of skill in careful planning, a discerning eye for subtle weakness in human nature and an ability to act he never much cared to expend that much thought and energy on, he didn't consider himself anywhere near a master scam artist. He did, though, give himself some credit for having worked the shrink enough to get his hands on an assault rifle.

One of the boys.

And all hell was set to break loose, the M-16 in his hands maybe the difference between life and death. His own.

Clear and present menace was in the air, in the faces of the men in black, even burning off the bodies of the civilians they were supposed to execute. He was stuck, for the moment, but he would find a way out of there, run like there was no tomorrow, assuming, of course, there was even a night to finish out. Armed and once free of the shadow men and the star children, he could at least wander the county, stick the muzzle of his assault rifle in some poor sap's face, relieve the victim of cash—hopefully—then boogie on in a stolen ride.

San Diego sounded pretty good. Close enough to the Mexican border, a few decent Yankee dollars in his pocket going light-years up against the measly peso, and he could start over.

That was still way in the future. Right now he was in the middle of the pack, marching down the steel-walled corridor, a view of the universal biohazard sign painted on the glass partition straight ahead.

The supersecret house of the truth Nixon so desperately sought didn't look like much at all to Collins, as he frantically racked his brain, searching for some avenue of escape. Steel walls, narrow corridors, a mounted camera here and there. Metal steps taking them to a lower level. Steel doors sealing off whatever lay beyond, as the group rolled ahead, led by two grim hardmen.

They rounded a corner and Nixon started bawling, "That's it? It's packed up, hidden!"

"Shut your hole! Do your job first!"

It was the guy from the house, snarling for the geeks to get their hands up. The setup was planned, Collins figured, all the workforce gathered now in some large room that looked more like a rubber pad at the nut house, but for the few bunks mounted into the walls, a steel table where frightened faces were framed in a glaring white light....

A dolly with some big gray box, probably made of lead, was being shouldered by two blacksuited men down an adjoining corridor. The hardman from the house barked for a few of the cultists to go help with the chore of pushing the miracle from heaven.

"I wanted to see it!"

"Not now," the man was shouting back at Nixon.

Collins felt it all but set to blow up in his face. The workforce was rising, maybe thirty or thirty-five guys, snapping out the questions, a half dozen with nothing more than white underwear covering the birthday suits, looking wet, towels falling as if they'd just stepped out of the shower.

Nixon, he saw, was at the limits of patience, his eyes fired up with a weird light, good and angry now, as if they had really planned to clue him in, Collins thought.

A look over his shoulder, and he saw three hardmen peeling off his rear. To his right—all clear—there was some sort of thick glass partition, leading back to the hall. This game was dead, he decided. Nixon and nuts had been led here by their noses, for reasons he didn't care to know.

Collins was taking a slow shuffle toward the partition when the sound of thunder rolled from up top. Someone upstairs was crashing the party.

Then the shooting started in earnest.

SPEED SAW Bolan reach a firepoint on the dome first. The soldier was taking up cover behind the last SUV in line when Taggart fell in. The former black op was sucking wind, body ripe with running sweat flushing out the poison. As far as Bolan was concerned, the man could tag along for the bloody charge. Actually there was little choice. If Taggart had wanted him dead, he'd already passed on two opportunities to put one through Bolan's head.

They whipped low around the corners of the hatch, autofire ripping loose when Bolan made his move to start bringing down the house. The Executioner tapped the M-203's trigger, aiming for a gray wall just beyond the shooters as his point of impact for maximum infliction of death and pain.

The buckshot round was special delivery. For Bolan's purpose at the moment, it was meant to cause a whole bunch of pain and horror when any standing guys found themselves flailing about, wailing to the indifferent heavens why they looked as if they'd just been shoved through a meat grinder, assuming they still had eyes left to see the ruins. The projectile streaked past the shooters, slammed into the wall, and the impact fuse on the warhead exploded the works of countless flying steel minirazors of fléchettes. A 40 mm frag bomb down the chute and Bolan dropped the hellbomb inside the opening of the dome, adding more punch to the mix.

They were shrieking up a storm inside, but the screams faded, a body toppling into sight as the second blast removed all concerned. Bolan was up and running for the smoke, Taggart huffing on his heels. The op was clearly in sorry shape, drowning his demons around the clock for years, keeping himself nothing more than a walking hump of formaldehyde. The soldier wasn't about to let the man become a liability, and he had no time to spare pondering Taggart's soul and personal sickness. Once inside, they were both on their own.

The toughest part, Bolan knew, would prove the first breaking charge into the dome. A whiff of the air beyond the slat, and his nose was full of a mixed bag of smells.

Not even a groan stirring the ripe air. All clear just beyond.

After that...

Taggart had his flask out, slugged one down the hatch for courage, or whatever else. "SWAT charge?"

Bolan shot an angry look at the man. Any number of listening devices could be planted in the vicinity, likewise eyes mounted in the rock or the dome. Bolan gestured with his hands that he would go first, a high charge, Taggart trailing low and breaking to the left.

Bolan filled the M-203 with a frag bomb and broke inside, surging past five corpses. No time to question Taggart about the layout, Bolan would have to keep rolling, watching, and shoot it down if it moved into his path.

The Executioner hit the edge of a rounded wall. A peek beyond, and the bullets came flying in a screen of lead that skidded off the steel. Two, maybe three down there. Bolan plucked a frag grenade off his webbing, released the spoon, dropped the bomb, the rattle of metal on metal lost to the chatter of weapons fire and screaming ricochets.

"Two count, and let's roll," the soldier said, mentally ticked off the numbers, hunched low and sent the lethal egg around the corner in a sideways whip of the

arm. He fell back to ride it out, hoping another drive
was about to clear the fences for the homer.

THORNTON GOT the slaughter started. A long sweep of
his HK subgun, and the first few bodies were mowed
down under his blazing lead finger. Seventy-One
jumped into the act next, standing tall and firing away
with his own subgun. The cultists had hesitated at first,
unsure what was really happening now that the bullets
were flying and guys were tumbling in crimson ruin
at their feet. But once a few heroes among the work
detail figured out they'd been rounded up for a massacre—and not for an emergency briefing on a security
leak as Thornton had told them—they started a bulldog charge for the cultists. Sparked by panic, the cultists cut loose with their subguns and assault rifles, hitting the work detail at point-blank range. Bodies were
spinning, guys bellowing out the rage and pain. Figures were slipping and sliding as blood rained to the
steel floor. Wild autofire was hammering the glass partition, Thornton glimpsed from his stand inside the
doorway, the whole thing groaning, pocked with giant
spiderwebs before a flying sack of leaking red went
through it headfirst.

Thornton growled to Seventy-One, "Let's go. They
can finish up."

Then the shrink was backing out of the riot, Thornton saw, raking his M-16 all around, taking out workers and a few of his own people in a blind panic.
"Wait!"

Thornton saw next they were straining to move the

lead container down the hall. They were checking the wheels on the cart, barking that the dolly felt locked up. A quick check by Seventy-One's shooters and they found the wheels weren't locked at all. One of the NSA black ops was angrily muttering how the container suddenly felt hot to the touch.

Thornton kept the knowledge to himself. The "thing," powered up to level ten now, was on the verge of acting on its own will. He didn't anticipate this problem, but the thing was caged up in six-inch walls of lead. No way in hell could it break out, and fly off for trip around the Vegas skies.

"Nixon," Thornton shouted over the din of autofire, the razor's edge cacophony of cursing and screaming slashing out the doorway, "grab four of your people and help us move this thing out of here!"

Thornton heard the explosions above. Even muffled by steel barriers, there was no mistaking the screams of, once again, men in terrible pain.

"Belasko," Thornton muttered to himself, and stood there, shaking his head, chuckling. If Cromman had just two guys like that...

"What the hell are you laughing about, Thornton! Give us a hand with this damn thing!"

Seventy-One snarled out the order, as if he were all of a sudden in charge of something. Thornton slung the subgun around his shoulder. They were still shooting up the work detail, autofire and hideous screams raking the air, when they finally had the container rolling around the corner, on the way out.

"Here, let me give you a hand."

Thornton looked over his shoulder from where the guy had run. He knew the man behind the face. The guy Braxton had used as a scout, he figured, had jumped out the window after it was shot to shards, waiting in the hall to make his escape. Just like that, everybody was looking out for number one when the going got rocky.

It figured, so why was he surprised?

Thornton stepped back and allowed the man room to aid in the pushing contest. He needed his hands free for the subgun, if Belasko popped in.

Check that, he thought. Not if, but when.

THREE MORE of the black ops were down and out, fragged to hell, when Bolan hit the steel door. The racket of ceaseless autofire was striking the other side of the door, shooting up in echoes and howls of pain down below. What was happening and why remained to be seen.

The soldier gave the hallway one last check. Clear.

Grasping the metal handle, he gave it a twist, cracked it open, braced for the bullets to start flying for his face. Apparently, he suspected, all hands were below, engaged in some slaughter feast.

"Watch our backs on the way down," Bolan told Taggart, who gave the soldier a nod.

The soldier hugged the wall, descending the short flight of steps, M-16 cradled and out front. The camera hung over his head didn't escape notice, but Bolan figured whatever was going on beyond the door at the landing had everybody's undivided attention.

Through the door, Bolan found a roaring gun battle waiting on the other side. It was a one-sided slaughter he walked into, and the cultists were blasting away with autofire on unarmed men and a few women. Briefly the warrior pondered the insanity of it all, then concluded this slaughter was designed, orchestrated by Thornton or Cromman or both, meant to heap blame on the heads of the cultists when the heist of the device was discovered, and those two had cleared the scene for parts unknown.

A quick search of the hallway running parallel to the room where the bloody scam was being acted out, and Bolan found he was in the clear to advance and dish back some justice. It looked nearly a clean sweep, the cultists consumed by some fanaticism as they shouted obscenities, hosing down the workforce, oblivious to the new arrival.

Bolan waded in and began to drop the hammer. He hit the dozen or so cultists with a long barrage of autofire just as two of them were admiring their handiwork as their last victim collapsed to the floor. The Executioner blew them all over the room, sent them falling over the bodies of their victims, flying this way and that, screaming out the shock and outrage. A few cultists, having shot their wad on overkill, were fumbling to ram home fresh clips when Bolan chopped them down, painting ragged tattoos across torsos, left to right.

Human dominoes, checked out to the unknown.

Taggart's assault rifle chimed in to the killing beat, the former op picking out two runners who thought they could dive out the hole where the glass partition had vanished under the original onslaught. He caught them in midflight, lead skewers that sent them slamming to the base of the wall as Bolan burned out the clip on the final two standing cultists.

The Executioner stepped into the slaughter, alert for possums, any mangled ruins still clinging to life. Reloading the assault rifle, he found a taker. Wild eyes, framed by a mop of long red hair, turned toward the Executioner. The cultist was crying something about how this wasn't the way it was supposed to be, when Bolan punched out his lights with a 3-round burst to the chest.

Life was tough all over.

"Devious bastard, that Cromman," the soldier heard Taggart rasping from just outside the doorway. "I can hear what they were told. Cromman conned these slobs to do his dirty work. I can hear the snow job how he would tell them the truth about Area 51 and extra—"

The sentence died on Taggart's lips as the autofire chewed into his side, his skull coming apart next in a rain of gore.

"BRING IT ON. Make it snappy, the house is burning down as I speak."

Thornton heard Cromman copy, on the way. He could already picture the freak, holding the harness in the doorway, the chopper probably as close as the hilltop above. His big moment of triumph.

And once again, Thornton found himself bearing

witness to more of Belasko's work. Seventy-One was looking more distressed by the minute, as he mouthed a curse at the sight of yet more of his best shooters mauled by Belasko's special touch of doom.

No matter. Seventy-One's ploy seemed to be holding up, if Thornton judged all the shooting coming from below. Belasko was mired down, two of Seventy-One's hitters left behind to make sure both the cultists finished their butcher's work and to mop any threat on their tails.

Belasko should keep until they were flying on. He hoped.

The cultists and two of Seventy-One's hitters had the big pushcart trundling outside when Thornton saw the chopper landing. The loading ramp already built into the aircraft was growing out past the skids on Cromman's push of a button. The man was beaming as he stood in the maw, waving them on, arms outstretched, an albino Moses, Thornton thought, parting the seas.

"Hurry up! Come on!"

Right. The pharoah's on the way, only Thornton wondered if their badass pursuer could walk on water when the walls crashed down.

Thornton turned and found Cromman and Seventy-One discussing something as the others strained to shove the container up the ramp. It was almost a magic moment, a psychic talent of sorts he never knew he possessed, buried but now rising, flashing the warning lights in his brain. He could almost read their lips, even as their faces were obscured by a thin, swirling screen of grit. Talking about the money in the mystery envelopes. Cromman naming a figure, and who else but he could know the amount? Seventy-One's expression changed, the mercenary coming to life, bowing now before the real feeding hand, as it all became clear who had been sending along the insurance money. Thornton cursed himself more than Cromman. He should have seen this coming.

Cromman shouted to make sure the punchline was clearly heard over the rotor wash. "Thanks for your help, Thornton!"

Thornton almost beat Seventy-One and the hitters to the punch. The subgun was up and jumping around in his fists, Thornton winging around the lead, when he felt four, maybe five rounds slam him in the gut, blasting holes out his ribs. Somehow he held on, pitching back through the hatch, sweeping the SMG in a wild hosing. They were scrambling up the ramp, Cromman's squeaky voice shouting, "He's history! Forget about him!"

The lights wanted to fade away, but the burning pain told Thornton he had a few minutes, the mist holding in his sight, the agony alone urging him on. He was on his back, saw the chopper rising beyond the hatchway, gone. If he could just hold on, he told himself, digging into his pants pocket.

CHAPTER TWENTY-FIVE

Bolan didn't know how many shooters were out there in the hall, but knew they'd come rushing any second, could even feel the living heat, smell the fear beyond the doorway where the dead were cooling off. Hardmen were gearing up, adrenaline kicking it to overdrive for the enemy, no doubt, a bulldog charge up and coming.

A heavy blanket of quiet had fallen after their nailing of Taggart, the calm before the next storm, then some gunner with more arrogance than good sense dropped the spoon to a grenade. The sound was unmistakable, loud and clear as it hit steel, alerting Bolan the steel ball was armed and good to go.

Shooting a look off to the side, nothing moving yet in front of the gutted window, and Bolan flung the M-16, low around the edge of the doorway, holding back on the trigger. It was nothing but spray and pray, winging the lead out there.

And he caught a lucky score.

A grunt hit the air as Bolan kept pounding out the lead, peering around the corner. Just in time, he found, to see he tagged the gunner with grenade.

Sometimes simple bravery alone, he had to figure, was rewarded by a smiling fate.

The steel egg slipped from the hardman's lifeless hand, his chest ventilated and pumping out the blood. His expression registered dumbfounded anger, as he toppled backward, knees folding like deflated rubber spindles. Bolan turned away, hugging the floor as the grenade erupted, spewing out fire and flying steel bits. Then he rose and broke from cover into the smoke, pumping it up into into a full-bore charge of his own, catching the angry moans of the unlucky who hadn't cleared ground zero quick enough.

On the fly past the mutilated slab of crimson flesh, Bolan found a blacksuited gunner holding his face with one hand, the blood running in thick rivulets to the floor, while the guy scrambled to grab up the sub-gun. The Executioner zipped a burst of autofire up the man's spine.

Finished.

The hall was empty but for the dead. His gut, and the silence, told Bolan it was clear sailing, at least until he got back up top. The same instincts warned the soldier Thornton and crew had slapped together a last-minute plan, using some alternate way to move the device out of the facility.

Bolan moved back for the flight of steps. It was too quiet up there, and he feared the worst when he topped out.

The Elvis of supertech wonder had, most likely, left the damn building.

JUST BEFORE the shooting started again, this time around the chopper, he'd dropped behind the laboring pack. They'd been too busy grunting, sweating and cursing the lead box up the ramp to notice he was slinking away, melting off into the shadows.

Goodbye, so long, have a nice life.

Whatever the damn thing they cherished so much really was, he didn't care. They could have it.

Screw it, and them. He was free and rolling.

It was either dumb luck, pure stupidity or simple arrogance on their part, but he'd found the keys hanging in the ignition to one of the SUVs.

Ernie Collins laughed. His only concern was getting the hell out of the valley of death, out of Nevada. From there on, he would figure it out, he always had.

The problem of the moment was the hills, the rough terrain seeming to dictate his course, forcing him southbound. Then the edge of some godforsaken cut in the land made him hit the wheel to the right, guiding him against his wishes westbound.

Then he saw the duped and the conned. The other half of Nixon's star children were quickly put behind, though, as the shadows started walking toward the bigger dome, no doubt wondering what the hell all the shooting was about.

Screw them, too.

Westward now, in the direction taken by the black chopper.

As soon as the desert hardpan allowed, he would adjust his run away from those people. Things were looking up, the future bright, for once, the hard part over. A free ride now, a gun by his side. Gifts were falling into his lap all over the place.

Christmas.

Now, if he could just find some out-of-the-way all-night hole, preferably one attended by a lonely desert rat with a few bucks in the till.

Beyond that, there was San Diego. He'd never been there, but he heard it was something of a sweet town, good times rolling, if a guy had a few bucks to spare.

Pretty much like anyplace else, only he'd never known a few extra dollars to sample all the good times he dreamed about.

He was going to change that, sure to run across someone with cash, an ATM card, something to line his empty pockets.

He watched as the chopper gathered speed, flying on into the night.

It sure looked as if everybody was happy, he thought, every man had what he had come here for.

Everyman's name penciled down in the fabled Book of Life.

Ernie Collins chuckled, and rolled on. The good times were as close as tomorrow.

"WHY IS IT doing that? What the hell is going on, Cromman! What is this goddamn thing?"

Cromman jumped back from the container, Seventy-One barking in his ear. It was a whisper at first, a dark, laughing voice in the caverns of his head he should recognize but couldn't pin down. The container was strapped to the wall, but the device was banging around in its hold, the lead shield...

A soft glow emanated from inside, like some beacon flaring on, out of the dark.

Cromman felt the nausea swelling his guts, a sickness that went far deeper, became more consuming than the affliction he suffered.

"Why is it doing that?"

The shrink, standing near the open fuselage door, was crying, some panicked child ready to grab on to mommy's skirt.

It was all he could do, but Cromman put some iron into rubber legs, walking past the container, toward the cockpit. They were skimming the desert, no more than twenty feet above the ground, three miles, he figured, from the facility. Another mile or so and the tractor trailer would be there, waiting to pick up the device.

"Cromman!"

He nearly puked as the chuckling voice came rolling louder out of his head, telling him he was screwed.

Thornton.

He turned and saw the container nearly break free of its restraints. He was vaguely aware of the scream rifling through the fuselage as the container lurched, hammered into the man called Nixon and sent him flying off into the night.

Gone, and forgotten, the scream whipped off into the dark, all eyes locked in, laser beams of pure fear aimed at the container.

"Cromman! What the fuck is happening?"

Seventy-One lifted his subgun, ready to toss it all away, edged out there beyond terror to murderous impulse.

It was a wrecking ball slamming him in the gut, as Cromman heard the sob rise from his throat, coming to a terrifying rest in his ears.

The dream was dead. Unless...

"The son of a... Thornton..."

"What? He did what?"

Panic rooted him in the cockpit doorway. The cultists, Seventy-One and the hitters looked like some absurd caricatures in a gruesome cartoon, gaping at him, the stupid, clueless peasants.

"Is Thornton dead?"

The container rose on its own, suspended in a white halo a few feet off the floorboard for a stretched second, then pounded down, jostling about like some enraged tiger.

"We shot him," Cromman heard Seventy-One shout. "You said to leave the guy, we did."

"Then...he might be still... Oh, God...oh, God."

"What?"

"He powered it up to level ten!" Cromman screamed.

"How do you know?"

"I was head of Special Security, you peasant! I had the means to destroy the thing. Before I was terminated... Now Thornton... Oh, God."

"You're telling me Thornton somehow primed this thing to blow up. That if he's still breathing he can push..."

"A button, yes, a button...five kilotons!"

NOTHING BUT THE DEAD and the damned were waiting for him when Bolan made his way back to the front gate. M-16 fanning the compass, poised for a corpse to rise from the dead, and the Executioner pinned the groan down.

Thornton, gut-shot and bleeding out near the hatch. The savages had begun, he knew, to consume one another in their darkest hour.

It figured. It fit.

The light was fading fast in Thornton's eyes, the man sensing Bolan's approach perhaps as he rolled over, almost appearing as if he expected the return of his worst nightmare. The soldier froze when he saw the small black box, clutched in a bloody mitt.

"You..."

No surprise. The guy made it sound, Bolan thought, as if in another time, another place, they would have been drinking buddies trading war stories, heaping on the bull for the glittering eye of the nearest and dearest sweet little barmaid.

Not now, or ever. A few savages, the soldier knew, were still on the loose.

The Executioner was checking the area, sure a bogeyman or two was ready to come rushing out of nowhere. Then he saw the open elevator car to his right. It was so perfectly built into the wall, it was damn near a magic act. No point now in kicking himself for having missed the sleight of hand on the way in.

The device was gone.

And then it happened.

It was apparent enough Thornton had triggered some doomsday package, a blinding light flaring beyond the hatch. No sound, not even a far-off rumble of thunder on the horizon, but the warrior braced himself for the superheated wind, the ride into oblivion that never came, squeezing his eyes shut as the light of some supernova blew beyond the screwed-tight cover of his lids.

A few eternal heartbeats later, and the light lost some of its intensity.

And then the wailing of the damned erupted beyond the hatch.

HE HEARD HIMSELF crying, calling out to a God he had never thought about, much less believed in, at some distant point beyond the ringing in his ears. He would never know how he'd been launched, free and clear of the chopper, when the light blew in his face.

It didn't matter now.

Cromman was blind, and the pain was a living fire racing through his body.

He staggered about, heard a pitiful wail or maybe two somewhere in the dark. He called out to the crying voice, anything, anybody who might come to him, take him by the hand, steer him to a safe abode.

Give him comfort.

Was there anybody out there?

He felt his hands reaching out, groping in the blackness. Who was that calling out to God? He recognized the voice.

Nixon.

''Here! I'm over here!'' Cromman shouted.

He stumbled ahead, focused on the crying man.

BOLAN HIT the first trio of living dead with a sweeping burst from the M-16. Moving on, he nailed another staggering shadow in the chest, then got his bearings.

Whatever the explosion or the device, Bolan would let it be, unexplained. Thornton had touched off the explosion, a planned stab in Cromman's back if it looked as if the man were going to leave him high and dry.

Which was exactly what Cromman had done before the world blew up in his face.

The blast had left behind blinded zombies, those cultists or black ops agents who had gone to the secondary dome, for whatever reason. They were crying out for answers, and for deliverance all over the valley.

A couple voices were even raised toward the heavens, calling out to God for help.

All the lonely people.

The Executioner looked at the halo of bluish-white light, a static charge of lightning breaking out from the shining umbrella to the west, only it appeared more like the spool of a great tornado upon longer study.

Before venturing beyond the dome, a check of his Geiger counter indicated no radiation. At first, judging how the blue jagged fingers of electricity had jumped from the engines beneath the bus and the SUVs, he was sure some electromagnetic superpulse had fouled up the works on anything with wires or computer chips. Now the needle flickered a little, fifty rads, and holding.

Not a problem. No spacesuit required.

The Executioner walked on, a burst of autofire here and there chopping down the zombies as he went. They pleaded to God, wanted answers, crying out they couldn't see. The last few living dead had to have figured out the stuttering of Bolan's M-16 for what it was, whispering words of wisdom. Two of them hit their knees before the Executioner, imploring to be spared.

Bolan put them out of their misery, sent them on their way.

Where did they all come from?

He still couldn't help but wonder what had happened and why, as he retraced his steps to the motor pool. Then he figured there was no point in trying to puzzle it out, as he caught the distant wail of still more zombies blinded by the light.

Westward.

Where the blue tornado now spiraled into the sky.

By the time he reached the SUVs, the static blue screen was gone from the engine housings. He piled in behind the wheel and twisted the ignition key.

Nothing.

A second try, and the engine coughed, something once near death attempting now to fight back.

It took a full minute of waiting and working the key, pumping a little gas into the works, and the soldier finally heard the engine sputter to life.

The Executioner began rolling out the valley of the damned.

Time for the mop-up encore.

"WHY? WHAT'S happened to me?"

He staggered on, zeroed in on the albino creature's bleating wail. The man with all the answers sounded like some terrified little child to Nixon.

"What have you done?" Nixon raged.

"Where are you?"

Nixon heard himself sobbing, unsure whether it was the fire eating up his insides, or the horrible truth he was blind that was bringing on the terror and the anguish. It would have been better, he thought, if he'd been killed outright when slamming to the desert after the evil thing had knocked him out the door.

The albino thing had lied to him; that much was now clear. There was no great truth, no mystery of the ages the creature would have revealed.

Nothing more than a small nuclear device had been smuggled out of their facility—he was sure of it. If that was true, though, he reconsidered, why had the thing inside the lead box bounced around?

Nixon heard the sound of an engine coming up from behind.

Life! Someone who could see and lead him out of this horror!

"Who is that?" Cromman cried out as the door opened and closed in the dark.

"Help us! We can't see!"

"Not a problem. I only came to help."

Nixon felt the freeze in the air, as Cromman dropped into silence.

"Belasko? You..."

Nixon wanted to know whom Cromman was talking about, but the venom scorching the words was suddenly cut off as an automatic weapon sounded from behind.

He didn't need to see to know Cromman was dead. Nixon turned, sensing the man close on him in the darkness. "Who...who are you?"

"Deliverance. Real temporary deliverance."

THE ONES WHO'D taken it in the face at ground zero had the eyes burned out of their skulls. There was also some shiny white aura over skulls burned clean of hair, a slick coating glossed over exposed flesh that had been cooked to raw meat, only there was no sweet odor of burned skin. A check of the Geiger counter, and it was still hovering in the fifty-rad neighborhood. Bolan would never be able to explain how—if it was a nuclear blast, even a small one—there was no fallout, no superheated wind, no nothing. Whatever the big mystery element, he had to figure it was some buffer against radiation, or something else...

The cleanup was over when he dropped the one who wanted to know who he was.

They had come close to delivery, the soldier saw, as he walked the hundred yards or so to the eighteen-wheeler.

Two bodies sat upright in the cab, black holes where the eyes used to be. Any ID, other than dental, would be impossible, since their features had also been burned away to the bone.

The immediate area surrounding Bolan was lit by the spiraling blue tornado. A search of the desert, and he spotted the main rotor blade impaled in the earth.

No sound, nothing moving for as far as he could see in the blue light.

It was a wrap, or was it? he wondered. If the blast hadn't turned them all into blind zombies...

Why was he troubled one or two of the damned was still prowling about? Why was he suddenly thinking about the two women and the boys?

CHAPTER TWENTY-SIX

She should have left when she and the boys first re-turned home. A number of setbacks, though, had stalled any flight out of the county. Betty couldn't raise any relatives or friends. And Tina Waylan didn't have any friends, all of them long since melting off into the distant horizon, going on with their own lives, after she'd married.

It was a three-hundred-yard-plus walk to Betty's mobile home on County Road C. Tina Waylan looked over her shoulder, checking on the boys as they dumped the suitcases and duffel bags into the bed of the Chevy. The flashlight was finally working, and she let the beam wander over her sons. Weird how the flashlight...

What was happening? she wondered.

The horror, shock and lingering fear of what they had survived had kept them up nearly twenty-four hours. She had cooked lasagna for the boys, meat loaf next, made sandwiches, something, anything to help them fall back into a normal routine. A while back, a bag of popcorn, the three of them just sitting on the couch, huddled in the safety and comfort of their own home, watching late night television.

Right up to when the lights had suddenly flickered, blinked out, some blue electricity crackling off the television, killing the picture. The same blue-white sparks came jumping out of the phone in the far corner of her living room, the microwave nearly leaping off the kitchen counter.

It was enough to get her moving, a bolt of human lightning, and packing her bags. She had no firm destination in mind, other than to get out of the county.

Drive.

Something terrible had happened, and she didn't need to wait around any longer to find herself and the boys marched into another horror show.

She knocked on Betty's door, called out her name when there was no answer. Something felt wrong; Betty's vehicle was still parked outside. The door was open, and she went inside the living room, the beam roving around.

She gasped, her knees buckling.

The phone was like some obscene object to her, looking as if it were glued to Betty's ear, her friend's eyes bulging and framed in the beam of her flashlight.

Tina Waylan was out the door, running back for the truck when a shadow boiled out of the night.

"Freeze, bitch!"

She nearly flung the flashlight at the shadow's face, but she found she was too paralyzed by fear at the sight of something she couldn't even believe was human.

"Get that off my eyes!"

She thought she recognized the voice.

"Give me that!"

It looked as if he'd been burned, only the skin was a flaming red ooze, as if he'd been baked under the sun or toasted in a microwave.

"You have money!"

It was the one from the restaurant, the scraggly guy from the bar. He wanted money. Good. There was hope, if that was all he wanted.

"Yes. Here. Just don't hurt my sons."

"Slow and easy, Mom. Let's see the bread, and it better be more than chump change."

She dug out the wad of hundreds the dark stranger had given her. His eyes nearly popped out, and she wondered if the man was laughing or sobbing as he snatched the money.

"I need a ride. Okay, listen. I'm not going to hurt you or the kids. I'm not that kinda guy."

She heard her sons crying out, saw them moving toward her.

"Tell them it's all right!"

"It's okay, boys, he just wants a ride, he's not going to hurt us."

Or so she found herself offering up a silent prayer. She felt his hand shoving her ahead.

"You drive!"

"I...I need to stop and get gas."

Now the voice of rage sounded. "You're shitting me! After what I been through...did you see the explosion out there?"

"No."

"If I hadn't closed my eyes…in the truck, you little brats!" he snarled, waving the assault rifle at her sons.

She took the wheel, imploring him not to hurt her sons, she would do what he wanted.

"Just drive and find the nearest gas pump, then I'm gone!"

BOLAN HAD BEEN unable to reach either woman. It was only a fleeting hope they had taken his advice and left the area, but he clung to the feeling. Still, something was sticking in his gut, warning him they had stayed.

An ill wind was blowing, and he was catching a bad whiff.

He would never be able to explain why, but for some reason Bolan felt drawn back to Shambala. It was on the way to where they told him they lived, and Bolan wanted to check in on the sheriff anyway, a loose end that needed wrapping up. Beyond plucking the tin off the man's chest and letting him know he was out of a job, Bolan would let the guy walk, puzzle it out, pick up the pieces, scurry around in some vain attempt to explain the unexplained to the locals.

There were no answers.

As soon as he knew the women and children were safe, the soldier was ready to leave the whole bizarre mess behind. If they came from Nellis, the Pentagon or wherever to investigate and fabricate a smoke job, well, it wasn't his problem.

But if something had happened to the women and children...

Unable to explain the dire urgency he felt, Bolan floored the gas, flying down the interstate and deeper into the dark heart of the desert night.

"WHAT HAPPENED to me!"

He was nearly in tears, staring at the smooth, almost shiny waxen face mirrored in the sideview mirror of her truck.

Tina Waylan rested a hand on Tommy's knee. "Mister, you need to go to a hospital."

Obviously, it was the wrong thing to say, since he erupted, the muzzle of the assault rifle coming up in her face. "You do what I tell you! I don't need nothin' but to get the hell outta here, this messed-up state!"

"Okay, okay, easy. I'm sorry."

"You're fucking sorry? Look at me! What did they do to me?"

"Who?"

If she kept him talking, showed a little compassion...

God, she silently prayed, please save us, do not let him hurt my sons. Not after everything that has happened.

"The spooks, that's who done this!" He nearly broke down in tears, then his eyes lit up as the sign was framed in the headlights. "That's it? That's where I gas up...is this a joke? Shambala?"

"It's the closest place. If they're asleep, I can wake them up."

"Just remember, anybody messes with me, I'll kill these brats!"

"I understand."

IT WAS a miracle of sorts, but any magic act was hardly on the table.

And any miracle would come from the barrel of his gun.

The soldier could have let a slew of questions tumble through his head, but kept moving toward the lights. Weed was snapping out the threats, near the gas pump, the smaller of the woman's two sons clutched to his chest, the guy waving around the M-16, holding the desert rats at bay.

Again, he couldn't puzzle out the warning that told him to park the SUV beyond the rise. They would know he was coming.

Maybe it had been his sighting of her truck, a half mile or so out as he closed in on the dirt track. Maybe it was the way in which he sensed some desperation behind the wheel as she made what appeared a hurried run over the road to Shambala.

No matter.

The warning rumble in his belly panned out. He had left the M-16 behind, opting for the precision, one-shot delivery of the Beretta when he read the situation.

"I'm telling you, lose the guns or I'll waste the kid!"

Bolan melted into the shadows behind the diner, homed in on the voice, moving ahead.

"Please, do what he wants! He just wants to leave!"

Tina Waylan. Then a desert rat saying, "Fine." Following up the release of guns by issuing his own warning.

"But you hurt these people you'll curse the mother gave birth to your sorry behind!"

"I'm already cussing her, moron! Just let me gas up and I'm gone."

And Bolan could well believe Weed was regretting the day he was born. He couldn't be positive, but he caught enough sighting of the raw flesh to know Weed had been torched by the blue tornado. Why he wasn't blinded...

Bolan crouched at the corner, lifted the Beretta and sighted down. Weed volunteered Tina Waylan to fuel up the truck, when Bolan gauged the range. Thirty yards, maybe less.

Chip shot.

Weed was a picture of impending doom as he stood in the light, the muzzle of his M-16 wandering around, but away from the boy.

The Executioner sighted in the target and stroked the trigger.

Weed never knew what hit him, as the slug cored through his temple. The man who wanted to leave so bad spasmed, jerking up on his toes, then toppled out of the light.

Already gone.

Some R and R, Bolan thought as he walked toward Tina and her sons, prepared to help them on their way to a better life. No rest for the weary, the man once said. And the Executioner had no doubts about that at all.

DEATH LANDS

**brings you a brand-new
look in June 2002!
Different look...
same exciting adventures!**

Salvation Road

Beneath the brutal sun of the nuke-ravaged southwest, the
Texas desert burns red-hot and merciless, commanding
agony and untold riches to those greedy and mad enough to
mine the slick black crude that lies beneath the scorched
earth. When a Gateway jump puts Ryan and the others deep
in the hell of Texas, they have no choice but to work for a
rogue baron in order to win their freedom. If they fail...they
face death.

In Deathlands, the unimaginable is a way of life.

A state-of-the-art conspiracy opens the gates of
Hell in the Middle East....

PRELUDE
TO WAR

A team of brilliant computer specialists and stategists
and a field force of battle-hardened commandos make
rapid-deployment repsonses to world crises. But now even
Stony Man has met its match: a techno-genius whose cyber
army has lit the fuse of war in the Middle East. Stony Man's
Phoenix Force hits the ground running at the scene, racing
against time to stop an all-out conflagration that promises
to trap America in the flames.

STONY
MAN

*Available in
June 2002
at your favorite
retail outlet.*

James Axler
Outlanders®

DRAGONEYE

Deep inside the moon two ancient beings live on—the sole survivors of two mighty races whose battle to rule earth and mankind is poised to end after millennia of struggle and subterfuge. Now, in a final conflict, they are prepared to unleash a blood sacrifice of truly monstrous proportions, a heaven-shaking Armageddon that will obliterate earth and its solar system. At last Kane, Grant and Brigid Baptiste will confront the true architects of mankind: their creators…and now, ultimately, their destroyers.

In the Outlands, the shocking truth is humanity's last hope.

Or order your copy now by sending your name, address, zip or postal code, along with a check or money order (please do not send cash) for $5.99 for each book ordered ($6.99 in Canada), plus 75¢ postage and handling ($1.00 in Canada), payable to Gold Eagle Books, to:

In the U.S.	**In Canada**
Gold Eagle Books	Gold Eagle Books
3010 Walden Avenue	P.O. Box 636
P.O. Box 9077	Fort Erie, Ontario
Buffalo, NY 14269-9077	L2A 5X3

Please specify book title with your order.
Canadian residents add applicable federal and provincial taxes.

GOUT22

Outlanders brings you a bold new look in May 2002! Different look… same exciting adventures with Kane, Brigid, Lakesh, Grant and Domi!

James Axler
·:· Outlanders®

The first of a brand-new two-book story arc—
The Dragon Kings:

DEVIL IN THE MOON

As the ruling oligarchy of nine barons rebuild what was once the United States after an internecine war for power, a mysterious entity is attempting to impose a dark destiny on Earth. But the tides of battle turn with the discovery of a functional pre-dark moon base, whose human defenders are all that stand between Earth and its obliteration.

In the Outlands, the shocking truth is humanity's last hope.

BOOK I

Watch for the second book of The Dragon Kings series, *Dragoneye* coming in August 2002.